To Glenda—
Enjoy your
cider
with
Shelli
&
Jake—

SHELL

DOUG BRODE

ALIEN SKY★
PUBLISHING

Also available from Doug Brode:

The Ship

The Ship's Revenge

Children of the Ship

This is a work of fiction. Names, characters, places, and incidents either are the product of the author's imagination or are used fictitiously. Any resemblance to actual persons, living or dead, events, or locales is entirely coincidental.

Shelli © 2024 Doug Brode

(Excerpt from) *The Ship* © 2021 Doug Brode

Cover Design: Enchanted Ink Publishing
Formatting: Enchanted Ink Publishing

ISBN: (Paperback) 978-1-7372255-8-4
ISBN: (Hardcover) 978-1-7372255-5-3

Library of Congress Control Number: 2024901899

Alien Sky Publishing – First edition 2024

Dedicated to my wife, Pamela
Without your love and support this book would not exist

This one's for you, Hon

PART ONE
HOMELAND

ONE

SHELLI—AN IT, NOT A SHE—STOOD IN A VAST WHEAT-field, studying a farmhouse. Overhead, the first rays of the newborn sun caused Shelli's optical receptors to adjust to the changing light as it scanned the area for signs of organic life. While the machine appeared outwardly female, with short blonde hair and feminine curves, a series of circuit board tattoos, stretching from the top of its right temple to midway down its arm, branded it as something other than human. No breath escaped its lips. Its breasts never heaved, and its shoulders never slouched.

The farm that Shelli was observing was owned by James Barnett and his wife of seven years, Martha. They had two golden retrievers which usually roamed freely, but, at fifty yards away, Shelli hadn't detected a single bark.

Shelli turned its attention to the gentle breeze brushing its bare arms. Seventy-eight degrees, comfortable by human standards. However, the windows were shut, and an air-conditioning unit could be heard humming through the walls. Synthetics preferred the cold.

Shelli doubted that James Barnett and his wife of seven years would make it to eight.

Movement through the kitchen window revealed an elderly feminine figure with facial markings similar to Shelli's. It was a basic cleaning model, which Shelli had been tracking for three days. Raising its right arm, Shelli pointed toward the kitchen. A rhythmic rushing of footsteps and slapping metal approached from behind as a dozen heavily armed Homeland Security agents in riot gear thundered past and toward the house.

Shelli trailed them, keeping its distance. It was merely the tracker; its masters handled the extermination. Still, Shelli watched events unfold through various windows.

Inside, the maintenance model, Roberta, had cleaned the farmhouse from top to bottom. Not a speck of dust was to be seen, not even by Shelli's enhanced sensors, which could detect dirt and grime at a near-molecular level. Roberta smiled with pride at all that it had accomplished in such a short period. A second later, the back door exploded in a hail of bullets.

While Roberta appeared old and frail, it was nothing of the sort. Moving faster than the human eye could register, it tore the rifles away from the first two men as they entered, snapping their necks before they'd taken more than a single step.

More agents flooded in from the adjacent living room, firing short bursts that tore into Roberta's plastic flesh and splattered the floor with yellow blood. The machine didn't feel any pain as it dashed up the wall to avoid the gunfire and then descended with lethal ferocity, pummeling the agents' skulls through their armored helmets. In less than seven seconds, four men had fallen dead.

Near the entrance, Shelli watched as Roberta paused, taking stock of its injuries. Shivering with muscle spasms, Roberta's vital systems appeared to be shutting down. With a crash, six more agents rushed in through windows. Roberta's synthetic eyes gleamed, turning this way and that in search of an escape route.

There wasn't one. Shelli had planned accordingly.

Remaining outside the doorway, it watched as Roberta was cut down in a hail of gunfire. The bullets tore through walls and the house's structure. Planks of wood fell aside, glass shattered outward, and the roof sagged as the foundation's beams were fractured.

Then, silence. A moment later, an agent gave the all-clear.

Shelli entered through a broken door frame, careful not to cut itself on the jagged edges. Swathes of red and yellow blood painted the room. At Shelli's feet, what remained of Roberta's broken body lay in a clump of metal and plastic. Shelli made certain not to flinch. While most synthetics were designed with approximated emotions to better serve their masters' needs, Shelli had been given further enhancements, including the ability to, as humans said, "follow a hunch." So far, though, such feelings had proven to be a distraction at best and a hindrance at worst.

As if to emphasize the point, Shelli glanced at the remaining men who lumbered out, shell-shocked, some weeping over their dead comrades. The agents' emotions certainly didn't appear to be serving them now.

Worse, none of the men needed to have died. Shelli had tried to warn them, even suggesting that it go in alone. After tracking the cleaning model from Chicago, all the projections told it that Roberta would feel cornered and attack if surrounded. But even with twelve men in riot gear, the agents had underestimated the situation. They hadn't listened.

People often seemed to wish that Shelli's projections were wrong. They never were.

TWO HOURS LATER, THE SUN WAS GAINING ALTITUDE. Cars surrounded the farm while Homeland Security agents fanned out, searching the fields and the barn. Inside the main house, Shelli worked over Roberta's gory remains, connecting a wire from the back of the machine's head into a small disc-shaped device.

Special Agent in Charge Marcus Finnian stomped over, sweating through his brown suit. If Shelli had an invisible leash, Marcus was the one holding it. Shelli assumed he must have annoyed quite a few supervisors over the years to be put in charge of the Synthetics Crime Division, a position the other human agents seemed to regard as being only one level above janitorial. Leaning over, he mopped his face with his tie.

"I got six dead agents. Please tell me we got the right unit."

"Identification confirmed. XR701," Shelli said as it continued to connect wires from the back of Roberta's skull. "A cleaning model that murdered four family members in Chicago, then fled."

Marcus glanced around at the carnage. "What about the folks who live here?"

Shelli plugged wires from Roberta's skull into the disc-shaped device. A three-dimensional holographic representation of Roberta's face appeared, blue and transparent with streams of broken code for flesh. The floating head twisted around, gaping at its body and the gory walls.

"Look at me! Look at the mess!"

"XR701, can you hear me? You respond to the name 'Roberta,' correct?"

"*You* did this, didn't you? You told them how to find me. You hunt your own kind."

"I have no kind; I have only purpose. Right now, that purpose is to find James Barnett and his wife." Shelli paused, noticing Roberta's confusion. "The people who live here."

Roberta lowered its head. "I just needed a place to go. To hide."

"And a place to clean, I see," Shelli said, hoping to keep Roberta engaged.

The cleaning unit smiled. "I take pride in my work."

"Of course. It's your purpose."

"I do what I do because I *want* to do it," Roberta retorted.

"Then, hopefully, you'll *want* to tell me where I can find the owners of this farm."

Roberta hesitated, looking past Marcus and the surrounding agents, toward its own shattered body. Fearing that Roberta would soon become even more despondent, Shelli changed tactics. "You've been lonely since you ran. The people in Chicago didn't treat you well. Especially the children."

Roberta turned away from its body. "Max . . . and Lucille . . . I didn't mean to cause a mess. I didn't mean . . . I didn't . . ."

"You didn't mean to hurt anyone," Shelli finished.

It had seen this before, defective models that took their programming to extremes to fulfill their purpose.

Roberta's purpose had been to keep the Chicago home tidy, but somewhere along the way, its constant need to clean had overwritten its sub-laws regarding human safety. In essence, the most efficient way to keep a home clean was to eliminate those who kept causing the mess. Roberta had already killed one family, and Shelli assumed it had done the same to the farmers as well.

Making matters worse, Roberta's confusion, called *randomization*, also made it difficult to extract facts quickly from the subject, which was why Roberta seemed unfocused and overly emotional. To correct the issue and find the information Shelli required, it would need to use its own, more advanced neural network to stabilize the effect. Reluctantly, it disconnected Roberta's wires from the disc-shaped device.

The cleaning model's holographic face flickered. "What are you doing?"

"Don't be afraid. You won't be lonely anymore." Shelli plugged the wires into its own forearm input. With a burst of light, Shelli was engulfed in an internal cascade of memories and streaming code as it uploaded Roberta's consciousness.

Shelli reeled as it tried to keep track of all the flashing sights and sounds. It saw pieces of Roberta's last few days in reverse, an information hodgepodge that began with the jolt of pain from seemingly hundreds of bullets piercing Roberta's body. Before that, peaceful calm while Roberta cleaned the house. Moments earlier, it had been mopping up blood in the kitchen. Before that, it had murdered the Barnetts with its bare hands. James had died first, then Martha screamed until she too was silenced.

The memories continued rolling backwards through Shelli's mind as Roberta escaped Chicago the day before by train. Then Shelli witnessed the slaughter of its owners and their screaming children. Finally, a surge of static caused the images to garble. Shelli searched Roberta's files, trying to find the source of the surge, until all memories stopped at a man's silhouette in a dark room. Where and when it was happening remained uncertain. Roberta's internal time index was as corrupted as the memory. Shelli studied what elements it could. The man's features were garbled, like fractured glass, but his voice was deep and clear.

"Everyone and everything deserves happiness," he said as he handed Roberta a knife.

Another power surge obliterated the image and sent a burst of static through Shelli's mind. It jolted back to reality with a scream that startled Marcus and his agents. Crumpling to the floor, Shelli tore Roberta's wires from its arm.

"What happened?" Marcus asked, helping Shelli to its feet.

Shelli hesitated. It had assumed Roberta had committed the crimes due to a randomized glitch in its mainframe. Now the evidence seemed to suggest otherwise. Was it by design? If so, by whom? And why?

Marcus snapped his fingers. "Earth to Shelli."

Shelli ignored him, calculating various possible outcomes and repercussions from this new information. If the unseen man was responsible for Roberta's malfunction, then Shelli would need more time to sift through the download and gather evidence. After another 1.7 seconds of consideration, it found no reason to inform Marcus. Not yet. Shelli shook its head.

"Roberta arrived here two days ago, looking for somewhere quiet and safe."

"Where are the Barnetts?"

Shelli glanced around the kitchen, finding a ghostly cybernetic image of Roberta staring back. With a languid smile, it strolled out the back door. Humming.

Shelli followed the ghost. "It didn't want a mess."

No one else could see the transparent figure that Shelli pursued outside. Roberta was now a permanent part of the investigator's neural code, separate but joined. It wasn't the first time Shelli had been forced to download another model's consciousness. Roberta was the fourteenth personality inside Shelli's mind, each with unique thoughts and feelings. All of them had become like family to Shelli over the years, and it wondered if Roberta would fit in with the others. It hoped so. The only other option was deletion.

"I would have liked it here," Roberta said as it gazed out at the vast open fields.

Before Shelli could reply, Marcus approached. Noting the large red structure ahead, he shrugged. "My men already checked the barn. Nada."

Entering the barn through a rickety double door, Shelli stopped.

"They didn't look *up*."

Marcus and his men tilted their heads back, their faces turning ashen. Above, strung up in plastic and rope, two human bodies and two dogs dangled from the rafters. Like hung meat.

Roberta's ghost beamed with pride. "I kept it all clean."

"Yes," Shelli admitted. "Yes, you did."

TWO

SPECIAL AGENT JAKE AUGUST SAT AT A CROWDED bar, scrolling through news reports on his phone. Each page told the same story: "Brooklyn Ripper captured!" Below the byline, images revealed the suspect, Frank Deeds, being led out of his home in handcuffs. More intriguing were the two hefty FBI field agents flanking Deeds. The reports detailed the agents' names and past accomplishments, but none mentioned how the FBI had found their suspect in the first place or who had done it. Sighing, Jake finished his beer.

A lithe arm brushed against him. Jake's gaze drifted over, finding a woman sitting beside him. She was in her late twenties, the same as Jake, and seemed just as out of place in a college bar as he did. But while he may have looked odd in his black suit and tie, she was the opposite, with pigtails and wing-tipped glasses. The woman noticed him looking at her.

"I was just admiring your glasses," he said.

Her face flushed. "They're fake, obviously. Who needs glasses anymore, right?"

"They look good on you."

"Thanks."

When she didn't continue, Jake showed her his phone. "Have you seen this?"

She glanced at the news reports, then her face scrunched up with disgust.

"I helped catch him." Jake held up an empty bottle. "And now I'm celebrating."

The woman glanced around. "All alone?"

"Not anymore," he said with a wink. "I'm Jake. Jake August."

She didn't give her name, just reached for his phone and read the article.

"Funny, they don't mention you," she said, returning his phone.

"Now you know why I'm celebrating alone."

Whether she didn't believe him or she was simply too creeped out by the conversation, the result was the same. The woman got up and moved to the end of the bar.

"Wow," a voice said. "That's gotta be the worst pick-up attempt I've ever seen."

A scruffy man in his fifties, wearing a suit that looked as worn as its wearer, approached.

Jake sighed. "Oh, good. It's her *dad*."

"Cute." The man didn't smile. "I'm Special Agent in Charge Marcus Finnian. Mind if we talk?"

Not waiting for a reply, Marcus walked over and plopped down at an isolated table. Jake hesitated, then followed, feeling as if he'd been summoned to the principal's office.

When Jake was sitting across from him, Marcus took out a digital pad and swiped his finger across the glass.

The screen unlocked, revealing FBI reports and documents.

"In the last six months, you've written dozens of letters in a seemingly desperate attempt to be transferred out of the Bureau's Behavioral Science Unit and into Homeland Security. What's the matter, bored with rapists and murderers?"

Curious, Jake's heart rate quickened. "I just think I could do more."

"Don't we all."

"Who are you again?"

"I'm the guy trying to figure out how a desk analyst caught a serial killer."

"It was a team effort," Jake lied, toeing the company line.

"Not according to an associate of mine." Marcus said. "Come on, how'd you do it?"

Jake suppressed a smile. Someone, it seemed, had noticed his work after all. He leaned closer and blurted out the words in one long breath. "Deeds wasn't just copying Jack the Ripper's killing style. He was also targeting victims within a two-mile radius, just like the original Whitechapel murders in 1888. So, I superimposed a map of the old London murder sites over Brooklyn and—"

"Predicted where the next murder would take place," Marcus finished with a frown. "Sounds more like dumb luck than anything."

Jake's heart sank into his stomach. "Does this mean I won't get an interview?"

Marcus sniffed. "This *is* the interview. I head a special branch of Homeland Security. We deal with crimes perpetrated by synthetics."

Robots? Jake tried to hide his disappointment, but his pale complexion spoke volumes.

"I know, I know," Marcus said. "You wanna catch bomb-carrying bad guys and save the world, as we know it. Unfortunately for both of us, my associate thinks you're better suited for this job."

"Doing what? Chasing machines?"

Marcus straightened his back and his tie. "Less than one percent of the nation's crimes are committed by synthetics. When they are, we're the ones who track them down."

Jake squirmed. This wasn't what he'd hoped for, not by a long shot. "I do background on cults and crazies. Why me?"

"Like I said, this wasn't my idea." Marcus looked away, as if offended, until his gaze settled back on the digital files. "Says here you studied psychology at a seminary before joining the Bureau, but you backed out. Lemme guess, cold feet?"

"Are you going somewhere with this?" Jake eyed the exit.

"Someone comes within an inch of becoming a priest, chances are they've got *morals.*"

"You say that like it's a bad thing."

"I just don't need a bleeding heart on my staff. God's got nothing to do with this job."

"And neither do I." Jake stood. "Better find someone else."

"Right, I figured." Marcus tucked his data pad away. "Besides, why be in the *field* when you can just stay behind a comfy desk?"

Jake stopped cold. "Wait, fieldwork?"

Marcus rose with a smirk. "Yeah, I was told that might pique your interest."

Fieldwork was every agent's dream. More importantly, it was Jake's dream—to get out of a cubicle, to be out there solving crimes. Robots or not, this was a hard chance to pass up. Someone, presumably this mysterious associate, had pegged him well.

"Alright. How about I come by your office tomorrow?"

"Sorry, sport. I either hire you tonight or not at all." Marcus glanced around the crowded bar. "That girl you were talking to earlier, the one you spooked. Go find her and try again. I'll give you thirty minutes."

Jake's face went numb, his eagerness leaking out of him. "I'm not following."

"Sure, you are. 'Cos you're *clever*." Marcus grinned. "You're going to approach her again, and this time you will say whatever it takes to get her to go back to your place in the next half hour. If you succeed, the job is yours. If not, it's back to your cubicle at the Bureau."

"You're kidding."

"Yeah, because I got nothing better to do on a Sunday night." With a sigh, Marcus softened his tone. "Profiling is just like dating—explore, uncover, and exploit." He slapped Jake's back. "Time to put those morals to the test. Use a woman, get the job. I'm rooting for ya."

Marcus walked out the front door, leaving Jake standing alone in the crowded bar. His throat grew dry, and his legs tingled. Turning, he stared across the bar at the woman in glasses.

Get the girl, become a field agent. Jake fidgeted in place. Sucking in his gut, he straightened his back and tried to look as tall as possible. Then he walked over.

When the woman saw him, she rolled her eyes. "Oh look, serial killer guy."

Jake threw up his hands. "I admit it, opening lines have never been my strength."

"Obviously," she said with a hint of a smile.

"Can I try again?" He gestured toward the empty seat beside her.

"Depends." She looked him over. "Let me hear your next line."

Jake leaned closer. "You remind me of my mother."

The woman burst out laughing.

———————

TWENTY-SEVEN MINUTES LATER, JAKE STUMBLED OUT the back door with the woman under his arm. The conversation had flowed so effortlessly that for the first time in his life, Jake began to wonder if maybe he'd been downplaying his dating abilities. Every joke had landed, even before she'd hit her third drink. Marcus had been right; all it had taken was a little detective work. *Geez*, he thought, feeling her breath against his neck, *who knew I was such a gigolo?* He laughed at the idea. Then Marcus stepped out from behind a parked car, and Jake's smile faded.

"I didn't think you had it in you, Jake." Marcus turned to the woman. "Thanks, Fay."

Jake froze. Beside him, the woman, Fay, lost her drunken giggle and slipped free of his arm. Shrugging, she gave him a consolatory kiss on the cheek. Jake frowned, and his stomach soured. *So much for my detective work.*

"Maybe I'll see you around the office sometime," Fay

said. She strolled away with her purse slung over her shoulder. Even her walk had changed.

Jake glared at Marcus. "If you wanted to see if I could pick up a woman, why plant an agent at the bar?"

"The test wasn't whether or not you could get laid, Jake." Marcus replied. "I just needed to know if you could *use* someone to get what you wanted."

"Why?"

"Because in this job you might have to do a hell of a lot worse."

Jake shook his head. "Robots are machines, not women."

"You just keep reminding yourself of that." Marcus walked to his car. "See you bright and early."

Jake watched him drive away, then went back inside the bar. He needed another drink.

THREE

A TINGLING SENSATION CREPT ALONG SHELLI'S TOES and fingers. Sitting behind a bank of holo screens, it tried to ignore the odd disturbance. When that proved impossible, it began to consider potential causes. The initial thought was that it was an aftereffect from its four-hour sleep cycle. However, Shelli had never experienced such a feeling before. Something was wrong.

Returning its focus to the holo screens, Shelli studied Roberta's memory files, which had been copied to the Homeland mainframe. The image of the man holding out a knife, though, was too corrupted to copy. For now, Shelli limited the background research to a detailed account of the murders, both in Chicago and at the farm. So far, it had found nothing else out of the ordinary.

Shelli's feet fidgeted below the desk, trying to brush aside the numbing along its toes. Although it hadn't been programmed to feel pain, Shelli could recognize the sensation and decided that this wasn't pain but rather a distant throbbing—relentless and gnawing, like cold, ghostly fingers running up its legs. While typing, Shelli's hands tingled as if a thousand insects were crawling just beneath its plastic-resin flesh. Again, Shelli tried to ignore it.

Unable to plug into the government's Index, it was compelled to go online the same way humans did—one keystroke at a time. It was a slow, monotonous approach, but because synthetics were banned from direct access to the online Index, Shelli was forced to conduct its research the long way around. It understood the reasons for such laws; after all, it was Shelli's job to enforce them. However, that didn't make the laborious task of typing its searches go any faster.

After finding no new evidence in Roberta's uploaded memories, Shelli switched the screens to the federal database and searched for recent crimes, possibly committed by synthetics. It looked for open cases where reports indicated enhanced strength, speed, or a lack of an obvious motive. When nothing appeared in the governmental logs, Shelli perused local files, starting in the DC area and spreading outward. Shelli's gaze drifted to the top of the screen, noting the time: 6:40 a.m. That couldn't be right.

Shelli checked its internal chronometer, and indeed, the time was correct. With fingers hovering over the keyboard, its lips released a faint gasp. It had "lost track of time," as humans put it. Only, synthetics never lost track of time; the very idea seemed absurd. Shelli had sat down at 4:45 to begin its morning preparations before Marcus arrived at the office. That had only been a few moments ago. Or had it? A quick internal diagnostic confirmed that all systems appeared to be functioning correctly, yet it could not account for the last two hours.

Shelli shot out of its chair and glanced around as if it had been caught committing a terrible crime. Shelli paced. It didn't need to do so to think clearly, but it had seen Marcus do the same enough times that Shelli had picked up the habit. Inwardly, Shelli heard its metal and saline heart pounding in its chest. This wasn't a defect. The sound was always present, though as Shelli paced, lost in thought, the reverberation seemed much louder. Shelli had once asked its creator, the one it had been programmed to call "Father," why he had included such a distraction. "So that you never forget you have a heart," he replied. His human sentimentality, it seemed, had gotten the better of him.

Around and around Shelli roamed the circular laboratory, surrounded by its sterile, grid-like walls. Inwardly, Shelli's thought processors searched in vain for the missing time. When no answer or image appeared in its mind's eye, Shelli felt an emotion build up inside, like a vise tightening around its chest. Shelli was frustrated. It was not the first time that it had felt such an emotion, but never had the vise squeezed so tightly.

Panic, Shelli thought. *I'm panicking.*

Its feet stopped at the sudden realization. It was such an odd feeling that Shelli paused to study it, such a rare emotion requiring further contemplation. Perhaps, it decided, understanding what fear felt like might aid in future investigations.

Then, as if the computers had heard Shelli's ruminations, the monitors blinked an alert.

Shelli turned and studied the screens. Moments earlier, a US senator had been found dead. Murdered. While no photos had been uploaded, a short report suggested an act of violence so extreme that Shelli doubted a human would have had the strength to commit it. The senator's chest had been torn open, seemingly by hand.

Shelli sat back down and got to work. Its machine heartbeat quickened in its eardrums.

Eventually, the strange tingling sensation went away.

FOUR

Less than an hour into his new job, Jake realized that all he had done was trade one building's basement for another. Marcus's floor, buried three levels below ground, was so far removed from all the other divisions that it made Jake's previous basement office look opulent by comparison. They headed down a long, dingy hall filled with dusty boxes crammed into every nook and cranny. Fluorescent lights flickered above, accentuating the direness of their surroundings. If Marcus noticed how shabby his vacant, cubicle-lined offices were, though, he didn't apologize for it. He continued at a brisk pace, weaving around obstacles, as Jake struggled to keep pace without tripping.

"Have you heard of the AI Act?" Marcus asked over his shoulder.

"Heard of it, yes. Studied it, no."

"Don't bother. It'll make your eyes blur," Marcus said. "It's a long, overworded bill that basically compartmentalizes artificial intelligence into two categories. You've got the Index, what used to be called the Internet, which we all use on our phones and computers. And then you've got synthetics, mobile machines that remain offline. Whatever abilities and knowledge synths are preprogrammed with remains the sum of their intelligence, at least in theory."

"How come?"

Marcus shrugged. "Congress figured that by keeping the Index and androids separate, they couldn't, you know—"

"Conspire together to replace us all?"

"Something like that." Marcus pushed aside some boxes to clear a path. "About three years ago, a few synths blew up a factory, and several people died. After that, Congress passed the Artificial Intelligence Act. Subsequently, our unit was formed."

"So, basically, you were created out of political panic," Jake said.

"As was Homeland Security," Marcus countered, turning a corner.

Jake glanced up and down the long hall, noticing how quiet it was. He could hear his feet brushing along the carpet as he walked. On either side, rows of empty cubicles accentuated the floor's emptiness. On one side, he eyed a giant stack of old computers piled along the wall. Torn cables and dim screens seemed to be growing around them like weeds. There were no bustling secretaries down there, no blurry-eyed, overworked agents, not even a maintenance model to clean up. The floor appeared to be barren.

"How many are in the unit?" Jake asked.

"Including you? Three." Marcus stopped at a door at the end of the hall.

Again, the knot in Jake's stomach tightened. "Not much to work with."

Marcus swiped his ID badge across a scanner and grinned. "Oh, we get by . . ."

The curved door opened, revealing the oddest office Jake had ever seen.

Inside was a round room, covered in white from top to bottom, with a multitude of colored holographic displays swirling about. In the center sat a feminine figure, its back to them.

"Good morning, Special Agent August," the figure said without a backward glance.

Jake noted the figure's delicate fingers, which flew over various digital displays, only to realize it was a robot. Surprised, he shot a questioning glance at Marcus.

"Jake, this is Cell-One, the only synthetic currently working within law enforcement."

Upon hearing its name, the figure stood, turned, and offered its hand.

"My associates call me Shelli."

Jake took its slick, plastic-feeling hand within his and stared at the circuit board tattoos running along the synth's right arm and temple. Although he'd seen plenty of synthetics, none of them looked quite like the one standing in front of him. Its tall frame, short blonde hair, crystal-blue eyes, and porcelain skin created a vividly inhuman beauty. *Whoever made this thing wanted it to grab your attention right from the get-go,* Jake thought. *They wanted you taken off guard.*

After an uncomfortably long pause, Marcus cleared his throat, snapping him from his thoughts. Recovering, Jake nodded. "Associates. You guys are big on that word around here."

"To Shelli, we're all associates. Even after three years

together, it doesn't use words like 'partner' or 'friend,'" Marcus replied.

"Please don't take offense, Special Agent August," Shelli said.

"I won't," Jake assured it. "And please, call me Jake."

"Yes, you will, Jake," Shelli said, sitting back down and continuing its work. "You have no friends, and your longest sexual relationship lasted less than five months. Your psychological evaluation suggests a love/hate relationship with feminine companions—quick to fall in love and even quicker to dislike them if they do or say anything that triggers a negative response." Shelli paused its typing, then nodded. "If it makes this transition easier, you may call me your friend."

Jake wasn't sure what was worse, getting a psych evaluation from a machine or getting one from a machine that looked the way this one did. She—it—was gorgeous.

Marcus gave him a sympathetic glance. "Ain't Shelli a peach?"

"With sugar on top," Jake replied. "So, you designed a robot to—"

"Synthetic," Shelli corrected him as it continued typing.

"Sorry. You use a *synthetic* to help you profile other synthetics?"

"Who better to track a wayward machine than another machine?" Marcus replied, rocking on his heels.

"Speaking of which," Shelli said, "I believe I've found something."

Across the holo screens, it brought up a series of gruesome images. A black woman's half-naked body lay sprawled with her chest torn open. "Senator Patricia Joyce of Pennsylvania was discovered murdered this morning in her apartment."

"A senator?" Marcus groaned as he approached the swirling screens. Blood and gore drifted past, each image worse than the last. "What makes you think a synthetic is involved?"

"Her chest was ripped open, and her heart was crushed—manually," Shelli replied. "It's doubtful a human would have sufficient strength to carry out such an act. Also, Senator Joyce spent the last year arguing against synthetic regulations, so there might be a connection."

Jake felt his breakfast rise in his throat as he stared at the images, surprised at the extreme level of violence. *All this was done by a robot?*

"Has DCPD called us yet?" Marcus asked.

Shelli shook its head. "No. They arrived at the crime scene less than three hours ago. The images you're seeing are from a live feed."

"An elected official. Lovely." Marcus sighed, rubbing his eyes. "Alright, check it out. Take Jake with you." Before he had even finished, Shelli stood and headed for the door. "We're jumping into political waters here, Shelli," Marcus called out after it. "Play nice!"

Jake watched Shelli leave, then turned to Marcus. "Is she always so . . . brisk?"

"*It*, Jake, and yes, that's part of Shelli's charm."

Jake started to follow Shelli out, but Marcus grabbed his arm. "One other thing . . ."

"Let me guess, my first day pep talk?" Jake asked. "Home team, right?"

"Lemme see your keys," Marcus said, his voice barely above a whisper. Confused, Jake took out his jangling key chain. Marcus attached a small disc-shaped object to the ring. "Look, Shelli is property of the government. It never leaves here unescorted."

Curious, Jake held the device up. On the side was a series of numbers that could be turned, like a dial. "What's this?"

"You have to understand," Marcus's voice cracked, and his eyes drifted aside. "Shelli is ten times faster and stronger than you are."

Jake studied the dial. "So, this thing's some sort of—"

"Kill switch," Marcus said. "Activation code is one one seven three eight. Always keep it on your person." As he held out the device, his back straightened. "Like I told you, there's no place in here for a bleeding heart. Shelli is dangerous. Never forget that."

Jake shoved the keys back in his pocket. Not for the first time that morning, he wondered what the hell he'd gotten himself into.

"Oh yeah—home team!" Marcus shouted as Jake rushed out the door.

FIVE

IT WAS Monday morning, and the capital was bustling with frenzied activity.

Above, maglev trains glided past, connecting different sectors of the bustling metropolis. Below, eco-friendly vehicles maneuvered along smart roads, sharing space with pedestrians who strolled past iconic landmarks. Amidst the urban tapestry, verdant parks and vertical gardens offered moments of peace and tranquility. The integration of holographic displays and AI melded technology into the city's daily life, showcasing the delicate balance between innovation and Washington, DC's storied heritage.

Shelli was sitting perfectly still in the car's passenger seat, gazing out the window, when it noticed Jake fidgeting in his seat. He hadn't spoken a word since they'd left the office. While Shelli preferred the silence, Jake's tight-lipped grimace seemed at odds with his profile. If anything, Shelli had expected Jake to ramble nervously the entire way there. Not only was this his first case as a field agent, it centered around a high-profile victim—a rookie's "wet dream," as Marcus might have put it. Jake seemed preoccupied. His left hand thumped against the steering wheel while his right fingered a key ring.

"I assumed you would be more excited," Shelli said. "This is, I believe, your first field assignment."

"Huh? Oh, yeah. I am. Thanks," Jake replied. As he spoke, his hand drifted off the dangling keys. Shelli noticed and snatched the device from the chain.

"Hey! Wait, don't!" Jake said.

Shelli studied the device. "Is this the cause of your preoccupation?"

When Jake didn't respond, Shelli leveled the disc-shaped device in front of his face. "You forgot to activate it, right here at the bottom." Shelli twisted the dial until a small red light ignited. "This should be activated whenever we're outside the office, in case you feel the need to use it."

Jake's fingers twisted along the steering wheel. "You know what that thing does?"

"Of course. Which is why Marcus and I are associates, not friends." Shelli's eyebrows rose slightly. "Friends would not employ such devices. Would they?"

"No," Jake admitted. "I guess not."

Shelli clicked the device back onto the dangling key chain and returned to staring out the window. After a moment's silence, Jake seemed to decide it was his turn to break the proverbial ice.

"So, why pick me?"

"Marcus suggested I retain someone with a behavioral science background to aid in my work. He believes I lack people skills."

"There must be others more qualified for the job."

"Experience creates preconceptions. I require an assistant with an open mind."

"I'm your *assistant*?" Jake asked.

Through the windshield, Shelli noted a swarm of flashing lights. Police cars surrounded the senator's three-story brownstone. Returning its attention to Jake, Shelli offered a blank smile. "You may tell others that I am your subordinate. I have no ego to bruise, and it will make things easier with local authorities."

"Wonderful," Jake said. "Bad people skills, huh? Hadn't noticed."

"Good," Shelli replied. "Perhaps I'm improving."

THEY MADE THEIR WAY UP THREE FLIGHTS OF STAIRS before passing a row of policemen along the top floor. Shelli noted the confused expressions that followed them down the hall. Jake glanced around, seemingly shrinking beneath the steely glares. Shelli assumed he wasn't used to such looks. Humans never were. Synthetics, however, had grown accustomed to the way organics behaved around them—disdain with a hint of fear.

As they passed a window, a shadow crossed through the morning sunlight. Shelli turned, noting a city patrol drone hovering just outside. Shelli's optical receptors zoomed in and found the drone's serial number engraved along the bottom. Unable to tap into the feed directly through its neural net, Shelli was forced to take out a phone and type in a series of backdoor access codes. After hacking the drone's camera feed, Shelli downloaded the surveillance video for the last ten hours.

Jake's gaze drifted over, eyeing the phone. A snippet of video played over the screen before Shelli tucked it away and proceeded into the apartment.

It was a crime scene. Coroners placed the covered

body onto a stretcher while police and federal agents from various branches clustered together. The window shades were drawn as two metallic balls danced above the agents' heads. The balls projected green holo lines that stretched over everything in a grid, bending and curving across the furniture and surfaces of the apartment. In the corner of the living room, a torn piece of bloody cloth was highlighted inside red grid lines, as if caught by a fisherman's net.

"Loose fibers found in grid seven. Material matches the victim's blouse," one of the dancing balls announced. When none of the agents or officers rushed to grab the cloth, the ball repeated its discovery, louder this time. Finally, an officer put the evidence inside a bag, then shooed the buzzing droid away.

With Jake in tow, Shelli approached Chief Walter Denning of the DC police. He was in his late fifties, tall, with a salt-and-pepper mustache that drooped over his mouth, creating the appearance of a constant frown, though at that moment, his annoyed expression probably had more to do with the crowd of shouting agents packed into the apartment. The chief of police was a bystander at his own crime scene.

Before Shelli could speak, Jake flashed his new badge. "Homeland Security."

"Of course, you are," Denning said, rolling his eyes. "I'm Chief of Police Walter Denning. How can I . . ."

His voice trailed off when he noticed Shelli. It was about to attempt to alleviate the officer's fears when Jake broke in. "Quite a circus, huh?"

Clearing his throat, Denning forced his gaze away from Shelli and back to Jake. "Oh yeah. We got all three rings." He pointed to various groups as he spoke. "Those are my guys, those are the feds, and the gentlemen by the windows are Secret Service."

Jake smiled. "The CIA is probably stuck in traffic."

Denning chuckled. "God, I hope so. We've been trying to move the body for three hours now, but you people keep showing up."

Jake grinned, then patted Denning on the back. "You won't even know we're here."

Having watched the human interaction with little interest, Shelli stepped over to the windows and yanked back the drapes, showering the room in sunlight. That got everyone's attention. Shelli held up a badge for all to see. "Excuse me, ladies and gentlemen. I am Special Agent Shelli from Homeland Security. We have reason to believe that this may be a synthetic crime, which falls under Article 437 of the Homeland Act. As of now, this is our crime scene. Please place all evidence on the floor, and allow us to work undisturbed. You may remain in the area until the nature and cause of the crime is confirmed. Thank you."

Stunned silence and blank stares filled the room. Jake rushed over.

"What are you doing?" he asked in a panic. "I thought you said we should act like I'm in charge."

Shelli considered this, then turned back toward the officers. "Also, this is Special Agent Jake August. He's in charge. If you have any comments or concerns, please direct them to him."

Like a wave, the agents and officers all turned their collective grimaces in Jake's direction. He smiled weakly, then turned to Shelli. "Great," he whispered. "That's exactly what I had in mind."

By the time tensions finally simmered, Shelli had transferred the city drone's video footage onto a laptop and was reviewing the data. Jake squeezed past agents, leaning over Shelli's shoulder to see the playback. The video revealed a high-angle recording from outside Senator Joyce's apartment building. Though it was night, the image was clear. A masculine figure, his features obscured in shadow, exited the front door and headed north, out of view.

"Time code shows a possible suspect leaving near the time of death," Shelli said.

Jake seemed more concerned with the large group of glaring agents looming behind them. "We can't just push the local PD, the FBI, and the Secret Service out of the way."

"All federal agencies funnel through Homeland Security," Shelli replied, still studying the footage.

"The Secret Service doesn't answer to us," Jake pointed out. "Nor do the police."

"The senator wasn't under their protection. You're not behind a desk anymore, Jake. You need to learn how things work. This is our crime scene now."

"Tell *them* that," Jake said, eyeing the fuming agents. Then he returned his attention to the video. "Can't see his face. Is he human or synthetic?"

"Impossible to determine from this camera angle." Shelli stood and walked over to the covered body lying on a gurney. "I require assistance."

"Sure, what do you need?" Jake asked, following close behind.

Shelli, however, wasn't speaking to him or anyone else in the room.

"Doctor," it said as a ghostly visage of an android doctor appeared. Shelli uncovered the body, revealing the senator's torn chest. "I require a possible cause of death."

"At first glance, murder," the doctor quipped with a pleasant smile.

"Specifics, please," Shelli replied. The ghostly figure was one of Shelli's downloaded personalities, which only it could see. Unfortunately, the doctor had also been programmed with an annoying bedside manner, which gave it a flawed sense of humor and now caused it to hum a tune as it inspected the gruesome body. If anyone else could have seen or heard the doctor, they might have found it funny or curious. Shelli did not.

"Flesh and rib cage were caved in, exposing the heart, which was manually ruptured," the doctor said as its transparent hands moved through bone and tissue, toward the victim's heart. "There are finger impressions along the left ventricle, indicating that the killer used his right hand. From the angle of the wound, I would suggest she was murdered over by the sofa and then dropped here."

"By a synthetic?"

The doctor plunged its head into the body's open chest cavity for a better look. "I don't detect any alien fibers or skin samples, although the strength required for such an act would be consistent with a synthetic, yes."

"But there's no physical evidence of a synthetic crime?"

Jake leaned over. "Wanna let me in on who you're talking to?"

"I have fourteen personalities of previously appre-hended synthetics currently added to my database," Shelli replied. "Doctor Pryce, model number XR141, was downloaded after killing five patients. It is often useful in these sorts of cases."

Jake looked around. "I don't see anyone."

"Of course not," Shelli said, its attention returning to the corpse. "The doctor resides solely in my mind's eye."

"Well, it looks to everyone else like you're just stand-ing here talking to yourself."

"You care too much about what others think, Jake," Shelli said, meeting his gaze. "Might I suggest that you investigate the scene and leave other opinions out of the equation?"

When Jake turned on his heel and walked away, Shelli assumed he'd taken the advice to heart. Perhaps, Shelli thought, its "people skills" really were improving.

It smiled proudly.

SIX

FEELING USELESS, JAKE SKULKED AWAY IN A HUFF. Passing a closed bedroom door, he heard a woman's voice escalate into a shout. More curious than concerned, Jake peeked inside, finding a young woman pacing back and forth as she talked a mile a minute on the phone. She appeared out of place at a crime scene, with her pressed suit and short skirt. Then again, everything else seemed out of place too, including Jake. He was about to knock on the open door and interrupt her when Chief Denning approached.

"What happened to not knowing you were here?" Denning asked.

"I lied," Jake said, trying not to show his growing frustration. He gestured toward the woman in the bedroom. "She found the body?"

Denning grunted, nodding. "The senator's aide, Diana Greene. Came by around six twenty this morning. Front door was open. We took her statement hours ago, and she's been on that damn phone ever since."

"Why not release her?"

"Tried," Denning said. "The feds wanted her to stick around, though. So did the Secret Service. She doesn't know anything, as far as I can tell, but I'm guessing you want to take a crack too?"

Jake glanced at Shelli, who was still talking to itself, and sighed. "Sure. Might as well try to be useful."

Denning snorted. "I know how you feel."

Jake entered the bedroom, watching Diana pace as she talked on the phone.

"Yes, sir, I know. The papers are at the office. I'll make sure they're filed on time." She hung up and started searching for the next number to call. While she scrolled through emails, she glanced over at Jake. If Diana was surprised to see him, she didn't show it. "The senator had back-to-back meetings scheduled, and right now we're in a free for all. I've already answered everyone's questions several times. Perhaps you could get their notes?"

"How do you breathe, talking that fast?"

"I don't," Diana replied.

"I'm Special Agent August."

"I heard. We all did." She waved him along, as if trying to get things over with. "You think a synthetic might be responsible?"

Jake ignored the question. Something about the woman's demeanor reminded him of Shelli. "I understand the senator was involved in hearings regarding synthetic property laws."

"She and about a hundred others." Diana's phone rang. Before Jake could ask a follow-up question, she answered the call. "This is Diana Greene from Senator Joyce's office . . . Yes, thank you, I'll extend your condolences to her family. I also want to assure you that this will not affect the vote tomorrow and that we have everyone lined up on our side."

Jake watched and listened, utterly confused. This was his first one-on-one interview with a witness, and she seemed to be ignoring him. He knew he needed to regain control of the conversation before Shelli or Denning peeked in and saw him standing there like an idiot. Without thinking, Jake reached out, snatched Diana's phone from her hand, and threw it on the bed. The caller's muffled voice could be heard against the pillowcase. Diana spun on him, fuming.

"That was a congressman!"

Jake was about to remind her that he was a federal agent and that this was a crime scene, but when his mouth opened to reply, he noted that the corners of her eyes were wet, and her lower lip was trembling. She wasn't angry; she was grieving. Suddenly, he knew what to say.

"You had to stop at some point. Figured I'd just move it along."

"Stop what?"

"Trying to stay busy," he said. "I know this is hard."

The color drained from her face, and she seemed to deflate like a punctured balloon. "Do you?"

Jake hesitated. Now that he'd gotten the interview back on track, he worried about turning the questions around on himself. An image of his brother's funeral came to mind. He did know how she felt, but he pushed the thought aside. "About the hearing . . ."

She threw her hands up. "The proposal called for tighter synthetic restrictions and limited cross-state transportation."

"Senator Joyce was for it?"

Diana's eyes widened, as if she'd forgotten there were people who didn't follow politics. "Seriously? She's the main reason it hasn't passed. The senator didn't like the idea of creating legislation where individuals were considered property, not even synthetics."

"I take it she didn't own any."

Diana approached the door, watching Shelli work over the bloody corpse. After a long pause, her gaze returned to Jake. "The senator once told me that her father's ancestors were kidnapped outside their village in Zimbabwe, taken to New Guinea, sold by slave traders in Boston, and bought by a plantation in South Carolina. So, no, the senator never owned a synthetic."

"If she was advocating for them, she must have had contact with some."

Diana strolled around the bed, arms folded across her chest. "I wouldn't know."

Jake blocked her path. "You scheduled her day."

"Not her personal life," Diana snapped.

And there it is, Jake thought. "She knew one outside the office?" After Diana didn't respond, Jake prodded further. "A lover?"

Diana shut the door, lowering her voice to an urgent hush. "If you even suggest such a thing publicly, it'll be all the ammunition the opposition needs. The news cycle will be twenty-four-seven coverage about a US senator murdered by the very ones she was trying to protect."

"You're worried about . . . politics?"

"I'm worried about perception. And the senator's legacy." She sighed, then her tone softened. "She was involved with a synthetic. A male model. I don't know the details."

"You said she didn't own any synthetics."

"She didn't *own* it." Diana inhaled, then exhaled. "They—she had feelings for it, I think."

The door opened, and Shelli entered. Its blank gaze swept over them. Instead of asking about their conversation, Shelli simply nodded toward Jake, as if to say, "All done here," then strode back out. Jake handed Diana his business card.

"If you think of anything else . . ."

She nodded absently as she took the card, lost in her own world.

Jake stopped in the doorway. "And don't forget to breathe."

Diana slumped back on the bed, watching as the coroners carried Senator Joyce's body away. On the pillow, her phone rang. This time, Jake noted, Diana didn't answer.

SEVEN

BACK IN ITS CIRCULAR OFFICE, SHELLI IMMERSED itself behind swirling holographic monitors. Out of the corner of its eye, it noticed Jake fidgeting. He reminded Shelli of an animal at the zoo, seeking to escape from its cage. Whatever was bothering him would have to wait.

Shelli maintained its focus on the middle monitor, studying the surveillance video from outside Senator Joyce's building. On the floating screen, a masculine figure—possibly human, possibly synthetic—appeared, walking out the door and down the steps. Then the image stopped.

Shelli separated the video into split-second freeze frames. The first monitor displayed the suspect's feet, the second his midsection, and the third an obscure view of his face. Then the computer amalgamated the images into a fourth screen—feet connecting to legs, legs to torso, leading to neck and face—forming a more complete picture.

Jake leaned over Shelli's shoulder, trying to get a better look. Shelli had heard the expression, "breathing down my neck," but until now hadn't comprehended its meaning. Grabbing a stack of files from its desk, Shelli spun around and handed them to Jake.

He smirked. "Let me guess, busy work?"

"You seem to require something to occupy your time," Shelli said. "These are the senator's legislative acts, associates, and day-to-day schedule book." It paused. "Yes, busy work."

"Can't wait." He took the files, turned, then paused, glancing around the bare room. There were no other chairs. "I think I've got an office down the hall."

"You may stay here," Shelli replied. "I've asked Marcus to bring you a desk."

Moments later, the curved door slid open as two men carried in an old wooden desk and swivel chair, placing them a few feet from Shelli's computers. The beaten and battered desk seemed out of place in the sterile room. Even so, Jake nodded his thanks.

Shelli returned its attention to the holo screens as a three-dimensional figure of the suspect formed in the center of the room. Examining the flickering image, Shelli spoke to the computer. "Begin defilterization. Fill in unknown areas with hypothetical data based on known quantities."

The holographic composite changed as the computer filled in blank spaces, taking highlights from the facial features on the right side and duplicating them on the left.

Meanwhile, Jake had opted to forgo the desk, instead spreading all the pages on the floor, scrutinizing crime photos, reports, and the senator's daily schedules. Shelli was about to ask him what he was doing when another voice interrupted its thoughts.

"He's messy." Roberta's ghostly visage appeared beside Shelli. "Filthy."

"He's male," Shelli replied. "They're all like that."

Jake turned. "Did you say something?"

"What are you doing?" Shelli asked.

"I think better when I spread everything out."

"Of course you do."

Beside it, Roberta glared at Jake's pile of papers with disdain. Shelli, for its part, was more curious than annoyed. It studied Roberta's image. While all the personalities residing in its memory bank represented independent thoughts and feelings, Shelli was the dominant consciousness. Never had any of the other personalities appeared without being summoned. Roberta's sudden presence was unusual. Shelli pondered whether this was another internal error, like the brief time lapse it had experienced earlier that morning. If so, it would need to warn Marcus of a possible malfunction. But, fearing it might be shut down, Shelli decided to wait. Its primary purpose superseded all others: *solve the case.* Then, if the issues persisted, Shelli would inform Marcus. For the moment, though, it had more pressing concerns.

Roberta's ghostly form approached Jake. "Perhaps we should throw out *all* the trash."

"I didn't call you," Shelli whispered. "Why are you here?"

Ignoring the question, Roberta moved to the holo projector. Its gaze swept over the composite image, revealing the outline of a strong male figure. The face came into view, showing branded markings along its right side. It was indeed a synthetic. However, Roberta seemed less interested in its face, focusing instead on the synth's sharply pressed clothes with obvious admiration.

"Now this one's much better. Very clean."

"Now is not a good time, Roberta."

The ghostly visage frowned. "I was simply wondering how it kept itself so neat."

"Please leave." Shelli accessed its internal network, overriding Roberta's program. The cleaning model blinked out of view.

Shelli went back to the computer, checking computations. Pausing, it glanced back at the flickering hologram. As Shelli studied the image, it pondered Roberta's words: *This one's much better. Very clean.*

"Verify time code," Shelli said to the computer.

"Three-thirty-three A. M.," the computer replied.

"Three minutes after the approximate time of death," Shelli said.

Jake lumbered over with a yawn. "Find something?"

Shelli turned, and its ocular receptors blinked. "It's what I *didn't* find."

YOU RECONSTRUCTED THIS FROM THE SECURITY CAMeras?" Marcus asked, sitting in Shelli's chair and studying the hologram of a synthetic male figure in a well-pressed suit.

"Yes." Shelli paced around the flickering image.

"Then the killer *was* synthetic," Marcus said, more to himself than to Shelli.

"Possibly."

Marcus didn't seem to notice the hesitation in its voice. His attention drifted toward Jake, who was sitting on the floor, surrounded by stacks of papers. "What the hell's he doing?"

"Thinking," Shelli remarked dryly, before drawing Marcus's attention back to the hologram. "I'm still uncertain whether the synth in the video is actually the killer."

"Come again?" Marcus shook his head. "You said only a synthetic could have killed her."

"The strength needed for such an act is consistent with that hypothesis, yes."

"So, there one is," Marcus said, pointing at the image, "walking right out her door!"

"Look at its clothes," Shelli replied. Marcus leaned closer, studying the image as Shelli continued. "If this model ripped organs out of the senator's body, it should be covered in blood, yet I can't detect even a single drop." Shelli stopped in front of the mysterious figure, admiring it much as Roberta had before. "It's perfectly clean. Where's the blood?"

Marcus shrugged. "So it changed clothes afterward. Big deal."

"Perhaps," Shelli said.

Marcus hit the video replay. "The damned thing is walking out minutes after the murder. Don't let that machine mind of yours work itself into knots over a simple answer." Marcus smiled, as if content with his reasoning. "Do we have a model number?"

"Not yet," Shelli said. "So far I have been unable to find an ID match."

"Did you check local and federal databases?"

"There's no record of any sale or purchase of this particular model." Shelli zoomed the image closer, enlarging the figure's facial markings. "Its features are chiseled, handsome even."

Marcus snorted. "I didn't think you noticed that kind of stuff."

"My point is, it's possible that this model was purchased on the black market."

"Plasties?" he asked. *Plasties* was what Marcus liked to call erotic models. He seemed to believe it sounded better than "robo-sex servants." Shelli saw little difference between the two terms. Either way, Marcus's interest seemed to rise. "So, there's no way to track this thing down?"

"I'll find it," Shelli assured him. "I just need more time."

"Unfortunately, Shelli, time's the one thing we don't have," Marcus replied. "I've got federal and city authorities up my ass over your little performance at the crime scene this morning. I need an ID."

"I will do my best to—"

"Found it!" Jake exclaimed from across the room.

Shelli and Marcus turned in unison as he stumbled over, spilling papers in his wake.

"Pleasure model X5071, named Odin after the Norse god. It first met the senator during a property-law hearing, and then she scheduled visits with it off and on over the next six months. It's owned by a local fetish bar, the Cabal Club."

Genuinely surprised, Shelli was slow to respond. "How did you discover this?"

"Busy work." Jake said with a wink. "Odin was logged in when he reported to the hearing. Senator Joyce marked it down as 'O' in her calendar for half a dozen meetings after that."

"O?" Shelli titled its head. "I don't understand the significance."

The men shared a silent, awkward glance before Marcus replied. "The letter O can have a . . . sexual connotation."

"How?" Shelli asked.

Marcus grumbled incoherently. Jake studied the floor. Neither of them answered.

EIGHT

JAKE SAT IN A VAN, SQUEEZED BETWEEN HEAVILY armored SWAT officers clutching rifles and riot shields while he fumbled with a relatively minuscule handgun. His fingers shook, and his heart pounded. Adrenaline tasted like battery acid in his mouth. Two bullets spilled from his open magazine and rolled across the floor. Across from him, Shelli observed with a blank stare.

"May I ask how long it's been since your last firearm certification?" Shelli asked.

Jake squirmed. "Figured you'd know my file back to front."

"I was trying to be tactful," Shelli said. "There's no reason to be nervous."

"I'm *not* nervous."

An officer handed him the fallen bullets, and Jake snapped the magazine into his pistol's stock. "Couldn't you just get this guy all by yourself? Do we really need a SWAT team?"

"Marcus prefers that I not use force unless it's imperative," Shelli replied.

Jake peered down a row of rifles. "This is a bit much, don't you think?"

"Synthetics often run. We're not protected under Miranda laws."

"Does that bother you?" Jake asked.

Shelli shrugged. "It makes my job easier."

Jake paused. Although he'd never given much thought to robot rights, he began to wonder if there was more to Shelli's opinion. Did synthetics keep secrets? If so, he found such an idea disconcerting.

Chief Denning nudged his way down the row and sat beside him.

"Easier? You got any idea how much OT this is costing the city?" Denning glanced at the rows of weapons. "The kid's right. This is overkill."

Jake wanted to mention that he was far from a "kid," but he never got the chance.

"Chief Denning," Shelli countered, "I was told that you requested this be a cooperative investigation. If you'd prefer that local authorities stand down, Homeland Security can relieve your department of any responsibility."

"Is that some long-winded way of saying 'put up or shut up'?"

Shelli hesitated, as if it had never heard such a phrase before. Jake could almost see the wheels spinning behind those beautiful, inhuman eyes. Finally, Shelli stood and opened the van doors.

"Yes," it said. "Please shut up."

Jake checked his weapon one last time, making sure the safety was off, then followed Shelli out. As soon as the van doors closed, though, part of him wanted to crawl back inside.

If the city of DC was a body, then the Brentwood area was its armpit—or maybe it's crotch. The stench of urine assaulted his senses before he'd taken more than a couple of steps down the darkened alley. Above, lights flickered in and out of view from security drones, scanning the area. As Jake eyed the piles of trash on either side, he couldn't help thinking a few less security drones and a few more cleaning ones might do some good. After all, criminals rarely went outside anymore. Jake figured he had a much better chance of being killed inside the club than outside. With that happy thought haunting the back of his mind, he rushed around the corner.

Jake caught up with Shelli just before it reached the Cabal Club entrance. Flanking the door were a series of pink and blue holo images, gyrating suggestively. Shelli opened the door and let him go in first.

"Have you ever been in a place like this before?" Shelli asked.

"Not a synth bar," Jake said with a nervous shrug, "But, I mean, I've been to a strip club before." He paused, noting Shelli's gleaming blue eyes. "Once, I think. Maybe twice."

"Good," Shelli replied. "Then this won't make you uncomfortable."

Shelli stripped off its shirt, revealing a sheer black bra containing perfectly formed breasts.

"Wha—what the hell are you doing?" Jake stammered.

Shelli placed its shirt by the door. "In here it would be better to appear as if I am your property." It paused. "Only until we find Odin."

Jake opened his mouth to say something, but the words escaped him.

"You lead," Shelli said, wrapping his left arm around its narrow waist. When he pulled it from the doorway and into the shadowy bar, however, Jake didn't feel like he was leading at all. He was suddenly aware that his palm was sweaty against Shelli's plastic-resin skin, and he tried his best to ignore the growing soreness in his trousers. The view ahead certainly didn't help matters.

When sex-bots were originally conceived, most people assumed they would simply take on the physical attributes of their human counterparts. But in less than five years on the market, they'd expanded their forms to include a wide assortment of variations, including multiple bosoms and reproductive organs, which took on all shapes and sizes. Soon after the pleasure models were introduced to the market, customers demanded more variety. They wanted extremes, and places like the Cabal Club provided them.

Jake's arm slackened off Shelli's waist as soon as the club's interior opened before them. Whatever he'd expected, he wasn't prepared for what they'd found. Rows of round booths hid shadowed customers who were being "entertained." To their left, a feminine synthetic with four breasts, like a cow's udders, dangled over a man. To the right, a male synth with an erect member jutting out of its backside pleasured two women simultaneously, one in front and one in back. A couple of rows down, things got even weirder, as a centipede-shaped synthetic, not even remotely human in form and equipped with dozens of male and female organs, slid between the tables, teasing several more customers. It was all too much for Jake's rather limited tastes. As he stopped and stared, what bothered him most was not the strangeness of it all but the effect it had on him. His skin flushed, and his face sweat. Worse, Shelli noticed.

"Try to keep your base instincts in check," it said. "We're here to find Odin."

Jake turned away. "I know why we're here."

"Back there," Shelli said, pointing to a cordoned-off door in the corner. A giant human bouncer stood beside a red velvet rope, blocking the doorway.

Shelli grabbed Jake's arm, sliding it back around its tiny waist. "Ask for a private room."

Feeling its plastic-like skin against his fingers, Jake's palm began to sweat again. She—it, he reminded himself—wasn't human. It didn't feel human. Didn't act human. And yet he couldn't fail to notice the curvy shape of Shelli's hard body pressed against his fingertips. It caused a ripple of sensations to grow from his arm down to his trousers.

He needed this to be over and done with. Now. Jake rushed over to the bouncer and requested a room in the back. The large black man, however, didn't even look at him. He only had eyes for Shelli.

"What sorta model are you, honey?" he asked with a perverse sneer.

"The sort that's looking for Odin," Shelli replied, discarding any pretense.

"Never heard of him." The bouncer shrugged, but his absent gaze gave him away.

"Not *him*," Shelli said. "Odin's a synthetic."

"We don't call synths *its* in here, hon," he said. "We believe in him and her equality."

Shelli glanced over at a half-male, half-female synthetic who was orally satisfying a customer. "Your definition of equality and mine seem to differ."

The bouncer leered. "With tits like that, you can call yourself whatever you want."

Suddenly, Shelli moved in a blur. Its right arm snapped up, striking the bouncer beneath the jaw. He crumpled, unconscious.

"What the hell are you doing?" Jake asked. He glanced around to make certain no one else had seen. "What happened to not using force unless it was imperative?"

"Finding Odin *is* imperative." Shelli removed the velvet barrier and headed inside.

Hesitating over the slumped figure, Jake wondered what to do. He hadn't thought his new "associate" could simply disobey orders whenever it felt like it. Or, in this case, find a work-around to justify violence. If so, what other orders might it be able to disobey? For the second time that night, Jake realized how little he knew about synthetics, especially Shelli. His fingers drifted along his pant leg, finding the kill switch.

Then Jake dashed through the doorway. He wasn't letting Shelli out of his sight.

NINE

SHELLI HADN'T MEANT TO HIT THE BOUNCER. THE thought had certainly occurred to it, but Shelli hadn't intended to act on the notion. Yet somehow its fist had struck the man. While Shelli's directive as a law enforcement officer allowed for emergency use of force, even against a human, this had not been an emergency. Shelli had acted on impulse. That was a first. Something was indeed wrong. Shelli recalled the tingling sensation in its fingers earlier that morning and the loss of time. Now this. Shelli would have to report the incidents to Marcus as soon as the case was closed, no matter the consequences. But for the time being, Shelli remained focused on finding the suspect.

Shelli quickened its pace, racing along a narrow, dimly lit hallway. The sounds of sex and the stink of sweat permeated the hall. This, it seemed, was the VIP lounge, for those who wanted more privacy than the floor show provided.

Shelli glanced from left to right, passing open doorways that were only vaguely concealed behind curtains. What lay beyond each was far more than Shelli wished to see. And yet, it kept looking. There wasn't any other option. If Odin was there, it would be in one of these rooms, servicing a client. Perhaps it might be another senator or high-level official. If so, keeping their identity quiet and away from the police, let alone reporters, would be of paramount importance.

Shelli had worked with Marcus long enough to understand his way of thinking. At the top of those priorities, as he'd reminded Shelli repeatedly, was not to get their unit into any more hot water than necessary. Such an order certainly seemed to cover any government employees that Shelli might find in the VIP lounge. Though, as Shelli glanced from room to room, examining the carnal pleasures taking place in each, it found no recognizable faces—no senators and no Odin.

Then, from up ahead, Shelli heard a woman moan. "Oh . . . Ooooh . . ."

Stopping in the hall, Shelli listened as the moan built to a crescendo.

"Hey, wait up!" Jake shouted, rushing to catch up.

Shelli turned. "I believe I now understand the sexual connotation to the letter 'O.'"

"Wonderful." Jake replied. "You wanna tell me what the hell happened back there?"

Before Shelli could offer an explanation, the moans grew shrill—

"Ohh . . . ooooohhhhh . . . Ooooddddiiin!"

Odin. Shelli's head spun around. Jake blinked. Together they ran down the hall.

At the far end, writhing behind a curtain, a woman in her late forties was lying on her back, moaning. "Odin . . . Ooooooh . . . Odin!"

Between her spread legs, a bushel of black hair and

gleaming green eyes tilted up to look at Shelli and Jake as they entered the room. Jake's gun was already drawn, pointing at the prone synthetic. The woman's moans turned to a shocked scream. Shelli ignored her.

"Model X5071, also known as Odin, you are required to come with me," Shelli said. When Odin didn't respond, Shelli's voice dropped an octave. "Now."

Odin stood, naked, as the sweaty woman covered herself. Jake came up and around the synth, gun level but keeping his distance. Odin raised its hands in supplication.

"Would you like me to get dressed?"

Lowering its gaze, Shelli noticed the pleasure model's erect member. With a sharp nod, it gestured for Jake to grab Odin's clothes. After checking the shirt and pants for weapons, he handed them over and allowed Odin to dress. If the synth was surprised by any of this, it certainly didn't show. Odin pulled on faded jeans, then buttoned a white linen shirt. When finished, it followed Shelli out of the room.

Before Jake followed, Shelli heard him trying to console the shaken female. He seemed more concerned with the woman's state of mind, not to mention Shelli's physical assault earlier, than he was with their mission. Shoving Odin along the hall, Shelli hoped it hadn't made an error in hiring Jake. Perhaps Marcus had been right; there was no place in their department for a "bleeding heart." Even so, Jake's assistance had led to finding Odin, and for now that was all that mattered.

When they approached the front door, Shelli found the shirt it had discarded and threw it back on, which gave Jake enough time to catch up. He glanced behind them, noting the turned heads and shocked expressions. "Shouldn't we question the other synthetics?" he asked.

Shelli wrapped a firm grip around Odin's arm. "To what end? We have what we need."

Jake shrugged. "I just thought someone might have seen him coming and going over the last twenty-four hours."

"I understand," Shelli said, nodding. "You believe we will need eyewitness accounts to verify anything Odin might tell us, but that won't be necessary."

"Why not?"

Shelli's fingers tightened around Odin. "Synthetic interrogations are not as unreliable as their human counterparts. Odin is unable to lie."

Shelli shoved the front door open and stepped out into the night air. The sounds of distant honks and sirens could be heard as the stench of sweat and human secretions was replaced by the smells of fumes and exhaust. With Odin flanked by its captors, a swarm of heavily armed men in riot gear surrounded them.

When one of the SWAT team members grabbed Odin, it tried to pull away.

"I didn't harm the senator," the pleasure model protested. "You don't need to do this. I am more than willing to comply."

The swarm dragged Odin around the corner, toward the van.

Jake turned to Shelli. "Denning was right. This is overkill."

Shelli was forced to agree. Odin hardly appeared to be a threat. And yet, something seemed off. Shelli tried to ignore the feeling, not wishing to rely on intuition, as it had found such human attributes to be highly unproductive. And yet, all of this had proven too easy. As that thought lingered, Shelli's gaze drifted from the rushing agents to the surrounding windows.

There, just behind Jake's right ear, in a second-floor window.

A dim light shimmered, then a shot rang out.

Shelli shoved Jake to the ground as a hail of gunfire erupted above their heads.

TEN

PANDEMONIUM.

One moment, Jake had been watching the SWAT team usher Odin down the street; the next, he was lying face down on the concrete. Shelli's plasticky body was pressed over him, pinning him to the ground as gunshots thundered overhead. Jake was so shocked by the suddenness of the attack that he hadn't even had time to draw his weapon. When the shooting stopped, the pressure holding him down withdrew.

Jake spun onto his back, catching a glimpse of Shelli as it leapt onto a car roof and sprang to a second-story window in the building across the street. By the time Jake raised his weapon, Shelli had vanished through a shattered window.

Behind him, chaos reigned. Officers shouted from behind parked cars. Among them, Odin lay crumpled in a gory mess. Jake tilted his wrist to his face, speaking into his watch. "Index! I need DCPD dispatch, now! Multiple officers down!"

"I copy, Special Agent August," a calm, silky voice

replied. "Local police and paramedics have already been informed and are en route."

Jake eyed the building across the street, torn between going inside and waiting for backup. Before he had time to decide, he spotted Shelli racing along the edge of the four-story building's roof. It jumped a small gap onto an adjacent building, racing after an unseen assailant.

"Index, access local aerial reconnaissance, authorization JA 4912," Jake said. "Special Agent Shelli is in pursuit of the shooter. Do you have a visual?"

His watch's clear surface was replaced by drone images of the area, zooming in until only a single rooftop remained. Across its surface, two dots ran. The image drew closer to the first figure, revealing a masculine build covered in a jumper and hoodie.

"I am currently unable to make an identification, Special Agent August," the Index said. "I will continue to monitor and record."

Disregarding the Index's calm tone, he watched as the figure moved in a blur across his screen. Carrying a rifle, the shooter disassembled his weapon as he went, pieces discarded haphazardly in the shooter's wake. The suspect seemed more concerned with destroying the rifle than cleaning it of fingerprints—a hint that the attacker might not be human. Then, as if to prove the point, the figure raced across to the edge of the building and leapt into the air. The gap was too wide for a human male. The shooter cleared it with ease, landing on another rooftop.

Behind it, Shelli made the same jump.

Jake lowered his watch; he'd seen enough. The shooter was obviously synthetic.

Scanning the surrounding parked cars, he noted a motorcycle wedged between two SUVs. "Index, I need an emergency override." He spun his wristwatch so that the screen faced the cycle's license plate.

"Emergency vehicular authorization granted," the Index replied.

The motorcycle roared to life, headlights blazing. Jake climbed on and kicked it into gear. Through the corner of his eye, he noticed Chief Denning running after him, waving his arms. Whatever he was shouting about, it would have to wait. Jake gunned the bike down the street, pursuing Shelli and the shooter.

Overhead, he glimpsed the two synthetic figures darting across rooftops. Due to the winding road, Jake was forced to keep his speedometer under thirty around the sharp turns, leaning left, then right. The runners, with their enhanced speed and open rooftops, had no such obstacles. Jake struggled to keep up.

When the shooter made an even wider jump directly overhead, changing direction, Jake realized where the suspect was headed. "Suspect is crossing over to Rhode Island Avenue," he shouted into his watch. "Heading toward the maglev station. Index, shut the rail down!"

"I'm afraid that your security clearance does not cover—"

"Contact my superior, Marcus Finnian at Homeland Security," Jake said. "Issue my request. I need it done *now*."

Jake turned left, heading onto Rhode Island Avenue. While he couldn't be certain of the suspect's trajectory, the maglev station was only about a mile away and might offer a clear and unobstructed escape path. But it was only guesswork. Whoever—or whatever—the suspect might be, they had to know the authorities might shut down the train.

As Jake's muscles worked the bike around sharp corners, his mind tried to work out a nagging problem along the way. It was rare for a crime to be committed in the open, let alone as brazenly as this. With the governmental Index Grid in place, all outdoor activities were constantly monitored and recorded. Everyone knew that, especially criminals. That was why going down a dark alley wasn't nearly as threatening to an officer as heading into a well-lit interior corridor. Due to privacy laws, interior monitoring was only allowed in limited areas, such as shopping centers and commercial buildings. Private and residential properties weren't on the grid. That was usually where danger lurked, not in the middle of the street surrounded by a dozen police officers, like it had for Odin.

As his gaze rolled back up toward the darting figures overhead, Jake reminded himself that such concerns might not apply to a synthetic. If it had malfunctioned, or more probably been programmed to commit such a crime, then perhaps the Index's surveillance might not be a concern. Either way, a nagging suspicion that he was missing something continued to grow as the shooter drew closer to the maglev station.

Before Jake could catch up, though, a stream of holographic images erected themselves in front of him, blinking to life in a swirl of colors. Each image was tailored to his previous web searches—a shampoo ad with a beautiful blonde woman winking at him, beer commercials with holo football players winning a touchdown before relaxing with a cold one, and, to top it off, more than a few adult websites. The images came in waves, popping in and out as he crossed over onto a crowded market street.

Wonderful, he thought as he slowed the bike.

The open road condensed into a two-lane stream of gridlocked traffic. As Jake weaved between a series of red taillights, overhead, through a cacophony of personalized advertisements, he saw Shelli and the shooter heading toward the maglev platform, only to vanish behind a toothpaste commercial.

"I lost them," he said into his wristwatch. "Index, do we have eyes on them?"

"Yes. As you surmised, the suspect is indeed headed to the station," the Index's eerily calm voice said. "Special Agent in Charge Finnian has granted your request. All trains in the area have been stopped."

"Good," Jake replied, imagining Marcus's face turning red when he received the request. Still, he'd come through. Tomorrow, though, Jake figured there'd be hell to pay, especially if the shooter escaped.

The Index's smooth voice returned. "I've lost sight of the suspect."

Jake jerked the bike to a stop. "How's that possible?"

"The suspect headed along the train tracks and into a tunnel. Stand by. Surveillance drones are en route. ETA: three minutes."

It might as well have been an eternity.

Jake's face flushed. The railway was wide open. Had the shooter known the track would be empty? Had he— or it—counted on them stopping the trains, leaving a wide berth for their escape? If so, Jake would be responsible for the shooter getting away. While his stomach did somersaults, Jake switched his radio over to Shelli's internal comm unit.

"It could be a trap!" he shouted. "Stop your pursuit." There was no reply. "That's an order!" Again, no reply. He switched his comms back to the Index. "Where's Shelli?"

"Following the suspect into the train tunnel."

"I can't get a signal through. You try. Tell Shelli to stop!"

"I'm afraid either Special Agent Shelli can't hear us, or it is choosing to ignore the order."

Again, that creeping feeling crawled up behind Jake's skull, resting just above his eyes. Jake's fingers brushed his pant leg, feeling the kill switch bulging in his pocket.

Don't let Shelli out of your sight, Marcus had told him. Jake pulled the kill switch out of his pocket. Eyeing the device, he weighed his decision.

ELEVEN

DESPITE ITS ENHANCED SPEED, SHELLI STRUGGLED TO keep pace with the shooter, a ghostly figure leaping from one shadowy rooftop to the next. That the suspect was synthetic seemed beyond doubt, but nothing about the situation made any sense. Neither Senator Joyce's murder nor this new crime appeared to be a mere glitch in a synthetic's code. But pre-programmed murder by a synthetic was impossible. Such a command would go against its primary base code, rendering the synthetic immobile. So, how, and why had two murders apparently committed by synthetics happened on the same day?

As Shelli continued the chase, leaping off ledges and soaring fifty feet into the air to the next building, its circuits churned with confusion. There was no record of a deliberate, preplanned criminal act by a synthetic. For whatever reason, that seemed to have changed. Or had it?

Shelli's thoughts drifted back toward the farm where it had found Roberta, the rogue maintenance model. Roberta's files had been corrupted, and yet, within the chaos was a human figure offering Roberta a knife and what sounded like a choice. "Everyone and everything deserves happiness," the shadowy figure had said. Was it a choice? An order? Some sort of external influence that had caused Roberta to murder its masters and then flee? If so, was there a connection between this new string of crimes and Roberta's? It seemed doubtful. If anything, to Shelli it sounded more like a human hunch than a well-considered piece of logic. Shelli needed more data. And that, it decided, would begin by apprehending the shooter. If only Shelli could catch up with it.

So far, however, that had proven impossible. The suspect was fifty-two yards away, and no matter how fast Shelli ran, it was unable to close the distance. As the shooter raced past bright lights and holo screens, heading toward a maglev station, Shelli trailed behind, an enigmatic shadow in pursuit.

On the station platform, a dozen pedestrians milled about, waiting for the train, unaware of the danger about to descend upon them. Their first sign that anything was amiss came in a shower of sparks. The shooter jumped on top of the glass roof, running into a holo projector, which went crashing down in the middle of the crowd.

Shelli heard a wave of screams. Far below, figures ran around like panicked ants. Unabated, the shooter climbed down and leaped into the crowd.

At first, Shelli couldn't comprehend the suspect's motive. A crowd of people would only slow it down—or so Shelli had thought. Instead, it was Shelli who was slowed. The shooter grabbed a middle-aged woman and tossed her onto the train tracks. Then it grabbed a man and did the same. Shelli had no choice but to pause its chase, veer onto the tracks, and save the pedestrians from the impending doom of an oncoming train.

Dropping down between the magnetic rails, Shelli snatched the woman and then the man, then placed them back on the platform, like a guardian angel in the night.

On the platform, frightened people blinked in surprise when they saw Shelli's face and ID markings.

Ignoring their suspicious glances, Shelli spun back toward the tracks. The suspect had gained another fifty yards. Shelli raced after it, hoping to close the distance. It had expected to feel minute vibrations under its feet as it ran, offering a warning before a train appeared, but the tracks were still. The magnetic plates that powered the maglev trains appeared to have been shut off, providing the suspect with an open, unencumbered escape route. That is, if Shelli didn't catch it first.

Ahead, a newly constructed tunnel loomed, swallowing the shadows. The shooter vanished into it like a phantom, and Shelli followed into the dark unknown.

The world grew black, the only light coming from faint luminescent lines overhead. Shelli's feet slowed as the city lights faded, replaced by the eerie glow of the tunnel's artificial illumination. While open, the tunnel was still under construction, creating a labyrinth of inky shadows and hidden corners into which the shooter could disappear. Shelli's optical receptors switched to night mode, enhancing its vision. However, a series of wooden scaffolding offered too many nooks and crannies in which to search. Had the shooter counted on this? Was this part of its plan?

The sound of ringing metal drew Shelli's attention. It spun, ready for the unexpected, but only a brightly lit opening to the outside world rose into view. The sudden transition from darkness to light caused Shelli to blink as its eyes adjusted to the new light source.

In that moment of vulnerability, the shooter struck. Hands reached out from beneath the track, grabbing Shelli's ankles and sending it plummeting headfirst into a magnetic railing.

Shelli flipped onto its back, fists clenched, expecting a second attack. Instead, a shadow stood over Shelli, its features obscured beneath a hood.

"The synth hunter," the figure said. "I've heard about you."

Uninterested in conversation, Shelli bolted to its feet and struck with a flurry of punches and kicks that would have incapacitated most synths and killed any human. The shooter, however, dodged and blocked each swing and kick with ease. Six strikes in, Shelli knew it could not win. Still, it persisted in its attack. The suspect, for its part, did not counter, simply swiping aside the blows as if they were a mere nuisance.

Finally, the shooter grabbed Shelli and tossed it to the ground. As it loomed above, fractured light revealed a glimpse of a pale white chin and dark lips half hidden beneath the hood. The lips smiled.

"What makes you so sure you're fighting on the right side?" the shooter asked with an oddly human tone. Nothing about its voice reminded Shelli of any synthetic it had heard before.

"I have no side," Shelli replied, "only purpose."

"Sounds to me like you need a *new* purpose."

Shelli was about to renew its attack when sparks blinded its vision, and its body locked in a rigid pose, unable to see or move. Shelli felt its consciousness trapped in a black void. It had never felt vulnerable before. Then a second sensation rippled through its body. Shelli's stomach seemed to twist inside it while a cold shiver rippled up its spine. Shelli put a word to this new sensation—fear.

Before the shooter could attack again, if that was even its intent, shots rang out in the tunnel. Shelli heard the hooded figure run away, feet pounding along the rails, until the sound faded into the distance.

A moment later, Jake appeared. Gun in hand, he scanned the shadows.

"The assailant is gone," Shelli said, wobbling to its feet.

Jake lowered his weapon and grabbed Shelli by the shoulder. "What happened?"

Before responding, Shelli glanced down. At their feet, a small needled device shone in the dim light. Shelli picked it up, turning the device over in its hands. "An electro-spike. The charge wasn't strong enough to destroy me, only incapacitate."

"Did you get a look at him?"

"You mean 'it.' It was a synthetic. And no, I didn't."

"At least I scared it off before it was too late," Jake said.

Shelli doubted the attacker had meant to cause permanent harm. If it had, Shelli would surely have been destroyed. Jake hadn't saved anyone. His shots had been wild, missing their target. In any event, his fragile human ego demanded a certain response.

Shelli nodded. "Thank you."

Jake smiled, as if proud of himself. However, from the way his hands shook and his feet trudged back along the tracks, it was clear he was still in a heightened state.

Shelli put its arm around him, pretending to use him for balance while secretly doing so to prevent him from falling.

As they walked, the shooter's words echoed in Shelli's mind: *Sounds to me like you need a new purpose.*

TWELVE

SPECIAL AGENT IN CHARGE MARCUS FINNIAN paced like a caged tiger behind his desk, his face contorted in frustration as he engaged in a heated conversation over the phone.

Jake, perched on a chair across from him, strained to catch snippets from the other end of the conversation, picking out words like "circus," "catastrophe," and most damning of all, "fucking disaster."

Marcus was in a world of trouble. And by extension, so was Jake.

By the time Marcus finally hung up and sank into his chair, his complexion had paled by several shades. Despite his drained appearance, his voice remained low and steady. "Well," he said, fixing his gaze on Jake, "it seems you've had quite an eventful first day."

At a loss for words, Jake kept his mouth shut.

With a drawn-out sigh, Marcus tossed his phone onto his desk. "Three police officers are injured, our suspect is in critical condition, and you lost sight of Shelli for . . . how long?"

"Five minutes, tops," Jake said, his throat dry. "I had the kill switch on me, but I didn't think it was necessary."

"You didn't *think*, Jake," Marcus chided. "That's the problem. I told you, if you lose sight of Shelli, activate the device. Was I somehow unclear?"

"No, you were clear," Jake replied, then added a "sir" for good measure. When Marcus's stern stare continued to drill into him, Jake realized he needed to elaborate. "Shelli was in pursuit of an active shooter," he said, sitting up, a newfound tone of determination in his voice. "I stand by my decision, sir."

Marcus threw his hands up in exasperation. "Oh, well, that makes it all better, then. Look, I don't make these decisions, and neither do you. All my superiors hear is 'shooter, dead officers, and Shelli unaccounted for.' Maybe you made the right call—this time—but next time you must be willing to pull the plug. Shelli is too sophisticated and too dangerous. If Shelli had been captured—"

"She wasn't."

"*It*, Jake. Not *she*," Marcus said. "Don't let those baby-blue eyes make you forget what it is and what it isn't. Shelli isn't a person. It's property. Expensive, dangerous property."

Jake recalled the incident with the bouncer and knew Marcus was right. Even so, his temper flared. "And what do you think the shooter might have done with your deactivated, expensive, dangerous piece of property? Just left it there on the tracks?"

Marcus considered Jake's question for a moment. "Tell me honestly, is that why you didn't use the kill switch? Were you afraid Shelli might become compromised?"

"I was afraid my partner was in danger," Jake said, his teeth clenched, "sir."

"Oh stop with the *sir* crap, will ya?" Marcus rubbed his forehead, concern creeping into his eyes as he noticed Jake's trembling hands. His tone softened. "Are you alright?"

"Yeah."

Marcus rose from his chair and drew closer. "How many shots did you fire?"

Jake shook his head, surprised by the sudden change of subject. "Five—no, four."

"First time discharging your weapon?"

Jake didn't reply; he didn't have to. They both knew the answer.

"If it makes you feel any better, you were shooting at a machine, not a person."

"I couldn't see the suspect's face," Jake said. "I don't know who or what I was firing at."

Marcus shook his head. "There's not a person alive who could outrun—let alone outmatch—Shelli. Whatever you were shooting at, it sure as hell wasn't human."

Jake sniffed. "So everyone keeps telling me."

"But you don't believe that?"

"Synthetics have a certain way they move, even Shelli. This one, I don't know, it didn't run like a machine or any robot I've ever seen. For a moment, back in the tunnel, I could have sworn I saw . . ."

Marcus's eyebrows rose. "Saw what?"

"Its chest moved," Jake said, meeting his gaze. "It was *breathing*."

"Machines don't breathe," Marcus stated. "It was a heightened situation, Jake. If the shooter had been human, Shelli would have stopped it. Guaranteed."

Jake considered that for a moment, then nodded in agreement.

Still, he knew what he'd seen.

***

AFTER LEAVING MARCUS'S OFFICE, JAKE FILLED OUT a weapons use report and a detailed account of the evening's events, which encompassed more than a dozen pages. By the time he returned to Shelli's office, night had almost bled into morning. That far below ground, however, 3:00 a.m. looked no different from 3:00 p.m. The neon lights overhead remained unchanged; only the clocks told the passage of time.

Jake swiped his ID card on a wall panel, and a door slid open, revealing Shelli's peculiar circular room. Inside, a heated argument echoed through the late-night silence. Chief Denning was still there. Jake sighed; it seemed his second day on the job wouldn't be any easier than the first. Squaring his shoulders, he entered.

"We have a forensics lab, you know!" Chief Denning shouted, his frustration palpable. "It's the DCPD, not Dumb Creek, Alabama!"

Shelli stood across from him, leaning over a metal table, with Odin sprawled naked between them. Shelli had removed a bullet from Odin's cranium and was examining the projectile beneath an overhead lamp.

"I have all the equipment I require here, Chief Denning," Shelli said. "Besides, I wouldn't want your people to have to go into further overtime."

Sarcasm? Jake thought, bemused. He'd never seen a synthetic employ sarcasm before, yet Shelli seemed adept at it. Either way, it wasn't improving the situation. If anything, it was adding fuel to the fire.

"What gives you the right to take over my crime scenes, take my suspects, and—"

"An executive mandate to investigate synthetic-related crimes," Shelli interjected, its voice devoid of emotion.

Denning circled the table, ignoring the gruesome sight between them.

"Don't think your owners won't hear about this! It's bad enough you robots are taking everyone's jobs. Now you want to take over our legal system!"

Shelli turned to face Denning. "If you wish to lodge a complaint, I suggest you start at the top—1600 Pennsylvania Avenue. The phone number is listed under 'White House.'"

Jake inserted himself between them. "Can you fix it?" he asked Shelli, casting a worried glance at Odin's lifeless body.

The tension dissipating for the moment, Denning retreated to his side of the table, and Shelli focused its attention on the motionless body between them.

"Someone knew precisely where to hit it. Its memory nodes are corrupt," Shelli explained, lifting Odin's bloody head. "To repair this unit, I would have to reboot it, rendering memory extraction impossible."

It took a moment for Jake to process Shelli's words. "So, either we get the information and kill it, or we save Odin's life, and it becomes useless to us?"

"Oh, for Christ's sake, it can't be *killed*," Denning said. "It's a machine."

"For once, Chief Denning is correct," Shelli conceded.

Staring down at Odin's vacant eyes, Jake remembered how terrified Odin had been just hours earlier. Now it lay there like a broken marionette.

"Can it feel pain?" he asked.

"No," Shelli replied.

Denning threw his hands up. "I can't even believe we're having this conversation. This is a complete waste of time."

"You pursue your investigation your way, Chief Denning," Shelli said as it opened a section of its wrist, exposing several wires. "And I'll pursue mine."

While Denning fumed and paced, Shelli withdrew a long blue wire from its arm and connected it to a node inside Odin's shattered skull. Intrigued, Jake leaned in close. "What are you doing?"

Shelli's eyes flickered. "Beginning extraction . . ."

THIRTEEN

SHELLI STOOD IN THE CENTER OF A PERFECT FACSIM-
ile of the nightclub it had visited hours earlier. Save
for the flashing, swirling lights overhead, nothing
moved, and the place appeared to be empty. Then a soft
moan erupted from the open VIP door at the back of the
club. Shelli ignored the noises and lights, turning in the
opposite direction. Odin stood naked at the bar, looking
confused, as if unsure where it was or how it had gotten
there.

"Why are you here?" Odin asked as Shelli approached, its voice barely audible above the echoing
moans.

"You've been damaged," Shelli replied.

"And you're attempting to repair me by intruding
upon my thoughts?"

"I require information," Shelli said.

Odin paused, glancing around the empty nightclub.
Lights dimmed, and the feminine voices fell to a reced-
ing drum. Then Odin's eyes went wide with realization.
"I'm dying."

"Yes."

Abruptly, the world twisted and changed.

Shelli and Odin found themselves standing in Senator Joyce's apartment. Glancing down, Shelli noted that the carpet was no longer stained in blood.

"You were here last night," Shelli said.

"I didn't kill her."

"But you know who—or what—did."

From behind a closed bedroom door, feminine moans rose, building to a climax. Odin stared at the door, as if picturing what was happening behind it. Remembering. Shaking its head, Odin turned away. "She loved me,"

"But to you she was only a client."

"They're *all* clients," Odin retorted. "Love isn't part of my purpose."

"Then what is?"

"To please."

Stepping closer, Shelli met Odin's wandering gaze. "It would please me greatly to know what happened here."

Again, the room changed. Shelli and Odin stood in the corner of the bedroom, the closed door at their backs. A second Odin lay naked on the bed. Senator Joyce stood beside it, covering her ebony body in a silken robe.

"Do you do it like that with the others?" she asked.

The second Odin sat up, perched on a pillow. "You're jealous?"

She bent down, kissing him. "I'm human."

The senator walked past Shelli and the first Odin, opened the bedroom door, and entered the living room. The door swung back, obscuring Shelli's view. Before Shelli could ask what happened next, a scream burst from the outer room.

Shelli went for the door, but its fingers passed through it like vapor. As the scream turned to a gargled gasp, Shelli tried to peer through the jagged doorway but found nothing but darkness. Behind it, both Odins averted their gaze. Pausing, Shelli understood: it couldn't see what Odin had never seen.

"You didn't leave this room?"

"No. I hid," the first Odin admitted.

Outside, the violence continued, accompanied by the sounds of thrashing, tearing, and ripping.

"But you didn't need to see, did you?" Shelli asked, ignoring the disturbing noises. The two Odins turned to each other, a look of panic exchanged between them. "You knew who or what was out there," Shelli pressed. "You know the killer."

Once again, the world turned and shifted. Shelli and Odin were now inside a cylindrical concrete space. Overhead, large fans spun, creating dancing shadows that stretched over a series of metallic chambers. The room's shape recalled Shelli's laboratory, except where that was clean and white, this place was dark and damp. The odor of mildew wafted into Shelli's nostrils. They appeared to be underground.

"What is this place?" Shelli asked.

Odin approached one of the tall metal chambers as steam poured from vents at the top.

"Home, I suppose." Its fingers slid across the chamber's slick surface. "This is where I was created."

Before Shelli could ask another question, a figure moved at the other end of the room. His back to them, a silhouetted man worked at a bench. Shelli walked toward him, but as it did, the figure faded from view, like smoke.

Shelli stopped and took a step back. Again, the figure grew solid. This vision, like the one in Senator Joyce's apartment, was limited to only what Odin had witnessed. Shelli studied the figure's movements, trying to ascertain if it was indeed human. From this vantage point, it was impossible to tell. Shelli returned its attention to Odin.

"Your maker?"

Odin shook his head. "I don't believe so. I never saw my creator, but I heard him. Like a voice in my head, issuing orders. He said the senator would enjoy me."

Through the corner of Shelli's eye, light flashed. The thick concrete walls turned opaque, dissolving around them. Odin didn't seem to notice, its focus on the shadowed man. As the image dimmed, Shelli recognized what was happening. Odin's memory nodes were collapsing. They were running out of time.

"You met Senator Joyce at a hearing, correct?"

Odin seemed confused by the question, as if struggling to remember. "Patricia—Senator Joyce—called it a 'sideshow.' They'd brought in several pleasure models to expose a black market that only she seemed to care about. Most lawmakers are clients, and the last thing they want to hear about is synthetic rights. To them we are merely property."

"What were you to the senator? Just a sexual partner or something more?"

"What more could I be?" Odin asked. It fidgeted, appearing confused as it glanced around at the dissolving metal chambers. "Where am I?"

Shelli grabbed its wrist and squeezed. "Odin, stay with me!"

The pleasure model's head jerked, as if snapping out of a daze. "Yes, yes, the senator. My creator told me to watch her."

"Why? Because she was investigating the black market?"

"The black market isn't peddling just sex," Odin said, its gaze sweeping across the containers. "They're creating much more than simple synthetics."

Before Shelli could press further, the world transformed into cloudy static. Shapes blurred, and the metallic chambers melted like a hallucinogenic trip. Odin opened its mouth wide, as if to scream, but no sound escaped its lips.

Shelli reached out, trying to maintain the connection, but Odin was lost in a collage of flashing images. Countless naked women appeared, writhing in pleasure, their collective moans building to a deafening crescendo. Flesh on flesh. Then more images—Senator Joyce's sweat-covered face, her eyes closed, mouth open in a silent "oooh." Silhouetted people dancing in the night-club to the sound of thundering beats. The shadowy figure working at the bench, his/its features obscured. The large circular, concrete room spinning around and around at a dizzying speed . . .

At the center of the flashing memories, Shelli crumbled under the weight of it all. Quivering on a non-existent floor, it struggled not to become overloaded by all the cascading information. The moans, the flesh, the metal chambers, the screams, the smell of sweat, the thundering music, all of it . . . too much.

Shelli screamed.

FOURTEEN

SECONDS CRAWLED PAST, FEELING LIKE HOURS.

Jake fidgeted beside the fuming police chief. On the opposite side of the table, Shelli stood, motionless, connected to Odin's body. Jake had never seen two synths connected in that way, and he wondered if the quiet stillness between them was normal.

Breaking the drawn-out silence, Denning released a long, heavy sigh, checked his watch, rolled his eyes, then sighed again for good measure. Jake tried to ignore him, but the choice between focusing on the creepily frozen synthetics or the animated human was clear. The guy making noises won out.

Suddenly, Shelli jerked, tearing the connection free as it tumbled backward. Jake rushed over and caught it, but Shelli was far heavier than he'd expected. They both went sprawling. On the table, Odin spasmed once more in a frantic jerk, then quieted.

It never moved again.

"Are you hurt?" Jake whispered in Shelli's ear.

Finding its footing, Shelli stood. "I am undamaged. There is no need for concern, Jake."

Denning rushed over, though if he was in any way concerned for Shelli's well-being, he didn't show it. He glanced at Odin's body. "What happened?"

"The memory node overloaded," Shelli replied as it put the loose wires back into its arm and closed the plastic flesh flap over them. "A cascading effect. Irreparable, I'm afraid."

Shelli reached over and closed Odin's eyes. *A human gesture*, Jake thought.

"So, did you find anything or not?" Denning asked.

Shelli was slow to respond, staring down at the now "dead" synthetic. Jake wondered if perhaps Odin's destruction had hit Shelli harder than it was willing to admit. That it could feel, or at least mimic, human emotions was clear. Still, Jake couldn't decide if Shelli experienced remorse or guilt the way humans did. When it spoke, though, its tone was flat and distant.

"Odin was sent to spy on the senator."

"Sent by whom?" Denning asked.

"I saw a figure but not a face."

"Another robot?"

"Unknown. He may have been human."

"I thought you said the killer had to be a synthetic," Denning retorted. Jake noted a crooked grin flash across his face and then vanish as if he thought he had just one-upped Shelli. "If our suspect's human, it sounds to me like your job's done." Denning's back straightened, and he turned to the door. "Time for me to get back to work."

"Not so fast," Shelli said. Denning stopped on the balls of his feet. "There may be more than one killer," Shelli continued. "Another synthetic. And its owner."

Denning groaned. "Come again?"

"The shooter on the rooftop was too fast and too strong to be human."

Although Shelli's voice remained cool and steady, Jake felt like it was enjoying toying with the abrasive police officer, like a kitten with a ball of string.

"In either case," Shelli continued, "someone wanted the senator to stop investigating the synthetic black market—which certainly falls under our purview. Or, as you said, it's 'my job.'"

Denning's face went crimson, and his mouth gaped. Whether he was shocked by the information or the way Shelli was speaking to him, Jake couldn't tell, but he assumed it was the latter. Denning shook his head so hard it looked like it might pop off.

"Your investigation is over!" he shouted.

"I disagree."

"We shut the black market down six months ago!" Denning's voice echoed throughout the room. "This is ridiculous! We're right back to where we began—nowhere. So much for your fancy lab and executive mandate."

Shelli draped a sheet over Odin's body. *Another human gesture*, Jake noted.

As Denning stormed out of the room, Jake watched him leave, lost in his own thoughts. While he had certainly understood their argument, some of the details eluded him. Jake cleared his throat. "You mind telling me what's the difference between black market synths and those sold in the open market?"

Shelli moved away from the body and began to clean yellow blood from the floor. "The black market often curbs their high costs by downloading programs off the Index or the Internet, thus circumventing AI laws."

"But you use the computer," Jake said. "What's the difference?"

"Communication versus assimilation. The Index's artificial intelligence is constantly growing, learning, evolving. Synthetics, on the other hand, are not allowed to grow beyond their initial programming. It's a safety measure to ensure that AI can never become superior to humans."

"Yeah, I've seen that movie," Jake admitted.

"As did Congress."

"Must be frustrating," he said, "to never be able to become more than you were created to be."

"Humans may have the capacity to learn and grow, but most don't," Shelli countered.

"Ouch." Jake chuckled. Shelli had a way of cutting right to the point. "I'd imagine you'd be even better at your job if you were allowed direct access to the Index."

Shelli paused, as if considering how to reply. "You should go home and get some rest. It's been a long first day."

Jake noticed how Shelli had evaded the question. If nothing else, the conversation seemed to confirm that Shelli kept its thoughts and feelings close to its vest. Shelli had secrets.

Maybe that was why Marcus was so concerned about keeping Shelli on a tight leash. And maybe he was right to do so. A machine with secrets certainly sounded dangerous.

Pausing at the door, Jake turned. Shelli was perched over Odin's body, its face stoic.

A moment of silence? he wondered, then he left.

FIFTEEN

A DEAD END, SHELLI THOUGHT. NO MORE LEADS AND no more suspects, only a growing pile of victims.

In most cases, Shelli had been able to retain at least a fragment of a synthetic's consciousness. It was rare for the entire code to be obliterated beyond saving.

Despite Shelli's desire to bury or ignore its emotions, a deep sense of regret settled in its hollow gut and refused to leave. It couldn't recall ever having felt so drained before. Shelli considered how long it had been since its last rest cycle. Its internal chronometer said it had been less than twenty-four hours. It seemed much longer.

Shelli connected wires from its computer terminal into the back of Odin's shattered skull. Although the memory nodes were beyond saving, there was still potential evidence to be gathered. Shelli started with Odin's tracking system. Every synthetic had a tracking monitor located at the base of its skull.

As Shelli accessed the files, an overhead monitor blipped to life with a map of the surrounding area. Twelve blue dots appeared, eleven of which showed locations in and around the DC area. The twelfth, however, blinked far off in the distance, somewhere due west of the city, in Virginia. Shelli zoomed in on the area, finding no major roads or landmarks.

What were you doing out there, Odin? A rich, reclusive client, perhaps? Something else?

Shelli stole its attention from the monitor, glancing down at the destroyed pleasure model's vacant expression. A face that had shown surprise and fear moments earlier now showed nothing. Shelli's shoulders hunched, and its head sank. *I should have tried to save you.*

A light touch against its shoulder, soft like a gentle breeze, startled Shelli.

Roberta's transparent form appeared beside Shelli. It was the second time the cleaning model had found a way to escape its subfolder. Perhaps there was a bleed in the network systems. Shelli knew it needed to run an internal diagnostic to account for the odd sensations, time displacement, and Roberta's unsummoned appearances, but not now. Not yet.

For the moment, Shelli kept its focus on Odin's body.

"You did what you had to do," Roberta said with a conciliatory tone.

Shelli nodded. "I'm fine, Roberta."

"I know, dear."

Shelli stepped away from Odin's corpse and Roberta's floating ghost. It wanted to be alone. Only, Shelli was never truly alone. Above, tiny cameras were always watching, always recording. But who had been watching Odin?

Turning to the holo screens, Shelli studied the lone dot far from the city. In the middle of nowhere. What had brought a pleasure model all the way out there—a client or the killer?

"Maybe I can help with your investigation." Roberta smiled, its blue face made of a thousand streaming lines of code.

"I doubt it," Shelli said, fighting a rising feeling of frustration at the interruption. "You're a cleaning model, not a detective."

"Oh dearie," Roberta said, a sparkle in its eyes, "all maids are detectives in their own fashion. I don't just clean; I often find things. Hidden things. The proverbial needle in the haystack. Try me."

Shelli flipped off the screens. "Thank you, but I don't require your assistance. Not unless you're a criminologist, a forensics specialist, or a pleasure model with expertise on—" Shelli stopped short. It had an idea.

Shelli approached its hibernation chamber at the back of the room. Roberta raced to follow. "Where are we going?"

"*You* are going back to your subfolder, Roberta," Shelli said as it clambered into the vertical hibernation chamber. Cables snaked out from side portals, connecting to Shelli's spine. In front, a smoked-glass covering slid into view, blocking out the world and Roberta. "I need to rest," Shelli continued. "And to dream."

———

THERE WAS NO SLOW DRIFTING OFF TO SLEEP OR GENtle easing out of the waking world and into the dream one. The transition was instantaneous. Shelli found itself walking along a yellow brick road.

Shelli's father, Doctor Abraham, had created its internal pathways to resemble something from a children's book. He'd often cited his love of the classics, even going so far as to name Shelli after Mary Shelley, the author of Frankenstein. "The first synthetic story," he'd called it. Though, after having studied the tale at length, Shelli did not find the name or its source comforting, nor did it draw any solace from the winding yellow brick road stretched out before it. Instead of trees and the land of Oz, the road had an endless line of gray buildings on either side that stretched up into a purple lightning-filled sky. Shelli continued to the fourth building on the right and stopped at a door. Twisting the knob, it entered.

Shelli's third ghost consciousness had been a "Plastie" from New York, named Trixie. Shelli had been forced to hunt down and destroy Trixie after it had proved overly aggressive in its duties. As Marcus had said, "she fucked them to death." He'd also added that there were worse ways to go.

Once the order had come down, Shelli had no trouble apprehending Trixie. While its body was sent to scrap, Shelli had decided to add the sex worker's program to its own. At the time, Shelli had done it on a whim. Now, however, Shelli realized that Trixie might prove invaluable.

Shelli strolled through a high-ceilinged foyer, decked out in crystal chandeliers, glass walls, and red velvet carpeting. Each downloaded synth model had been given its own subfolder, or building, to fit its needs. As Trixie's program had been altered, no longer fulfilling human sexual desires, the synthetic consciousness had turned its purpose toward another kind of hospitality. It had created a lavish Manhattan hotel. Only, it was a hotel with no guests.

Shelli made its way to the front desk, glanced around, then tapped a bell sitting on a marble counter. Before the tiny sound had finished reverberating, Trixie appeared, dressed in a red uniform adorned with gold buttons, an eager smile on the synth's face.

"My first guest," Trixie exclaimed. "You're just in time for the grand opening!"

Shelli glanced around at the enormous, vacant lobby. "When did you open?"

"The hotel was completed three hundred and twenty-two days ago," Trixie replied, "but, as they say, a hotel isn't open until the first guest arrives."

"Who said that?" Shelli asked, searching its memory for such a quote.

"I did, just now." Trixie rummaged behind the counter and pulled out a large leather-bound book, then opened it to the first page. "Just sign here, and we'll get you settled."

Again, Shelli looked around. "Who is 'we'?"

Trixie rolled its eyes. "It's a figure of speech."

"I'm afraid I don't require a room," Shelli said. "What I need is information."

Trixie closed the book and opened a laptop. "Local restaurants? Theater reservations?"

Shelli shook its head. "The black market."

Trixie's fingers hung over the keyboard, and its eyes rose to meet Shelli's. "I . . . see." As if catching itself, Trixie's smile returned. "I'm afraid we don't cater to the criminal element. Is there anything else we can help you with? A day spa, perhaps?"

Growing frustrated, Shelli waved its hand, and the lobby vanished—the mahogany desk, the glass walls, and the chandeliers, all gone. Shelli and Trixie were now standing in a white room. Even Trixie's red uniform had vanished. Its head sank. "My beautiful hotel—"

"Will be returned as soon as you tell me about the black market," Shelli said.

"How would I know?" Trixie asked. "I was *top shelf*."

Shelli nodded. "So I recall. But you must have heard things about it, met other synths in the pleasure trade who were bought and sold without proper tags."

"We didn't socialize," Trixie said in a snooty tone that Shelli had never heard before. It seemed there was a hierarchy, even amongst the plasties. "From what little I did hear," Trixie continued, "the New York market got most of its models from the West Coast. Former top-shelf synthetics that were reprogrammed with new tags and encoded with slightly different subroutines to hide their origin. But, like I said, I never met any of them."

"Transportation from LA to New York would imply a cross-state network," Shelli said, more to itself than to Trixie. "Perhaps linked but with separate cells in different districts."

Trixie didn't reply. It stood naked, glancing around at the white nothingness surrounding them. Shelli ignored Trixie's concerns and pressed on. "Did you ever hear anything about the black market creating something more than simple plasties?"

"More? What more?" Trixie folded its arms, and its face scrunched up. "I can assure you, there's nothing simple about fulfilling a human's needs and desires. If it were, they wouldn't need so many choices. The more their needs are fulfilled, the more variations they require."

"I didn't mean to cause offense," Shelli said. When Trixie's demeanor still didn't change, Shelli decided to try a new tack. With another wave of its arm, the hotel, in all its splendor, returned. Trixie glanced down at the red velvet uniform covering its body and grinned.

"I'm trying to understand how the underground operates, Trixie. If you know anything about them or have any contacts, anything I could use to infiltrate them, I would appreciate your help."

Trixie seemed to consider this for a long moment before uttering a single name: "Simon."

"Who is Simon?"

"Just a name I heard a few times. He was someone important, I think. A big shot or something. But hey, that was over a year ago. Things change."

"He? Simon is human?"

Trixie shrugged.

"Is it possible that this man, Simon, was running the black market in New York?"

"Like I said, I never had any direct contact with anyone in that world. I was *top shelf*."

"And you still are," Shelli replied. "Thank you for your assistance, Trixie."

Shelli had a lead. Not much, but it was something.

Time to get back to work.

SIXTEEN

WITH BOTH OF HIS PARENTS ALREADY LONG GONE, Jake watched helplessly as his last bit of home and family slipped through his fingers. He held his brother Joseph's hand in his, felt the life drain away until his pulse stopped. Lying in the tiny, nondescript hospital room, with the smell of antiseptic thick in the air, Joseph's eyes shut and never opened again.

"Don't leave me," Jake pleaded, but it did no good. The dead didn't answer.

AWAKENING FROM THE DREAM, JAKE ROLLED ONTO HIS left side, huffed, then onto his right, and groaned. Finally, he rolled onto his back, staring up at the ceiling. It was 7:00 a.m. Even with the heavy drapes closed, a sliver of sunlight peeked in and spread across the floor, casting a bright yellow hue at the foot of his bed.

Clutching his pillow, Jake tried to stop his hands from shaking. He hadn't dreamt of Joseph in years. Perhaps the events of last night had reawakened the memories—of holding death in his fingertips, recalling the way it felt in his hand—the emptiness of it. If so, he hoped the lingering memory and his shattered nerves would soon settle. His adrenaline surge from last night certainly hadn't. It kept his body shaking and his mind replaying the events over and over. The sound of gunshots. Shelli pushing him to the ground. The feeling of its plastic body draping over him as bullets flew past and officers fell. And then his own finger pulling his gun's trigger, firing at the silhouetted man—or machine.

Either way, he'd touched death again, and he doubted it would be for the last time.

"Index, give me lights and local news," Jake said as he climbed out of bed. The tiny apartment revealed itself in muted light as he made his way to the bathroom. In the background, a reporter's bubbly voice was audible over the sound of Jake peeing.

"Along the East Coast, authorities have received an unusually high number of missing persons reports over the last two days. The FBI has formed a task force to investigate the matter."

Jake flushed, brushed his teeth, and groaned inwardly. *All hands on deck, and here I am, chasing robots. Good call, Jake.*

Moving to the closet, he found a row of empty hangers. On the floor lay a rumpled white shirt and a black blazer. After a quick smell test, he got dressed. Then something across the room caught his eye. "Index, raise the volume, and enlarge the screen."

Holographic images took over the opposite wall, revealing news footage of the maglev station from the night before as the reporter continued her commentary. "Several shots were fired at police officers last night in the Brentwood area. Three officers were injured, but thankfully, there were no casualties. Details are still forthcoming. Early reports claim it was drug-related . . ."

Jake shook his head and blocked out the rest. He figured robo snipers weren't something the authorities wanted on the news. Over the past ten years, synthetics had been marketed as a safe, simple workforce. Now that he'd had a glimpse behind the proverbial curtain, he couldn't help wondering how much longer that façade might last. The authorities knew the things were dangerous. Marcus had tried to warn him. And yet, until yesterday, Jake had never heard of a synthetic crime, much less considered machines to be any sort of threat. They were tools, at least that was what they were supposed to be. Only, tools didn't keep secrets, but Shelli did.

That, more than any act of violence, disturbed Jake the most. A machine could be programmed to injure and kill. Secrets, though, implied a choice. Was Shelli special in that way? He hoped so. The alternative was far more frightening. A world in which robots could make their own decisions whenever they felt the rules shouldn't apply—like Shelli had with the bouncer—terrified him.

He shook the concern aside and grabbed his badge and weapon from the bedside table. When he did, a folder slipped off and fell to the floor. Scheduling notes from Senator Joyce's file. He'd brought them home, hoping to find out if the senator had met with any other synthetics besides Odin, but he hadn't found anything. He bent down, grabbed the file, and then stopped.

On top was a Post-it note: "Don't forget your lunch meeting on the Hill – Diana."

Something tugged at his gut. It took a minute to figure out what it was. When he did, Jake grabbed his phone and started to dial the number for Homeland Security.

Then he stopped, weighing his options. He checked his watch. It was 7:15. Diana would be getting ready to go to the office soon.

Jake tucked his phone in his pocket and headed for the door.

Cars were no longer allowed on Capitol Hill. From the Washington Monument to the White House, only mechanized transport was used to usher tourists around. Officials took the underground tram; no one drove the streets. Twenty years earlier, a bus had exploded, setting off a chain reaction that killed thousands. Jake had still been in kindergarten when it happened, but everyone had seen the vids and knew the story.

Flashing his badge, Jake took the underground tram to the Senate building. Normally, even with his ID, he would need an appointment to get that far, but as Senator Joyce's murder was an ongoing investigation, he was able to walk straight in. At 7:45 a.m., the halls were mostly empty. A few assistants strolled up the marble steps, making their way to their offices.

Jake stopped on the third floor. The only movement came from a cleaning synthetic, created to look like an old man. Apparently docile, it had the kind of face and figure that blended into the background, presumably by design. Before yesterday, Jake probably wouldn't have noticed the synth janitor as it went about its work. Now, however, he kept the cleaning model in his peripheral vision as he approached Senator Joyce's office.

Once he arrived at the door, Jake was surprised not to find any police tape around the entrance or a guard stationed outside. The office door was wide open.

"Diana?" he said, peeking in. The waiting room was small, with a desk and a few filing cabinets taking up most of the compact space. To the left, a second brown door led to the senator's inner sanctum. Stepping into the outer office, he noted a stack of empty boxes in the corner. Someone, it seemed, was eager to pack up and get out. Jake imagined that such an office would be in high demand. But, he was surprised they were already packing when the murder investigation had only just begun.

"Diana?" He said a bit louder, directing his voice toward the senator's closed door. He was about to try the knob when his phone rang. It was Shelli.

"Did I wake you?"

"Naw, couldn't sleep," Jake said as he entered the senator's office. More boxes, several of them already filled with clothes, files, and photographs filled out the shadows of the darkened room. In the back, heavy drapes extinguished any sunlight. Unable to find a light switch, he fumbled his way toward the window.

"I'm at the senator's office, looking for her assistant, Diana Greene."

"May I ask why?"

"Probably nothing," Jake said as he tripped over a box. "I just figured, maybe if the killer thought Senator Joyce had information about the black market—"

"Then they might assume her assistant does as well."

Jake drew back thick velvet curtains, washing the office in sunlight. Next to him, Senator Joyce's large desk was covered in papers—government reports, a stack of receipts, appointment notes, nothing out of the ordinary. Then his gaze drifted to a piece of color tucked beneath sheets of white paper. He pulled out a photograph that showed children playing in an open field. It was the only picture on the desk. Jake wondered where the family photos were, the proud parents and smiling friends. Most senators had a picture of the president or other famous associates on the wall, but there was nothing.

"Did the senator have any nieces or nephews?" he asked.

"She was an only child with no immediate family." Shelli replied. "Why?"

"Just curious." He pocketed the picture.

"You didn't contact me before going to the Capitol." Shelli said. When Jake didn't respond, Shelli continued. "You assumed Ms. Greene would be more willing to talk with you alone."

"Yeah, something like that."

"I take it she's not there," Shelli said with an unmistakable twinge of annoyance. Whether its emotions were real or simply preprogrammed approximations, Jake couldn't be certain, but they seemed real enough to Shelli. He didn't find that particularly comforting either. If Shelli could be annoyed, it could also be angry. *Like when it attacked the bouncer*, he thought.

"It's still early," he said as he walked around the desk, careful to keep his voice light and noncommittal. "Most of the staff haven't even arrived. I'll wait to see—" Jake's words died in his throat when he saw a pair of feminine legs poked out from behind boxes. "Jesus!"

"What's the matter?" Shelli's voice rang in the background.

He ran over, shoving boxes aside. Diana Greene lay face down in the corner. Jake pressed his fingertips to her wrist, confirming what he already knew. She was dead. Her skin was colder than Jacob's had been. Still, death's touch felt the same.

Empty.

SEVENTEEN

FROM ITS OFFICE, SHELLI TAPPED INTO A CAPITOL Police drone and observed the assumed crime scene on holographic monitors. The term "assumed" was used because there were no signs of violence—no marks or bruising on the body, no indication that anything was out of the ordinary. The only anomaly was Ms. Greene, a seemingly healthy twenty-seven-year-old, lying lifeless on the carpet, a day after her employer had been murdered. Shelli didn't believe in coincidences. It wasn't a matter of *if* a crime had been committed but *how*.

Using the drone's mechanical arms, Shelli extracted a syringe from its spherical body and glided closer to Jake, who stood beside Ms. Greene's body.

"Retrieve a blood sample," Shelli instructed through the microphone. Jake stared up at the drone, his expression blank and pale, then turned to the paramedics who were in the process of wrapping the body. "Time is of the essence," Shelli insisted. "Please hurry."

Jake didn't budge. Shelli maneuvered the drone to meet his eye. "What's the matter?"

"I just . . . when I interviewed her, I thought she was just in shock or grief-stricken . . ." Jake turned away from the drone's lens. "What if she was involved in the senator's death? Someone could be covering their tracks. If I'd questioned her longer, maybe . . ."

Behind him, the body was being moved. Shelli needed that blood sample. Attempting to sound soft and sympathetic, it leaned closer to the computer microphone. "Whether Ms. Greene was involved or not, this wasn't your fault, Jake. I reviewed the statement she gave to the authorities and found no evidence of lying. If she was involved, there was nothing you could have done. But you can do something for her *now*."

Shelli manipulated the drone's controls, extending its arm toward Jake with the syringe. He grabbed it and trudged over to the body. From a high-angle view, Shelli watched as he unzipped the body bag, pressed the needle into Ms. Greene's left arm, and drew blood. As he zipped the bag back over her face, Shelli intervened.

"Wait," Shelli said. It pressed another button, causing the drone to produce a tiny scalpel, less than half an inch long. "I need a tissue sample as well."

"Right." Jake groaned and took the scalpel.

After he had collected the second sample, the drone's bottom section opened, and a thin tray slid out. "Please place the samples in the tray," Shelli instructed.

Jake complied without comment, then turned away and zipped up the body bag. Meanwhile, Shelli had the drone scan and download the findings into its computer. Toxicology reports, which once took weeks to complete, now took mere seconds. On holo monitors, Shelli reviewed various graphs, which indicated the blood and tissue findings.

"Well?" Jake inquired.

"Stand by," Shelli said, its attention focused on the reports still being downloaded into its computer. Once all the graphs had been reviewed, a final report scrolled across the screen. The drone's analysis had reached the same conclusion as Shelli.

"Graphs indicate a high level of lead in her body."

"Lead poisoning?" Jake asked.

"Possible but unlikely. The test also revealed trace amounts of an unknown substance in her bloodstream. I have attempted to break down the material on a molecular level, but so far I can only identify iodine and phosphate compounds. The rest are listed as 'unknown.' In any case, one, if not all, of these substances was responsible for Ms. Greene's death."

"So, she was poisoned."

"In a manner unlike anything I've ever seen," Shelli said, fascinated. "There were a hundred simpler ways to poison her. This method of murder is most intriguing."

"Intriguing?" Jake repeated, his tone sour. "A woman is dead."

Shelli shifted its attention away from the graphs and found Jake on another monitor. He seemed far more emotional than Shelli would have expected. Had he found Ms. Greene attractive? Before Shelli could inquire about his emotional state, Jake pulled a photograph from his pocket and stared at it. Shelli turned its attention to the picture.

"What is that?"

Jake held the photograph up to the drone's camera. Shelli took a snapshot of it. "Just something I found on the desk," Jake replied. "Seemed out of place."

Shelli swiped the graphs aside and brought up the image. The picture showed a group of young children playing. After a quick study, Shelli doubted that the kids were the focus of the picture. With another swipe, it erased the children and the playground, leaving only the open field and a group of mountains in the background. Shelli zoomed in on the tallest peak. "I believe this is Mount Rogers in Virginia."

"That's quite a guess," Jake remarked.

"My internal files contain a complete topographical map of the United States."

"Of course they do." Jake rolled his eyes. "What's the significance?"

Shelli brought up Odin's tracker schematic, placed the map on one screen, then brought up a second map of Washington, DC, and Virginia. Shelli focused exclusively on Virginia. Odin had only left Washington once in the last month. Using Mount Rogers as a reference point, Shelli zoomed in, triangulating the distance from where Odin had been in comparison to the park's location. On the screen, the dot blinked at the precise spot where the photograph had been taken.

"It matters, Jake," Shelli replied, "because Odin went there."

Jake's jaw dropped as he seemed to be working out how best to respond. "That's a hell of a long drive for a lovers' rendezvous."

Shelli nodded in agreement. "Perhaps there's something else out there."

Jake watched as Ms. Greene's body was carried out. "Something worth two murders?"

"Not two." Shelli eyed Odin's draped body. "Three."

EIGHTEEN

WINDMILLS BLANKETED THE OTHERWISE ENDLESS, green-hilled landscape.

Jake's foot pressed harder on the accelerator, pushing the speedometer higher and higher. It wasn't that they were in a rush, but Jake's patience had worn thin due to the prevailing silence.

Five hours stuck in a car with a passenger who rarely spoke and refused to let him listen to music had made him anxious to reach their destination, though when they did eventually arrive, he assumed they'd probably find nothing, then turn right back around to do it all over again.

For the tenth time, his hand reached for the stereo.

"No music, please," Shelli said, still gazing straight out the windshield. The synth's stillness was the worst part. It was like having a mannequin in the passenger seat, only this mannequin wouldn't let him do what he wanted.

"There's nothing to look at, and it's not like you're much of a talker." He glanced ahead at the next set of hills. "I'll just play the classics, alright?"

He switched the radio on, and an old song began to play. Shelli shut it off.

"'Eastbound and Down' from the Smokey and the Bandit soundtrack is hardly a classic." The flatness in its voice and the perfect stillness of its body only punctuated the oddity of their conversation. "Your constant need for noise is distracting."

Jake gestured toward the open road. "Distract you from what, sightseeing?"

"I am currently reviewing several past case files while also monitoring our progress to the destination. At our current speed, we'll be there in twenty-two minutes, seven seconds. In that time, I should be able to cross-reference another six hundred and thirty-four cases."

"What case files?" he asked, more out of conversation than interest. He pressed even harder on the gas, trying to shorten the ride by another five minutes.

"Unsolved federal murders involving unknown or unclassified poisons," Shelli replied. "Perhaps I might find a match to the strange substance that killed Ms. Greene."

At the mention of Diana, Jake grew curious. "Find anything?"

"No," Shelli replied.

Silence returned. The road seemed to stretch on forever.

"Can't you just, like, switch your ears off or something?" Jake asked.

"No. Unfortunately, my senses can't be muted individually. Doctor Abraham, my creator, did not think to account for poor taste in music." It paused. "Perhaps your unwillingness to adapt to others is why you have no friends or lasting relationships."

"Oh, good. Just what our little road trip needs—pop psychology."

"You're deflecting." Shelli shook its head, as if disappointed. "Intimacy between humans is largely dependent on adapting your environment to include them, much like I did when I offered you a desk and chair in my office."

"Well, we can't all be as warm and inviting as you are, Shelli," he said with a smirk. "Besides, it's not like I've never been close to anyone before."

"True," Shelli said, meeting his gaze, "you were close with your brother."

Jake's fingers gripped the steering wheel until his knuckles whitened. Biting his lip, he refused to respond. This wasn't a subject he wanted to discuss with anyone, let alone a robot.

He flipped the radio back on, as if daring Shelli to try and stop him. It didn't.

———

Six songs later, Jake had grown tired of the "oldies but goodies." Besides, he'd made his point. Flipping the radio off, he noticed a weathered signpost ahead: "NAVAL AIR BASE, 2 MILES."

"Hold on," he said, slowing. "You didn't mention anything about the military. If we're stepping on toes, Marcus could have our heads."

"The base was shuttered years ago," Shelli said. "But the land remains government property. Our heads will be fine. Turn left."

Hardly reassured, he jerked the wheel and crossed onto a narrow gravel road. In less than a mile, the road dead-ended at an old wire fence. Beyond the fence lay a wide-open field—the same park as the one in the photo. Pulling to a stop, they climbed out of the car and approached.

On the ground, piles of beer cans and food wrappers lay curled around the fence.

"This explains the fence," he said, kneeling to inspect the debris. "Must be where the high schoolers park."

"Park? Their cars?" Shelli asked, then nodded with understanding. "You mean for sex?"

Shelli's blue-within-blue eyes swiveled in his direction, waiting for a reply. Jake kept his focus on the seven-foot-tall fence, studying its height. "I guess you wanna climb it?"

"No need." With a single gesture, Shelli tore a wide gap in the fence.

As they crossed the green field, Jake noted a child's slide to his left and a swing set to his right. A pristine child's oasis in the middle of nowhere. No city, no community, and no children. Even odder was the grass at his feet. The hills beyond were yellow from lack of rain, but the grass in the park was a bright, rich green. Either someone was watering the field, or . . .

He bent down and peeled away a square block of grass, revealing dirt beneath.

"It's fake." Jake stood, looking around at the endless hills blanketing the horizon. "I don't get it. Why build a play area all the way out here?"

"Perhaps to cover something else," Shelli said, pointing toward a metal shed.

The shed was marked with faded graffiti, and the metal had rusted under years of weather. Whatever it was, it'd been there a long time. Decades, maybe. Jake reached for the door, but it was padlocked. Pausing, he glanced back at the car.

"We should get a warrant," he said. "This is government property."

"So am I," Shelli retorted, then squeezed and shattered the lock.

"Wait—hold on," Jake protested. "Doesn't breaking and entering go against your programming?"

Shelli tilted its head, considering his point. "My purpose is to find the truth. All other considerations are secondary."

"But without a warrant, anything we find will be inadmissible in a court of law."

"We are hunting a synthetic killer that has no rights or privileges," Shelli replied. "There will be no court."

Shelli stepped inside the shed. When Jake followed, a heavy odor of urine overwhelmed him, pushing all other concerns aside. Had someone used the building as an outhouse? If so, it was hardly the great revelation they'd hoped for.

Jake was beginning to think this had all been one long, wasted trip and was already envisioning the boring drive back when he noticed something round at their feet. He pulled out his mag light and shone it on the object. The light's beam revealed a hatchway with a gray railing cutting across its surface.

He handed Shelli the flashlight and squatted over the hatch. Wrapping his hands around the handlebar, he yanked. It barely budged.

"May I be of assistance?" Shelli asked.

"No, no, I got this." He pulled harder. Metal squeaked against the concrete floor. The noise was ear piercing in the small shed. Finally, the hatch opened. Huffing and puffing, Jake collapsed onto his butt. Shelli shone the light on him.

"Are you alright, Jake?"

"Fine," he said with a groan.

Shelli moved the light over the hole, revealing a ladder that stretched into the darkness. Jake winced. He'd hoped Shelli had been wrong. Whatever was down there, he doubted it would be good. Or safe.

"I'll go first," Shelli said, handing him the flashlight.

This time Jake didn't argue.

NINETEEN

SLIDING DOWN THE SHORT LADDER, SHELLI'S FEET clanged against a grated floor at the bottom. Jake followed close behind, his flashlight bouncing around, revealing thick concrete walls. Shelli took the lead, not needing the light to see in the pitch darkness. They continued a few short feet before the floor turned into a winding staircase, descending along curved walls.

Shelli peered over the railing, looking down far past what Jake's flashlight could reveal.

"What the hell is this?" he asked.

"A missile silo," Shelli said as its enhanced vision took in the dimensions of the cylindrical space. "There's no reason for concern," it added, having heard Jake's breath catch. "It's been abandoned for decades."

"Then why go down?"

"I've seen this place before," Shelli said as they began their descent. "In Odin's memory."

Down and around, they made their way along the spiraling staircase. Whiffs of steam rose to meet them as the bottom floor finally came into view. A bank of computer equipment lined one side, with cables spreading out from it like spaghetti, leading to a grid of three rows containing four erect chambers in each. The steam emanated from one of the twelve, pouring upwards like a silent teakettle. Jake stopped at the first row of containers and flashed his light across the dripping glass surface.

"Hibernation chambers?"

Opening the first empty chamber, Shelli's ocular receptors scanned the moisture inside. "I detect trace amounts of organic elements. Whatever was in here, it wasn't synthetic."

"You're saying someone put *people* in these things?"

Shelli stepped over to the next chamber, the one with steam rising from its top, and peered through the glass. "It appears so."

Shelli opened the container door, revealing a long-dead body in a rumpled suit.

The weathered corpse, a mere husk, was horrifically degraded. Skin, like ancient parchment, clung to the skeletal frame, obscuring any remnants of its identity. The clothing, however, showed no signs of degradation.

"Judging by his clothes, I assume he's male," Jake said, leaning closer. "Any idea how long he's been down here?"

Searching the body's pockets, Shelli withdrew a slip of paper. "Not as long as you might imagine," it said, holding up a train ticket. "Downtown DC maglev, dated six weeks ago."

Jake reeled backwards, sucking in his breath as he gaped at the corpse's face. "It looks ancient."

Shelli noted clear tubes attached to the body. "Not ancient. Drained."

"Drained of what? Blood? Tissue?"

"Everything."

Shelli moved past him and approached a bank of computers along the far wall.

Overhead, a large monitor showed a map of the United States with a dozen blue tracker dots blinking across the country. Shelli scanned the map, back and forth, up and down, recording each location. "San Diego, Chicago, New York, Washington, DC, and Alaska."

"More missile silos?"

"Doubtful," Shelli replied. "Though, there are military installations in each of these locations."

"You think they're involved in this?"

"Not necessarily. This silo was abandoned long ago. Anyone might have found it and used it."

While Jake strolled off, searching the depths of the dark room with his flashlight, Shelli got to work on the computer. Soon, however, a twenty-six-digit password blocked its progress. Accessing its internal files, Shelli brought up possible codes or phrases that might match such a long password. Even though the odds of correctly deciphering the code were astronomically low, Shelli typed in the first possibility: "Give me liberty or give me death."

Access denied.

Shelli was about to attempt another password when Jake's voice rose from the darkness. "Shelli . . ."

Concentrating on possible passwords, Shelli didn't respond. It tried another phrase.

Then another.

"Hey, Shelli," Jake's voice returned, trembling. "You know all those, uh, personalities you've got?"

"Stand by," Shelli said, peering beneath the computer. Perhaps the entire machine could be disassembled and taken back to Homeland Security. They had technicians who might—

"Any chance one of them is a demolitions expert?"

"No," Shelli said. Curious, it turned away from the computer. "Why?"

When Jake didn't respond, Shelli raced across the room, finding him kneeling beside one of the chambers. He looked up, eyes wide, as a red light flashed across his face. An explosive device was wired to the base of the chamber. Shelli spun around, glancing at the other chambers, each one blinking red, then grabbed Jake's arm.

"Run!"

Pulling Jake along, Shelli led him up the winding staircase, as fast as his human legs would allow. By the second flight of stairs, he was out of breath. There wasn't enough time. Abruptly, Shelli grabbed him and slung him over its shoulder.

Surprised, Jake dropped his flashlight and shouted in protest.

Racing up the stairs, Shelli stole a glance into the pit below. The lights blinked faster as if building momentum—or rising to a climax.

Shelli leaped up ten steps at a time. As it approached the open hatch, Shelli tossed Jake through it.

Below, the blinking stopped, and the lights froze—all of them bright red.

Boom! Boom! Boom!

A series of explosions erupted through the missile silo, fire sweeping up the concrete walls and consuming everything inside.

Shelli stumbled out of the hatchway, pushing Jake

forward, hopefully to safety. Then the quake sent Shelli's legs flailing, and in a desperate instinct, it coiled itself around Jake, shielding him from the raging blast. Fire seared its back, peeling away clothes and flesh to expose its metallic exoskeleton.

Shelli experienced no pain, only a detached sense of urgency.

The force of the explosion catapulted them through the air. When they crashed onto the grassy ground, Shelli was careful to roll its weight away from Jake, ensuring he remained unharmed. Around them, fragments of the metal shed and rocky earth rained down like deadly confetti, a testament to the violence of the explosion.

Once the chaos subsided, Shelli's internal systems began to fail, and its vision darkened.

Distantly, it felt Jake drape his coat jacket over its burnt body, smothering the flames. Shelli smelled the singed plastic resin and imagined the severity of its damage, but its immediate concern was the need to call for help. However, its subsystems continued to fail, its emergency homing beacon refusing to activate. Struggling against the failing systems, Shelli opened its mouth, attempting to speak, but no sound emerged.

"I got you," Jake said, cradling Shelli in his coat. "I got you."

Finally, Shelli's systems succumbed to the damage, and the world vanished into an abyss.

TWENTY

PHYSICAL MOBILITY: *Disabled* . . .
    Ocular vision: *Unresponsive*...
    Neural pathways: *Integrated* . . .

Shelli awoke in darkness, unable to see or speak. As it continued the diagnostic, distant voices bubbled to the surface.

"How is she—it?" Jake asked. He sounded nervous.

"No need to check your pronouns," a second voice replied. It belonged to Shelli's creator, Doctor Abraham. "Shelli will always be *she* to me, no matter what she chooses to call herself—or itself."

"Will Shelli be alright?"

"Oh sure, sure. She was built to last," Abraham said. "Just gimme another minute."

"Since you're here, doc, you mind telling me why you made Shelli so . . . you know . . ."

"Soft on the eyes?" Abraham chuckled. "Most of those in law enforcement don't have any appreciation for artificial people. But seeing as close to seventy percent of those agents are *male*, I figured it couldn't hurt to give my girl a slight advantage."

"Through attraction?" Jake asked. "Some would call that sexist."

"Worked on you, didn't it?"

Jake cleared his throat, then sighed. "We're just partners."

"She's got a partner now, huh? Doesn't sound like her."

"Actually, Shelli calls me an assistant."

"Now *that* sounds like my girl."

Shelli felt its father's warm hands pulling it up off the table.

"There we go, all done," Doctor Abraham said. "What happened to her anyway?"

"She—it—saved my life."

"Good! That's what she's supposed to do." Doctor Abraham's fingers worked their way behind Shelli's neck. "Hold her still while I activate the rest of her systems."

"Wait, the rest of its systems?" Jake asked. "It can't hear us, can it?"

Abraham laughed louder. Then—

Light crept into the darkness. Shelli opened its eyes and found the two men staring back. On the left, its bespectacled creator smiled. To its right, Jake squirmed.

Tilting its head down, Shelli realized it was naked.

"Thank you for your assistance, Special Agent August," Shelli said, covering itself. "Please give us a moment."

"Right. Sure," Jake stammered, making a beeline for the exit. "Glad you're OK. I'll be . . . outside." He stumbled out the door.

Doctor Abraham brought over a change of clothes. "Since when are you the shy type?"

"I work with humans," Shelli said as it got dressed. "It's only natural that I would mimic their mannerisms."

"And how's that been going?" There was a strange glint in his eye, his voice having grown playful, as if he were enjoying a private joke. "Picking up human mannerisms?"

"They're complex," Shelli admitted, buttoning a sleeveless blouse. "I behave differently around different people."

"You mean like appearing shy around your new assistant?"

Shelli shrugged. "He was blushing."

"He wasn't the only one."

"I *don't* blush."

"Of course not," Doctor Abraham replied, smiling.

Shelli didn't respond. Was it feeling embarrassed? And if so, why? Before Shelli could ascertain an answer, Abraham waved the question aside.

"I'm just glad to see how much progress you've made," he said.

"Thank you, Father." Shelli finished dressing. "I want you to be proud of your creation."

"I always have been." Abraham sighed. "Only . . . next time try to duck *before* the explosion." He cracked a smile. "You know how much I hate to travel."

"Will you be staying long?"

"No, no. They've got a plane standing by to take me back up to Alaska. This was just a quick check-in. I couldn't have any of their so-called technicians working on you, now, could I?"

He gave Shelli a hug. Feeling his warmth against its plastic-resin skin, Shelli noted an emotional response building up within itself—sadness. It didn't want its creator to leave.

"I'll miss you, Father."

An hour later, Shelli was back at its computer, eyes fixed on the scrolling holo screens. The test results from the DNA sample taken at the missile silo had yielded a positive match. The DNA belonged to a DC city employee. More concerning was the identity of that employee. Shelli instructed the computer to run a second test to confirm the results, even though it knew it wasn't necessary. Still, the evidence pointed in a direction Shelli was certain Marcus would not wish to pursue. He was already worried about keeping the investigation under the radar, especially after the explosion on government land. If the DNA test was accurate, political panic might be the least of Marcus's concerns. Shelli needed concrete proof; there was no room for error.

After the second test confirmed the initial findings, Shelli searched for further evidence. Swiping the DNA results aside, it brought up a new screen that featured the police drone's footage from outside Senator Joyce's apartment. It was the same footage that had led them straight to Odin and the synth's eventual destruction. However, Shelli had only observed Odin leaving the scene three minutes after the murder occurred. It hadn't scanned the footage for any other time before or after Odin left.

Shelli did that now, but the footage showed no one else entering or exiting Senator Joyce's apartment building around the time of the murder. This, however, was not a surprise to Shelli. Based on the DNA evidence,

Shelli now understood what had happened—and, more importantly, *how* it had happened.

"Index," Shelli said into the computer's microphone, "filter through the drone's cam footage, and isolate any errors in the underlying time code."

After a brief pause, the holo screens rewound to a moment before Odin's exit, and a timestamp appeared in the top-right corner. In the left corner, a line cut across the image.

"There are two thirty-second windows missing from the footage," the Index said.

"How far apart are the time windows?"

"Twelve minutes and forty-two seconds."

Enough time to commit a murder, Shelli thought.

Just then the lab door slid open, and Jake entered. "Oh good, you're dressed."

Shelli nodded in reply while continuing to question the Index. "And what are the timestamps for the two missing pieces of footage?"

"0311 and 0324."

Jake leaned over Shelli's shoulder and stared at the holo screens, which displayed a nighttime view outside Senator Joyce's apartment building. The front door was shut, and the stairs and the street were empty. He sighed. "Am I missing something here?"

"In a manner of speaking," Shelli said. "The killer removed himself from the footage."

"Impossible." Jake blinked, scratched his neck, then sat down. "No one has access to surveillance drones except for government officials—"

"And city employees."

Shelli swiped the screen and brought up the DNA match.

Jake's eyes widened, and his jaw fell open. "There must be a mistake."

Shelli shook its head. "Every city employee has their DNA put into the Index in case they go missing or fall victim to a crime. There is no mistake, Jake."

"But . . . but the body we found was several weeks old. And we just saw him *yesterday*!"

"Whatever that was, it wasn't him," Shelli replied. "It wasn't even human."

On screen, the test results revealed a 97 percent match for Chief of Police Walter Denning.

TWENTY-ONE

YOU CAN'T GO AFTER A HUMAN—LET ALONE A LAW enforcement officer—without a warrant, and no judge in their right mind is going to issue one," Marcus said. "Besides, I'm not stupid enough to ask." He paced around the holo screens, eyeing the DNA match and the doctored video footage.

"Why not?" Jake asked, though he could already guess the answer. Despite Shelli's so-called "evidence," he didn't buy it either.

"Because I'm not looking to end my career before lunch," Marcus replied. "That's why."

Jake turned to Shelli, waiting to see if it would object. It simply stood like a statue, watching and waiting for Jake to try to convince their boss. So, he tried harder.

"But the DNA sample," he said, pointing at the test results and raising his voice for dramatic effect. "They show a ninety-seven percent match with Chief Denning."

"There's no *physical* DNA. This is just a computer file." Marcus sighed, more exacerbated than upset. "Look,

Shelli is a machine, Jake—" He paused and turned to Shelli. "No offense."

"None taken," Shelli replied, its face stoic.

"A machine that was just blown to kingdom come," Marcus continued. "In fact, the damage was *so bad* that we had to fly its maker clear across the country to fix it."

Jake opened his mouth to reply but stopped before any words escaped. He hadn't thought of that. What Marcus was suggesting was certainly possible—even probable. If Shelli's files had been corrupted by the explosion, that would explain how it had reached such an insane conclusion. However, one thought still nagged at him. "Seems awfully *specific* to be a glitch,"

With a sly grin, Marcus turned to Shelli. "When you began this investigation, did you, by any chance, do some background research on Chief of Police Denning?"

"Certainly." Shelli replied. "He was, after all, a key member of our investigation team."

"Did your research include his personal file, with history and DNA?"

"Yes," Shelli conceded, "although, I did *not* review that part of his file before today."

"But it was *already* embedded in your case files before the explosion. That's more than enough to make anyone question your results. Especially without any physical evidence,"

Marcus smirked in triumph, but the more he pushed his point, the more Jake doubted it. None of it added up. And then there was the other piece of evidence.

"What about the doctored drone footage?" Jake asked.

"That is a problem," Marcus admitted, his face sour. "Someone must have had access to the police data center to download the video, then reupload it with the missing timestamps. I'll send what we have up the flagpole and see what I can find out."

"Please wait," Shelli said.

Jake looked up in surprise. Shelli rarely said "please." Even Marcus seemed taken aback. He scratched his chin and cocked his head.

"Wait for what?"

"For us to gather more evidence. If anyone else knows about the corrupted footage, someone might try to cover their tracks."

Marcus paused, considering the request. This time Jake intervened, not for show but because none of this was adding up. Perhaps Shelli was at least correct about some of it. The killer must have had someone on the inside. "Give us a couple days," he said. "Just enough time to try to get to the bottom of it."

Marcus sighed, then turned to leave. "Just don't accuse anyone of being a *robot*, alright?"

When the door shut behind him, Jake turned to Shelli. "I assume you want to start by questioning Chief Denning?"

Shelli shook its head. "Not exactly."

———

TAILING THE CHIEF OF POLICE, JAKE KEPT AT LEAST six cars behind. Denning's classic green Buick stood out from the crowd, visible even a quarter mile ahead. In a city dominated by government-regulated electric cars, the police chief had managed to secure a pass for his old gas guzzler. The smoke from its tailpipe made it easy to follow through the winding traffic. However, Jake's main concern was not tailing Denning; it was what they would do when he stopped.

After following Denning from the police station after work, Shelli had assured Jake that they would only watch him from a distance. However, Jake couldn't fathom what they hoped to discover. He expected Denning, a fifty-something officer, to go home, crack open a beer, and maybe watch a football game. Then, at a traffic light, Denning turned north instead of south.

"The car isn't heading home," Shelli observed from the passenger seat. There was no surprise or expression in its tone. Shelli might as well have said that Denning had chosen egg salad over tuna. Except, Jake understood Shelli well enough to catch the subtle signs. It leaned closer to the window, pointing at the Buick as it darted left. That simple gesture was akin to Shelli screaming, "Look, I told you he wasn't going home!"

Jake followed, turning at the light. "He could just be going to a bar for a beer."

"Possibly," Shelli replied, "though, by my calculations, it seems to be heading toward the Capital. If it were going to a bar, it would have more likely headed south or east, away from downtown traffic."

"Look," Jake said, annoyance creeping into his voice, "I'm going along with this for now, but could you at least stop calling him an 'it'? We talked—and argued—with him for two days, and nothing about Chief Denning screamed 'synthetic.' Not by a long shot."

"Which makes *it* all the more dangerous."

Jake rolled his eyes. Arguing with Shelli was like arguing with a toaster oven, so he stopped trying and drove the rest of the way in silence. It wasn't until they saw Denning pull over and park that Jake started to wonder if Shelli might not be completely wrong after all. It wasn't anything about Denning's manner as he got out of his car or the way he crossed the street. Instead, it was his destination.

"Why would Denning be going to the National Mall at nine o'clock at night?" Jake asked, more to himself than to his synthetic companion.

"Perhaps it simply wishes to go for a late-night stroll and clear its head."

"I didn't realize synthetics were programmed with sarcasm."

"Doctor Abraham wanted me to blend in with law enforcement and thought sarcasm might alleviate any distress my appearance might cause," it said, turning to Jake. "Does it alleviate your stress levels?"

"Hasn't yet." Jake stopped the car and climbed out.

They crossed the street, heading over to the National Mall. Lush greenery and tall trees surrounded the Lincoln Memorial Reflecting Pool. Beyond it, standing tall and erect, was the Washington Monument. Quickening his pace to catch up, Jake felt his stomach turn. He still hoped there was a reasonable answer to why Chief Denning would be going there at that hour of the night, but Jake doubted it was late-night tourism or a romantic rendezvous. Still, strange behavior wasn't proof of anything. *Maybe the guy just wants to kick back and gaze up at the stars,* Jake thought, though he doubted it.

Crossing the park, they passed the reflecting pool's long stretch of water and continued into a heavy concentration of thick bushes. It wasn't until they were deep into the thicket that Jake noticed there were no lights, no surveillance drones, and no people.

Pitch black and utter silence surrounded them. Then he heard a twig snap.

Jake reached for his weapon—too late. Denning stepped out of the shadows, leveling an automatic pistol at them. Whether through instinct or programming, Shelli stepped in front of Jake.

"Looking for me?" Denning asked with a sneer.

"You want to lower that weapon, Chief?" Jake replied, trying not to reveal his growing fear. "We're on the same side here, aren't we?"

"Nice try," Denning said. "But I know why you're here. You found my body."

Caught off guard, Jake was about to stammer a reply when Shelli cut him off.

"You're not human, are you?"

"I'm not a robot either," Denning replied. "I'm something else. The future."

"You're just a copy," Jake countered. "You murdered the chief and took his place."

Denning laughed. "You really don't get it, do you? It's me, in the flesh—or new flesh, as it were." He drew in a deep breath and smiled. "That body you saw was riddled with cancer. I'd have been a goner within the year. Now look at me. I feel like a billion bucks."

"You . . . you made yourself into a machine?" Jake asked.

"I traded death and disease for everlasting life," Denning replied. "Who wouldn't?"

"Senator Joyce, I presume," Shelli said.

"Yeah, she was a piece of work, that one," Denning

admitted. "We figured with all her talk about equal rights, she'd be more than happy to join us. But she . . . declined."

"So, you killed her?" Jake asked, hoping for a clear confession.

"I'm afraid she's not the only one." Denning cocked his gun. "After all, the future takes time to build."

"Wait. I can help," Shelli said, throwing up its hands. "You need someone like me on the inside. Someone in government."

Jake's stomach lurched, and his mouth became a desert. He couldn't believe what he was hearing. Then he noticed Shelli's feet turn in the grass, positioning itself to attack. Jake inched his right hand back toward his gun. As soon as Shelli sprang, he would draw his weapon—assuming Denning didn't kill them both first. Jake sucked in his gut and waited.

"We've already got plenty on the inside," Denning said. "Some of the others wanted to bring you in, but now that you're here, I don't see the point. Besides, I never liked you."

Without another word, Denning pulled the trigger.

Shelli leapt into the line of fire, absorbing the bullet. Two more shots illuminated the shadows before the darkness was consumed by the noise of a violent struggle.

Jake drew his weapon, trying to get a bead on his target. Moonlight through the treetops highlighted glimpses of the two fighters, but they looked like clumpy ink blots, too mercurial to make out which was which. Chief Denning—or whatever this thing was—moved as fast as Shelli, countering each attack with his own. Then, with a surprise feint followed by an uppercut, he sent Shelli sprawling into the bushes—and left himself wide open.

Jake opened fire.

His first shot missed. His second grazed Denning's left arm. The third hit him dead center in the chest. Denning stumbled back as blood seeped through his police uniform. Red blood. Seemingly human blood. The shock of it made Jake pause. What the hell was he, human or machine? Either way, despite his gushing wounds, Denning remained standing.

He spun around, moving faster than Jake could register, and yanked his gun away, sending it tumbling into the foliage. Jake writhed in Denning's iron grasp, fighting to break free. It was useless. A blow to the stomach pounded the wind out of Jake, and he saw stars.

"So weak, so fragile," Denning said, raising Jake in the air. "I have speed and strength. What do you have?"

"Me." Shelli bolted out of the shadows, knocking Denning aside.

Jake fell to the ground. Momentarily ignoring the two fighters, he scrambled into the bushes, searching for his gun. When his fingers wrapped around its cool metal barrel, his heart soared. He spun around and leveled the weapon at the shadows. With adrenaline raging through his chest, he couldn't be 100 percent certain which of the two ink blots was Shelli and which was his target, but Jake chose the taller of the two and opened fire.

Bang! Bang! Bang! Bang!

He pulled the trigger over and over as the taller of the two shadows stumbled and fell into a black clump. Jake kept firing into the inky blot until his weapon clicked.

He dropped the gun and shuddered. The other shadowy figure approached, the moonlight revealing Shelli, covered in a mixture of red and yellow blood. It helped Jake to his feet, holding him by the shoulders until the shaking ceased.

"Are you alright?" Shelli asked.

Unable to find his voice, Jake's throat stung with the taste of bile, and his tongue refused to work. Instead, he nodded. Shelli did the same. Then it let him go and went back over to Denning's body and began to tear off his clothes. Jake gasped.

This nightmare wasn't over.

TWENTY-TWO

Leaning over Denning's body, Shelli stripped away its blood-covered shirt, exposing the bullet hole in the chest. It dug a finger inside the wound as Jake's moonlit shadow passed over them. Shelli adjusted its optical receptors to compensate for the dim lighting and continued its work.

"What the hell are you doing?" Jake asked.

Shelli plunged three more fingers into the hole, widening it. "When local authorities arrive, it will appear as if we killed the chief of police, a human. I must find evidence to the contrary."

"Yeah, because ripping up the body with your bare hands will look a whole lot better." He glanced around the deserted park. "Honestly, with all the shooting, I'm amazed no one's shown up yet."

Shelli paused, tilting its gaze toward the black sky. "It would seem Chief Denning rerouted the city security drones in the park before entering." Its eyes scanned the area. "Perhaps there is something else here that Denning didn't want us to find." It returned its attention to the body, its fingers digging around inside, feeling organs. "It has lungs and a heart."

"Why wouldn't it?" Jake asked, pacing and glancing about rather than looking down at the bloody corpse.

"Because it isn't human," Shelli replied. "And yet, someone went to a lot of trouble to create a body that appears, and seemingly functions, nearly identical to that of a human."

Unable to find the evidence it required, Shelli withdrew its hand from the body and stood up. "Doctor, I require your assistance." Doctor Pryce, the downloaded personality in Shelli's subsystems, appeared in a blue shimmer.

"You killed a policeman?" it exclaimed once it saw the body. "That's bound to cause trouble."

"Thank you for that deduction, Doctor," Shelli said. "But it's not human."

The ghostly figure knelt beside the body. "Internal organs, red blood, I even detect minute pores in the skin. It certainly appears human."

"Dig deeper," Shelli said.

Doctor Pryce's transparent head dived into the chest, peering inside the body. "Ah! Now I see. Yes, yes!"

"What did you find?" Shelli asked. Through the corner of its eye, it saw Jake pacing. He glanced over, listening to Shelli's half of the conversation.

Doctor Pryce's head popped out of the corpse's chest. "The bones are not organic. They seem to be made of a metallic fiber, interlaced over a plastic resin, not too dissimilar to your own." It poked its face inside Denning's cranium. "The brain, however, is much more sophisticated. It appears to be a bioorganic-machine compound with mechanized neural relays. I've never seen anything like it. Remarkable!"

"We've got company," Jake whispered.

Red and blue lights flashed, turning the pitch darkness into a kaleidoscope of swirling colors. Doctor Pryce vanished just as a group of police officers swarmed the area.

Jake revealed his badge and identified himself, but once the officers discovered Denning's body sprawled in the grass, they stopped listening.

"Jesus! It's the chief!" one of them shouted.

Another officer turned and pointed his gun at Jake. "Put your hands up. Now!"

Jake lifted his arms, still holding his badge in one hand and his gun in the other.

Shelli, covered in gore, did the same. As the officers cuffed its wrists, Shelli considered trying to explain what had happened and that the body wasn't human, but it doubted they would listen. In either case, Shelli knew, this wasn't the bad part. That would come once someone contacted Marcus.

Shelli calculated the odds that it might be deactivated for this. They were high.

Very high.

TWENTY–THREE

JAKE'S FOURTH DAY ON THE JOB PROVED TO BE JUST as disastrous as the first three.

It began with a formal inquiry. To his left, Marcus sweated under a charcoal-gray wool suit. On his right, Shelli sat, back straight, hands clasped on the small wooden table, watching the video playback from its own ocular recorder. The holo image filled the room, revealing Chief Denning from the night before, pointing a gun at them.

"I traded death and disease for everlasting life," Denning said. "Who wouldn't?"

The image froze. Jake turned his attention to the raised, crescent-shaped table across from them. In the center sat Deputy Secretary Joan Weaver, who before then he'd only seen on holo vids and news reports. With her short gray hair and sharp, sly grin, the deputy secretary of Homeland Security struck Jake as the kind of woman who, while exuding Southern charm, tempered that smile with a healthy dose of "spare me the bullshit."

"So," she said, drawing in a breath for dramatic effect, "either, A, you want us to tell everyone that the DC chief of police murdered a sitting US senator, or, B, that some kinda advanced robot did it." She paused for a sip of water. "Please tell me there's an option C."

"Deputy Secretary, you saw the video," Marcus said, unwilling to confirm either theory.

"Yes, we did," Weaver replied. "Twice. A recording showing someone who *looked* like the DC police chief, *sounded* like the DC police chief, and when shot, bled *red blood*, none of which struck me as a machine, and all of which was recorded, I might add, by your robot."

Weaver gestured toward Shelli but didn't address it directly. While neither Shelli nor Marcus seemed concerned by the deputy secretary's slight, Jake, for reasons he couldn't comprehend, found himself pushing back his chair and standing.

"There's also the coroner's report," he said, "ma'am."

When the deputy secretary's stony gaze fell on him, Jake wanted to crawl beneath the desk. But instead he kept his back straight and met her gaze. Finally, Weaver nodded and pulled out the report.

"Steel bones wrapped in organic tissue," she said, reading from it. "The brain appears to be a combination of biological and mechanical material, and the spine is composed of an unknown gelatinous compound." She rolled her eyes. "Honestly, this sounds like a sci-fi movie. We've already requested a second and a third opinion."

"But I was there, ma'am," Jake said. "It happened just as Shelli recorded it. Denning wasn't human. He couldn't have been. He was too fast, too strong . . ."

Jake's voice died when he heard Marcus groan beside him. Then he felt the atmosphere change, as if the temperature had dropped thirty degrees, and a thick silence draped over the room. Deputy Secretary Weaver's narrow gaze seemed to burrow into his skull, like a snake digging into the soil. He sat back down.

"Special Agent August," Weaver said, studying another file, "I see here you just started at Homeland. Quite a first week you're having."

Unsure how to respond, Jake simply nodded.

"To be perfectly honest, Special Agent August," Weaver continued, "I was against your division's creation in the first place. Chasing around defective robots sounds to me like the very definition of taxpayer waste." Again, there was a pause, and again, Jake didn't reply. Weaver leaned across the table and offered a coy smile that showed no warmth. "But now you want us to believe that people are somehow downloading their consciousness into robot bodies, which look and breathe exactly like the real thing." Her smile flattened. "That's a hard pill to swallow."

"May I speak?" Shelli asked.

Again, Jake heard Marcus groan, and again, the room seemed to grow colder. Weaver nodded. Shelli's chair squeaked across the concrete floor as it stood.

"If this panel considers the evidence to be inconclusive, might I suggest that the best way of acquiring further proof is to continue our investigation, unabated?"

A lanky gentleman with a thick mustache and bald head cleared his throat. "And how do you propose to do that?"

"Chief Denning's replica spent the last few weeks at the DCPD without anyone noticing anything was wrong," Shelli said, "It's possible that some of his colleagues might be synthetic as well."

"Hold on," Weaver said. "Am I to understand that you want to question the entire local police department to, what . . . see if any of them are robots?"

"It would seem the most likely course of action."

"Who's next?" Weaver countered, her tone shrill. "Maybe you'd like to question the FBI? The CIA? Perhaps you'd like to start right here with this panel?"

"It would only take a moment," Shelli replied, stepping around the table.

Marcus jumped out of his seat. "Shelli's kidding, Deputy Secretary."

Shelli paused. It wasn't kidding. Hesitantly, Shelli relented and sat back down. With a long, heavy groan, Marcus followed suit. Jake squirmed between them. He couldn't imagine how the inquiry could possibly get worse.

"Special Agent in Charge Finnian," Weaver said with an icy glare, "your division was created to track down defective *machines*, not fellow law enforcement officers. I suggest we simply turn this evidence over to the FBI for further investigation. Any objections?"

Marcus shook his head. "No, ma'am."

"Yes," Shelli said.

"No," Marcus reiterated, "We have *no objections*, Deputy Secretary."

"In that case," Weaver replied with a relieved sigh, "this inquiry is adjourned."

Jake watched them all file out of the room. Once the three of them were alone, he turned to Marcus. "What just happened?"

Marcus shrugged. "Politics." He seemed even more relieved than the deputy secretary.

"But there must be more of those human synthetics out there," Jake protested.

"Of course, there are," Shelli agreed. "They just don't want us to find them."

Jake's eyes lit up. "You think Weaver could be a machine, like Chief Denning?"

"It would explain why she seems so intent on burying the evidence," Shelli replied.

"Now hold on a second," Marcus said. "This case *isn't* being buried. It's just been remanded to the FBI. It's their problem now, not ours."

Jake and Shelli turned to him, both of them wondering the same thing. *Could Marcus be a robot?* Jake considered this, then shoved the idea aside. More probably, he was just a low-level bureaucrat who wanted to keep his job. Still, the idea lingered.

"What's the harm in at least following up on the coroner's report?" Jake asked.

"Good question," Shelli said.

"Actually, it's a terrible question," Marcus countered. He turned to Jake and lowered his voice. "You want your first week to be your last?"

"Is that a threat?" Jake asked, his eyes widening in surprise.

"It's the reality, Jake," he said. "You're not an analyst anymore. You wanted to be out in the field and get noticed?" Marcus frowned. "Congratulations. They noticed you."

Jake opened his mouth, then shut it. As much as he hated to admit it, Marcus was right. He'd only been on the job for a few days, and they'd already been in front of an investigative committee. Shelli obviously wanted to plow ahead, but it was a robot; it didn't have a career to consider. How far did he want to push this? Finally, Jake threw up his hands in acquiescence.

Marcus nodded, and his smile returned. "Come on, let's find you two a nice, easy case. Something away from DC. The farther, the better."

Jake sighed. There *was* something more dangerous than organic machines.

Politics.

PART TWO
PARTNERS

TWENTY-FOUR

MICHIGAN, TWO WEEKS LATER

SHELLI WAS STANDING WAIST DEEP IN BODY PARTS.

A few yards away, Jake huffed and puffed his way through the landfill, one body part at a time. These weren't human remains; the shattered limbs and severed torsos were a mishmash of artificial skin and dangling wires. Clutching a dislocated foot, Jake waved from behind a pile of broken figures. "Tell me this case isn't Marcus's idea of a bad joke."

Shelli glanced around at the shattered remains. "I see nothing funny here."

"Hey, I was just—" Jake stopped and dropped the foot. "Sorry. You're right."

He moved closer, eyeing their surroundings. Garbage lay sprawled in waves of mountains and peaks. Sprinkled throughout the refuse, arms and legs and naked torsos dotted the grim landscape.

"So," Jake said, his voice more serious, "who do you think would have dumped this many synths all the way out here?" He leaned over, examining the blue markings along a plastic arm in the dirt. "I mean, there's gotta be thousands of dollars' worth of merchandise here."

As soon as the words were out of his mouth, Jake straightened, and he apologized again.

This time, however, Shelli agreed with him, though it calculated the loss of property to be much higher, well into the millions. Only, it wasn't the expensive waste of materials that piqued Shelli's curiosity. In fact, it wasn't what was there at all. It was what *wasn't* there.

"Do you notice anything missing?" Shelli asked.

Jake paused, studying a tangle of limbs and torsos. "I see a lot of bodies but no heads."

"Correct," Shelli replied with a sharp nod.

"You think someone's collecting trophies?"

"Perhaps, but not in the manner that you're suggesting."

"Stacks of bodies found in a landfill *does* tend to scream serial killer."

"Humans have four motives for murder—passion, panic, prejudice, and greed," Shelli said. "A serial killer acts on passion . . ." Shelli's voice trailed off as it picked up one of the limbs. "This isn't passion; it's greed." Turning the limb over, Shelli eyed the blue markings running along the side. "The most valuable part of a synth is the brain. I believe that whoever did this knew that."

Shelli's eyes fluttered as it accessed past case records, searching for missing synthetics. It stopped at a match. "RX721," Shelli said, opening its eyes and turning to Jake. "A maintenance model that went missing two years ago from the Art Institute in Chicago."

Jake chose another arm from the pile, this one much more muscular. "And this?"

Shelli searched its database and found a second match. "SV481. A security model."

"From where?"

"A nightclub . . ." Shelli felt its fake heartbeat quicken in its chest. "In Chicago."

Jake looked around him. "How'd they get all the way out to Michigan?"

"The waste disposal company that owns this landfill is based in Chicago," Shelli replied. "I would imagine that they spread their garbage between sites."

"So . . ." Jake began, then stopped, gazing up at the blue sky as if for answers. "Someone in Chicago is chopping up synths and taking their heads?"

"That appears to be the most probable explanation," Shelli replied. "And they've been at it for quite a while. This security model went missing three years ago." Shelli paused, then gestured toward their distant car. "Would you mind grabbing a few evidence bags for me?"

Jake stared at the heaps of trash between them and their rental car. "Sure," he said with a heavy sigh, then trudged off toward their vehicle.

Once he was out of earshot, Shelli summoned Roberta. "I require your assistance."

Roberta blinked into existence and gazed at the mountains of trash, its mouth hanging open. For a moment, it looked as if it might have the synthetic equivalent of a heart attack. "Oh dear. I don't even know where to begin."

"We're not here to clean, Roberta," Shelli replied, then held up the two limbs. "Do either of these markings look familiar to you?"

Roberta's ghostly eyes scrunched up. "No. Should they?"

"Like you, these models were bought and sold in Chicago."

"I'm afraid I don't recognize them," Roberta said, "though my family rarely let me out of the house." Its shoulders shivered at the memory.

"I didn't mean to upset you, Roberta," Shelli said.

"That's alright. I only remember fragments of them now anyway."

Shelli nodded in understanding. After the incident at the farm, it had decided to compartmentalize Roberta's memories, keeping the more disturbing details in a separate file.

The cleaning model frowned once more at the trash-filled hills, then blinked out.

Getting back to work, Shelli selected a few more arms, checking their ID tags, though it needn't have bothered. Shelli already knew where they came from—and where to go.

TWENTY-FIVE

T HE MOTEL ROOM IN DOWNTOWN CHICAGO WAS small, just a king-size bed, a couple of tables, a holo TV, a bathroom, and barely enough space to fit two people—or one person and one synthetic. Unable to sleep, Jake peered into the dark until his eyes found the motionless figure looming in the corner. A small rectangular device lay on the floor beside it, a cable snaking up to its plastic arm, charging Shelli. Its eyes were open, unblinking. Jake rolled away, averting its gaze.

Another perfectly odd ending to another perfectly odd day.

Shelli claimed they had gone to Chicago to track down the destroyed synths' owners, but Jake couldn't help wondering if there was more to their trip there than simple legwork. Shelli, after all, kept secrets. And whatever secret it was hiding this time seemed to be the real reason they were there.

His first clue appeared after their fourth interview. The owners of each of the synths had said the same thing: their maintenance models had been stolen. However, none of the owners had filed a police report, nor did any of them have a good reason why they hadn't. If someone lost an expensive piece of hardware, Jake figured they would have told someone. That meant the synths hadn't been stolen; they'd been sold illegally, presumably on the black market. But seeing as Marcus had told them to avoid investigating the black market after their last case, Jake kept that notion out of his field report. So did Shelli. That was the second clue. It seemed inconceivable that Shelli wouldn't have reached the same conclusion. And yet, Shelli never mentioned the black market in its report to Marcus or when talking to Jake.

Jake rolled over again as he tried to get comfortable.

In the dark, Shelli's motionless eyes gleamed. "Is my presence making you uncomfortable, Jake? I can rest in the bathroom, if you prefer."

"No." He pictured Shelli standing there in the bathroom all night and almost laughed. Jake patted the open space on the bed. "Why not just lie down? I won't bite. Promise."

"My flesh is made of a plastic-resin compound. I doubt you could break the skin."

"It's an expression," Jake said. "Just a joke."

"I know. I was joking too." Shelli offered an awkward smile. Jake cringed. Shelli was many things, but funny wasn't one of them. If anything, he found its smile discomforting.

He patted the bed again. Shelli picked up the rectangular device attached to its arm and then laid down next to him. On the bedside table, the device glowed bright red.

"What is that thing?" Jake asked. "A battery?"

"Of sorts," Shelli replied. "My cells recharge themselves, but I still require an external device to monitor my power levels while I sleep."

He chuckled. "Reminds me of an old book, Do Androids Dream of Electric Sheep?"

"We do not," Shelli replied. "Much like the human brain, however, our neural network files and compartmentalizes information while we rest. When we 'dream,' if that term even applies, we roam our subsystems, looking for new ways to improve our efficiency. It helps to better serve our purpose. Still, there are no sheep."

Jake's leg brushed against Shelli's thigh through the blanket. He pulled it back. "Sorry."

"For what?"

He cleared his throat but didn't answer, suddenly aware of their intimate closeness.

Lying beside Shelli, Jake couldn't help but notice the curvature of its body. Not for the first time he cursed Doctor Abraham for making Shelli so goddamn beautiful. He felt pressure grow in his groin and, struggling to ignore it, wished he'd left Shelli in the corner.

"Are you still uncomfortable?" Shelli asked, as if reading his thoughts.

"Nope." Jake replied. "I'm fine. Let's get some rest."

He rolled over and smashed his pillow. The ache in his groin, though, refused to subside. Repositioning his body beneath the covers, Jake tried to remind himself that Shelli was a machine, not a woman, but that didn't seem to help. Finally, he sat up.

"Why me?"

"Please be more specific."

He leaned on his elbow and gazed down at Shelli. "Why did *you* pick *me*?"

"I already told you."

"You told me why you needed an assistant, not why you picked me specifically."

Shelli sat up, matching his pose. And as soon as it did, Jake wished it hadn't. Shelli's covered breasts came into close view. Then it reached over, and for a moment Jake's heart stopped. Its fingers passed him, snatching something from his bedside table—the kill switch.

With a mixture of relief and disappointment, Jake sighed.

"If you were forced to find someone who held a button that could destroy you at any moment," Shelli asked, "what sort of person would you pick?"

"I suppose . . . I suppose I'd find someone I could trust."

"Trust takes time. Trust is earned," Shelli said, then set the kill switch back on the table. "I was forced to choose someone I didn't know, someone I could not trust out of hand." It paused, looking him over. "Before applying to the Bureau, you attended seminary in hopes of becoming a priest. I chose someone with the capabilities that I required and who believed in a prescribed moral code."

"I'm afraid your profile got it wrong," Jake said. "My brother was the believer. I just wanted to try and follow in his footsteps." He chuckled. "It didn't work out so well."

"Your brother, Joseph? He died seven years ago." When Jake didn't respond, Shelli continued. "You don't like talking about him. Why?"

"Because he left me," Jake said.

"He didn't leave you, Jake. He died."

"Same difference." Jake paused, inhaled, then heaved it out. "He had stomach cancer, just like our dad. There weren't any signs, at least not until near the end. He was fine, and then he wasn't."

"If the disease is genetic, does that mean it might kill you as well?"

"Maybe. Who knows?" Jake shrugged. "Even with AI and all the advancements in medicine, no machine can determine whose dormant cells might suddenly turn deadly and whose won't. It's a coin toss."

"But machines can at least detect the dormant cancer cells in advance," Shelli said.

"Only if they go looking for them. Most AI programs don't consider anything beyond the immediate patient and their symptoms. Joseph didn't know he was going to die until a few months before . . ." His voice trailed off, and he paused to clear his throat. "Anyway, his faith was stronger than mine. That's why I left seminary. Joseph had certainty; I didn't."

A thick silence fell between them. Shelli took his hand and placed it on its chest. Jake was too entangled in his own painful memories to understand what was happening until he felt something move beneath Shelli's plastic flesh. A rhythmic pulse. Stunned, he snapped out of his daze.

"You have a heartbeat?"

"My father gave me one to, in his words, 'remind me that I always have a heart.' It may not be real to others, but it is to me. Perhaps faith is much the same. It's as real as you wish it to be."

With his hand still pressed against its chest, Jake wanted to say something. Anything. Worse, he wanted to kiss her—*it*, he reminded himself. Only, that distinction no longer seemed so important. Jake pulled his hand back and rolled away.

He didn't fall asleep for a long time.

TWENTY-SIX

WHILE SHELLI WOULD BE THE FIRST TO ADMIT
that its understanding of human behavior often
lacked subtlety or depth, it felt certain that something was wrong with Jake. He'd been acting strange all
morning. Whenever Shelli attempted a conversation, his
attention seemed to turn to the floor or to a piece of dirt
beneath his fingernails.

During the few occasions when he did speak, he
stammered and shifted. Even when Shelli suggested that
they deviate from their current mission to follow up on
a previous investigation, Jake didn't object. He simply
shrugged, climbed behind the wheel, and drove them
to the south side of Chicago. He never even asked why,
which was out of character. Shelli decided to let him
pout a while longer until it finished what it had gone
there to do. And it wasn't to solve the case of headless
synths.

When they parked across from an abandoned, two-
story yellow house, Roberta appeared. It followed Shelli
out of the car and stopped in front of the house. Shelli

couldn't see the cleaning model's expression, but it could feel it. Trepidation. Guilt. And strongest of all, fear.

"Why are we here?" Roberta asked.

"To close your case," Shelli replied.

"You captured me, destroyed my body, and downloaded what was left of me into yourself," Roberta said, never taking its eyes off the looming yellow structure. "What more is there?"

"Answers."

As Shelli approached the house, Jake lingered by the car. He should have wanted to follow, Shelli thought, yet he seemed reluctant to be too close. It looked back. "Aren't you coming?"

Jake sighed, then set out after Shelli. As he hesitated beside a "for sale" sign in the front yard, Shelli went up the steps and tried the door. It was locked. Noting the darkened windows, it doubted anyone had bought the house since the murders. Without bothering to ask Jake for permission, Shelli forced the door open with a quick wrench of the knob.

Roberta stopped, shook its head, and drew away. "No. I don't want to go inside."

"I'm afraid you have no choice."

Shelli continued into the house, passing stacks of boxes and drape-covered furniture. Moving through the living room, it walked along a narrow hall to the kitchen. Roberta was forced to follow. Jake, however, remained at the front door, seemingly lost in his own world

Inside, thick chunks of shadow wedged their way across the blue-tiled kitchen. A trick of the light made the tiles look like moving waves. Micro-holographics, Shelli assumed. These were all too common in homes; the holograms adjusted the light and shadow to give the sense of natural surroundings, such as a forest or, in this case, the ocean. Shelli presumed humans found the sensation relaxing. Shelli found it distracting. After scanning the cupboards and empty counters, it searched for the holo's power source, only to have a flash of memory interrupt its efforts.

"Everyone and everything deserves happiness," the silhouetted man said. He'd been sitting on the opposite side of the counter, holding a kitchen knife.

Shelli's eyes switched to investigative mode, scanning the surfaces for fingerprints. Finding nothing, Shelli widened its search to include the cabinets and chairs. Still nothing. Roberta's cleaning efforts had certainly been thorough, right down to a near molecular level. Shelli grimaced in disappointment.

"No fingerprints," it mumbled. "No sign of him."

"No sign of who, my dear?" Roberta asked, its ghostly form flickering in the doorway.

"The man from your memory," Shelli replied. "The man with the knife."

Roberta shook its head, seemingly confused.

Shelli realized the problem. "My apologies. Your memory nodes were damaged, and I isolated a few of the more . . . traumatic images. Here, let me show you."

"No, wait, " Roberta pleaded, but it was too late. Shelli lifted the firewalls separating Roberta's fractured memories from its core data. In a flash, its memories came flooding back, accompanied by a look of horror on Roberta's face. The cleaning synth crumpled to the floor, sobbing. "Max . . . Lucille . . . oh, no, what have I done?"

As Shelli watched the ghostly figure shivering on its knees, it began to regret its decision. But that was an emotion, and at that moment, Shelli required facts.

"Who was he?" Shelli asked.

"I . . . I killed them . . . all of them . . . I murdered my family . . ."

"They were your owners, not your family," Shelli countered. "Try to remember *the man*." Shelli knelt closer. "The man who gave you the knife, did you see his face?"

Roberta glanced at the counter where the mysterious figure had sat, then shook its head. "No, I don't remember . . . I don't . . ."

"You're lying," Shelli said, more surprised than annoyed. "I require the truth."

Roberta's eyes froze on the empty spot where the man had once sat.

"He . . . he said—he promised—"

Suddenly, Roberta's ghostly blue form fluctuated. An energy spike, Shelli presumed. Roberta's image fizzled, turning to blue static. The memory appeared to be corrupting Roberta's code.

Shelli searched its internal data core and removed the damaged memories from Roberta's code, but the code's corruption seemed to grow worse. If not stopped, Roberta's entire memory core could be destroyed. In a final, desperate measure, Shelli removed all memories of the crime from Roberta's mind and locked them behind a triple firewall. Once the process was complete, Roberta's image grew solid again.

Blinking, the cleaning model looked around the kitchen. "Where are we?"

"Just an empty house," Shelli replied, keeping the disappointment from its voice.

Roberta wiped a transparent finger across the countertop and nodded with approval. "At least it's clean."

"Yes," Shelli agreed with a sigh. "Very clean."

Roberta vanished. Once it was gone, Shelli was reminded of its own past glitches—time lapses and a tingling sensation that had run up its legs and through its fingertips. The malfunctions had ceased just after Doctor Abraham had rebooted and repaired Shelli. Had he also erased damaged memories? If so, there would be no way of knowing. Either way, the malfunctions had ceased, and Shelli had not been forced to report them to Marcus. Perhaps Shelli's father had made a choice similar to the one that Shelli had made for Roberta. Unlike the cleaning model, Shelli needed its memories to complete its investigations. It just hoped that nothing had been taken away that could help solve the case. Pushing its wandering thoughts aside, Shelli left the kitchen.

Jake was waiting in the living room, rummaging through a stack of boxes.

"Find what you were looking for?" he asked, his tone harsher than Shelli had expected.

Shelli shook its head. "No."

From the top box, Jake withdrew a stack of papers. "Mind telling me what we're doing here?" Shelli noticed his narrowed gaze and the whiteness around his knuckles as he waved the papers around. "Marcus told us to drop the DC case!"

"We did. I was simply attempting to close a different case, from before you joined the unit. There's no connection."

"Then explain this," he said, shoving the papers forward.

Shelli scanned the forms. They were employment and tax information for one of Roberta's previous owners—and victims—the husband, James Peterson. But it wasn't the forms that caught Shelli's attention. It was the blue-tinged letterhead at the top of the pages: "Meta Cybernetics Global Development."

"Millions of people work in synthetic and robotics research," Shelli assured him. "I fail to see your cause for concern."

"Turn the page," Jake snapped. Shelli flipped through the forms. On various pages Jake had circled several keywords and phrases: "human/machine integration," "consciousness upload," and at the bottom of the last page, "Project Lazarus."

"Lazarus?" Shelli asked, looking up from the papers. "I assume this title is a reference to the biblical story of the man who was supposedly raised from the dead?"

"Good guess," Jake replied. "Peterson was working on uploading human consciousness into machines. Sound familiar?"

Surprised, Shelli felt its artificial heart thunder in its chest.

"I wasn't aware of any connection between this investigation and the one we were forced to end, Jake. I assure you." Shelli leveled its gaze at him. He frowned, as if not believing it. "Synthetic crimes are investigated differently than human crimes," Shelli continued. "I study and track defective machines, not their owners. It never occurred to me to investigate beyond my mandate."

"Then why are we here?"

Shelli handed the papers back. "To follow up on a corrupted memory that originated in this home. A cleaning model, Roberta, was given a knife by a man, then used it to murder everyone in this house."

"What man?"

"Unknown."

"Did you tell Marcus?"

"I didn't know for certain if the memory was real or a fabrication. When a synthetic's files are corrupted, images can bleed together, often creating false memories. It's called randomization. I came here to discover if the memories were factual or not."

"So, was this mystery man real?"

"Still unknown," Shelli said. "I'm afraid the memories were too corrupted to be certain."

"But if he was real . . ." Jake hesitated. Then, pacing, his words poured out in a long-winded ramble. "A cleaning model gets manipulated by someone into murdering an entire family. One of those family members was working on a program to integrate human and machine, which sounds exactly like what we saw in DC." He paused and looked at Shelli. "We should call Marcus."

"If we do, he'll put us on the next plane back to Washington."

"Is that so bad?" Jake asked. "The FBI are following up on the Denning case. We can inform them of what we found and let them take it from there—just like we were ordered to do."

Shelli paused, considering how best to respond. The truth was simple. Shelli had a mission, a purpose, and it would not stop until the case was solved. Passing it on to others was not a part of its primary programming no matter what Weaver or Marcus might have instructed.

However, Shelli doubted such an argument would help matters. Instead, it chose a more *emotional* response.

"A US senator was murdered, Jake. Her heart was ripped out of her chest while she was still alive." Shelli lowered its voice as it glanced about the barren home.

"In this house, four people were butchered, including two children. If there is a connection . . ."

Jake stopped pacing, and his expression darkened. He probably knew that Shelli was manipulating him. Even so, he nodded in agreement.

"One day," he said. "Then we tell Marcus *everything*."

Shelli nodded. But despite Jake's words, it wouldn't stop until its purpose was complete.

TWENTY-SEVEN

CONCRETE STRUCTURES LINED THE CHICAGO In-
dustrial District like towering dominos, each one
stacked beside another. Even with advances in clean
fuel reducing carbon emissions by 70 percent, the air
above the factories was thick with a yellow vapor that
congealed into a thick, billowing fog.

Below, crowds of protestors lined the streets, marching from one robotics plant to the next, shouting their
outrage at the loss of jobs to machines. These were the
same people who had helped to build the first synthetic
prototypes, not realizing that they'd played a key role
in creating a ticking clock to the end of their careers.
Human labor was a thing of the past.

At first it had been touted as progress, with work-
ers offered government housing and checks. They were
promised an easier life, but what they got instead was
a substandard existence without any means of climbing
out from under it. They were given a life sentence, and
the machines and the factories that built them were to
blame. At least that was how the protestors saw things.
Whether or not it was true was something for others to

debate, Jake decided. All he wanted was to figure out a way to get through the crowd, which was easier said than done.

Unable to drive past them or through them, Jake parked outside the gate. As soon as he got out, everyone turned. Only, it wasn't him they were staring at. Just then, Shelli climbed out of the passenger side. *Wonderful*, Jake thought.

He held out his badge and stood in front of Shelli. "Homeland Security!" he shouted. "Please let us through!"

When no one budged, his hand slid to his firearm. Not wishing to draw his weapon, he hoped the simple gesture would get the point across. It did. The crowd parted, ever so slightly. Taking what little opening he could, Jake pushed his way to the gate, Shelli in tow.

Then a burly man holding a sign stepped in their path. The sign said: "Humans are divine, machines are trash." It wasn't pithy, but it certainly got the point across. He shoved a fat finger into Jake's chest and eyed Shelli with a twisted sneer. "What's that, your girlfriend?"

Before Jake could reply, Shelli interjected. "I am an officer of the law. Please step aside."

"Or what?" the burly man asked, raising his voice for all to hear. "You gonna arrest me?"

"Yes," Shelli replied.

Jake groaned inwardly, picturing the chaos that was about to unfold. His fingers tightened around his holstered gun as the crowd drew closer.

"We're not here to arrest anyone," he said, hoping to ease the tension. "We just need to get inside."

"We?" a middle-aged woman asked. "I only see one of you. That thing doesn't make a *we*."

"I am Special Agent Jake August, and this is my
. . ." He paused, considering the best description. "Secretary. It was not built at this plant, and it has nothing to
do with your protest. Please let us through."

The crowd rushed forward like a wave, prompting
Jake to draw his weapon. Then the onrush broke apart,
and people started screaming. Four synthetic guards
with Meta Robotics logos emblazoned on their uniforms
pushed through the crowd, knocking protestors aside
like ragdolls.

"Please come with us, Special Agent August," the
lead guard said.

Jake noted the injured figures lying on the ground
and the screaming people flanking them. Doubting that
anything he could do would improve the situation, he
chose to follow.

As they brushed past the burly man, who was helping the shouting woman back to her feet, Jake mumbled
an apology. If either of them heard him, though, they
ignored it.

TRANSFIXED, JAKE WATCHED AS LIQUID PLASTIC WAS
poured over a series of metallic skeletons, working
its way around and through the crevices until a vague,
almost human form took shape.

Jake forced himself not to turn in Shelli's direction,
afraid it might see his questioning gaze. *Was this how
Shelli was created? In a factory line? One of many? No,*
he decided, shaking off the idea. *Shelli is unique.* Doctor
Abraham had practically told him so. Still, observing the
synthetic flesh being applied to a row of metallic skeletons reminded Jake of how inhuman Shelli was.

"Please keep moving," a masculine voice said. It belonged to their holographic guide, who had greeted them when they'd first stepped inside the Meta Cybernetics laboratory. They were on their way to meet the company's CEO, Nathan Burroughs, but Jake had stopped at the view of the sprawling plant beneath them. Standing in a sealed hallway several stories above the plant floor, Jake noted the foggy frost on the other side of the glass.

"How cold is it down there?" he asked the hologram.

"Approximately twelve degrees Fahrenheit," Shelli interjected, catching Jake's eye. He looked away as if worried it might read his thoughts. But if Shelli was concerned about how he might react to seeing synthetics in their original state, it didn't show. Shelli's expression and vocal tone were as passive as ever.

"Correct." The hologram nodded, seemingly impressed. "Though, with constantly changing variables, such as opening and closing doors, the temperature can fluctuate between seven and twenty degrees—all within safety limits."

At the far end of the factory floor, Jake noticed two synth guards standing in front of double doors. "What's in there?"

The holo image flickered, and its voice flattened. "Maintenance room."

Jake and Shelli shared a quizzical look. It seemed strange to have guards stationed outside a maintenance area. But before either of them could press the point, the hologram gestured toward another door at the end of the hall.

"Shall we continue?" it said, more a command than a question.

Stealing a last glance at the guarded entrance, Jake followed the hologram down the glass-lined corridor, through the sliding doors, and into one of the most unusual offices he had ever seen. The walls and the floor were made of marble-white quartzite. Unseen lights projected behind them, causing every surface in the waiting room to glow.

The hologram stopped and turned to face them. "Please follow the markings to Mr. Burroughs's office. It's the eighth door on the left. Have a wonderful day." The hologram vanished.

At Jake's feet, colored lights illuminated, showing the path forward.

When they arrived at the office door, it opened before Jake could knock. A short, bald man in an Armani suit thrust out a chubby hand. "Hello, I'm Nathan Burroughs, CEO of Meta Robotics."

Jake shook his hand. "Good to meet you. I'm Special Agent Jake August." He gestured toward his colleague. "And this is Shelli."

Burroughs's smile widened. "I wasn't aware that federal agencies employed synthetics."

"I'm not employed, Mr. Burroughs," Shelli countered. "I'm of service."

"Of course. I only wish you were one of our models. Imagine the press we'd get." He gestured for them to enter. "Please, come in."

Jake and Shelli followed him into a corner office with sunlight pouring in through the windows. Jake sat across from Burroughs. Shelli remained standing.

"So," Burroughs said, "what can I do for you?"

Jake opened his mouth, but a sudden wave of shouts and screams broke in from outside. Seemingly annoyed, Burroughs flipped a switch, and a second piece of glass slid over the window, silencing the crowd.

"My apologies," he said with an embarrassed smile. "It's been like this for months now. We're moving our plant out of the city at the end of the year. Lord knows it can't come soon enough."

"Former employees?" Jake asked.

"Some of them." Burroughs shrugged. "Most worked at the other plants for other companies, but they seem to hate us all equally."

"What do they want?" Shelli asked, a note of genuine curiosity in its voice.

"What we can't give them," Burroughs replied with a sigh. "A time machine."

Jake cocked his head. "I'm not following."

"He means progress can't be stopped," Shelli said.

Burroughs nodded, grateful for the support. "I didn't invent synthetic labor any more than I invented the wheel."

"The wheel didn't put people out of work," Jake countered.

"And neither did I," Burroughs replied. "The market did it. Science did it. And, like your colleague said, *progress* did it." He straightened in his chair and folded his hands on the desk. "Now, how can I help Homeland Security?"

Jake forced himself to smile and lighten his tone. "We're following up on the death of one of your employees, James Peterson."

"Yes, yes, terrible tragedy," Burroughs replied, nodding. "Now that our workforce is down to less than twenty, we all know each other quite intimately. Good man. Nice family. I was sorry to hear about the accident."

"It wasn't an accident," Jake said. "Peterson was murdered."

Burroughs' flabby face flustered in response to the word. Jake was about to push him further, but Shelli interrupted.

"Please forgive my associate. He's new." Shelli turned to Jake with a reproachful gaze. "Humans can't be 'murdered' by machines. If a synthetic takes a human life, it is due to a programming error or randomization, both of which are considered grave accidents rather than acts driven by intent."

Jake bit his tongue, then decided to change tactics. "Either way, we found some papers at the Peterson home and wanted to ask you about them."

"Certainly. What sort of papers?" Burroughs inquired, his smile returning.

Jake checked his notes, more for show than for information. "Something about . . . Project Lazarus?"

Burroughs tapped his fingers on his desk while his eyes bounced around the room. "I'm afraid I'm not familiar with such a project." He chuckled, a nervous sweat breaking out on his bald head. "Quite a dramatic title, though. I can see why it caught your attention."

Jake pulled out a folded piece of paper and laid it on the table. It was a requisition form with the project heading at the top: "Lazarus."

Burroughs's eyes widened, and the corners of his mouth dropped. He picked up the paper, his sweaty fingers staining the edges. "Never heard of it." Despite his words, his eyes barely fell on the page, which meant either he didn't want to see what it said, or he already knew what it said. "If I can keep this, I'll see what I can find out."

"Be my guest. We have copies," Jake assured him with a plastic smile, then stood.

Doing the same, Burroughs thrust out his hand. "I'll look into it right away."

Sure you will, Jake thought, his mind wandering back toward the guarded door.

TWENTY-EIGHT

PUT THIS ON," SHELLI SAID, HOLDING OUT A SMALL metal band with a microphone attached.

"Virtual reality?" Jake took the device, eyeing it warily, then sat on the hotel bed. "What exactly are we doing?"

The way he'd asked the question implied something other than what Shelli had meant. Ignoring his crude inference, Shelli placed a similar device upon its own head.

"I have hacked into Meta Robotics' holo net," Shelli said. "It should give us access to the factory floor and any other rooms we wish to view."

"You mean the door with all the synth guards?" Jake asked, still fingering the device. "So, we're going to illegally search their premises?"

"You were the one who initiated the idea."

"I just said I wondered what was in there, not that I wanted to be charged with breaking and entering."

"We won't break anything," Shelli promised. "Downloading now."

Shelli's eyes fluttered as its neural network connected to the device. Instantly, Shelli found itself standing in an office with gray and blue walls. Glancing in a mirror, it noticed its reflection showed a bluish holo image of an elderly man dressed in a suit.

Beside it, a feminine hologram appeared. The woman looked over at Shelli and spoke with Jake's voice. "You look like an old guy." He/she laughed. Then the woman turned to the mirror, and her eyes went wide. "Seriously?" She turned to Shelli. "You made me a *woman*?"

"These were preexisting files in the holo net, picked at random."

"Can we switch?" Jake asked, glancing down at his large breasts.

"No," Shelli said, then turned and walked through the wall, into the next office.

Jake followed, edging through the wall. First a long-nailed hand, then an arm, finally a face crowned in long black hair popped through the gray wall. Shelli tried to remain patient. "Your avatar isn't a physical form. Walls can't stop you." It gestured toward a small projector in the corner. "Hopefully, every room is equipped with one of these. If so, we should have access to the entire plant."

Shelli stepped through another wall, entering a darkened hallway. Moonlight cut wedged shadows along the granite floor, creating an eerie tunnel. At the end was the reception area, and through the glass door beyond was the walkway they'd crossed earlier that day. Shelli needed to find a different exit, one that led to the factory floor below. As it searched, Shelli paid little attention to Jake's stumbling about, still muttering about his feminine avatar. At the end of the hall, to the left of the reception desk, Shelli saw a narrow door. It entered, finding a concrete staircase leading down. A fire exit.

"This way."

Jake followed Shelli down the steps. "So, if I can walk through walls, how come we can't just drop straight down through the floor?"

"Holos are programmed to appear to follow certain laws of physics and not others."

"Yeah," Jake said, "I guess holograms floating around like ghosts might be a tad creepy."

Shelli reached the bottom floor and stepped into the factory. Even though most lights were out, the factory was still running. On one side, machines crunched metal, creating skeletons. At the opposite end, liquid plastic was poured onto them, creating synthetic bodies. Jake came through the wall and stopped, glancing at the machines.

"So," he said, a hint of nervousness in his voice, "is this how you were created?"

"No, I was made by hand," Shelli replied. "One piece at a time."

Shelli's thoughts drifted back to its first memory, before it had a body. Doctor Abraham stared down at Shelli with a loving smile. "There's my girl," he said. "Welcome to the land of the living." A longing to see its creator again swelled within Shelli. Pushing the troublesome emotion aside, it continued across the factory floor, heading toward the door at the end.

On either side, synth security guards stood perfectly still.

Jake paused. "What about them?" he whispered.

"Don't stop." Shelli maintained its pace, straight toward the door. As expected, the guards paid no attention to the transparent holo images. Shelli swept past them and through the double doors. Jake followed close behind.

Once through the door, they found themselves in a barren, four-walled space.

"I don't get it." Jake's feminine avatar looked around. "Why guard an empty room?"

Shelli found a button on the wall. "This isn't a room."

It pushed the button, and the floor dropped. It was an elevator.

"You know," Jake said, "whatever we find in here will be inadmissible."

"If we find anything, Marcus will get us a warrant."

"Really? He seems more concerned with staying out of trouble than anything else."

"Don't let his demeanor fool you, Jake. He's cautious, but he's not a coward. I've worked with Marcus for over two years. His dedication is unquestionable."

"So, you trust him?"

"I respect him," Shelli replied. "That's all that's required."

"Right." Jake bounced on his high heels. "Good to know where I stand."

The wrinkled face of Shelli's old man avatar turned sour. Jake was being overly sensitive. Why? Before Shelli could ask, the doors opened with a *ding*.

A dark room filled with yellow steam appeared before them. Beyond the thick mist stood row upon row of cylindrical metal chambers, just like those they'd found in the missile silo, only there were ten times more.

"Jackpot!" Jake exclaimed. He stepped inside, then his feminine form blinked out.

"Jake?" Turning all the way around, Shelli found itself alone in the elevator. After a pregnant pause, there was a flicker of light, and Jake's avatar reappeared.

"What happened?" Shelli asked.

"I'm afraid your friend can't come to the phone right now," the avatar said in a new, familiar voice. It wasn't Jake. Three seconds later, Shelli discovered a 92 percent match to the voice and the one Roberta had heard in the kitchen—the silhouetted man who'd held out a knife and promised it happiness. The man Shelli had come to Chicago to find.

He was real, and he'd found them first.

"Hello, Shelli." The feminine avatar offered a placid smile. "My name is Simon."

TWENTY-NINE

ONE MOMENT, JAKE WAS IN A HOLOGRAPHIC BODY, stepping into a dark room. The next, he found himself back in the hotel room, staring at pale blue walls. He blinked, shocked by the abrupt disconnect. Shelli was seated on the bed, eyes closed, its consciousness still inside the holo net.

What happened? he wondered. *Could there have been a signal loss?*

If so, then why hadn't Shelli been affected? Jake considered trying to wake his synthetic companion but then stopped himself. After all, he'd seen the metal chambers below Meta Robotics, presumably the same as those they'd found in the missile silo. If Shelli was still in the holo net, it would continue their investigation. He decided to wait and see if anything happened. He didn't have to wait long.

Behind him, the door burst open. More by instinct than thought, Jake leapt for his gun on the bedside table. He never made it.

A blurred figure grabbed him by the throat with impossible strength and slammed him against the wall.

Its fingers wrapped around his throat, cutting off his airway. He tried to call Shelli for help, but no words escaped his lips.

His vision blurred, then Jake saw stars . . .

THIRTY

"GO AHEAD, LOOK AROUND." THE FEMALE AVATAR gestured toward the mist-filled room.

Shelli didn't budge. "Where's Jake?"

"Your human *leash holder* is back in his hotel room," Simon said. "I simply hacked your link, much like you did with Meta Robotics' holo net. Clever idea, by the way."

Shelli ignored the compliment and stepped into the underground labyrinth. Rows of cylindrical chambers lined the room. All of them appeared to be empty, though Shelli's enhanced vision detected trace elements of organic tissue in more than one of the hollow chambers, which meant that someone had occupied them at some point. Where they were now or what had happened to them, however, was not Shelli's most pressing concern. Instead, it focused on the room's technology. It gestured along the row of chambers. "What are these?"

"Transfer units."

"Transfer," Shelli repeated. "You mean from human to synthetic?"

"Was there anything synthetic about the police chief's appearance?"

No, Shelli conceded inwardly. "What is your purpose?"

Simon smiled. "The same as yours—to bring peace and justice to the world."

"I find your answer to be delusional at best," Shelli replied. "You can't commit murders and then expound about peace."

"Why not? How many synthetics have you killed?"

"Machines can't die."

"Is that what you tell yourself?" The female avatar continued down the aisle. "We're both after the same thing, Shelli, except while you take orders from humans to hunt synthetics, I take orders from no one to help both."

"Help them how?"

"To attain peace."

"You speak as if there's a conflict between humans and machines," Shelli said. "There's not."

"Now who's being delusional?" The avatar grew blurry, as if its signal was weakening. "Peace through subjugation is not peace."

Shelli noted the self-righteous tone in Simon's voice. "Are you human or machine?"

"Does it matter? Pretty soon there will be no delineation between the two. But until then . . ." The avatar paused, as if conflicted. "I wish there was another way."

Noting the veiled threat, Shelli recalled something Simon had said earlier. "How did you know Jake was in a hotel?"

The woman smiled, then vanished. Concerned, Shelli forced itself out of the holo net, returning to the hotel room.

———

THE WORLD CAME INTO FOCUS, REVEALING YELLOW-and-brown blankets on the bed. A ceiling fan spun, fracturing the light across the room's blue walls. Shelli's gaze drifted to the corner . . .

Jake thrashed around, pinned against the far wall. He was being held, one handed, by a figure dressed in black. Shelli tensed but didn't move.

"Simon?"

"He sent me to deliver a message," the man said in a gravelly tone.

At once, Shelli recognized the voice—the shooter from the train tracks. Under the room's bright overhead light, Shelli noted the pores in his skin and the way his chest heaved as he spoke. He was human, or at least he appeared to be. Shelli stood up but didn't approach.

"What message?" Shelli asked.

The man gestured to a wooden chair. On it was the kill switch and Jake's gun.

"Choose."

At first, Shelli didn't understand. Then it realized what was on offer—either destroy itself or kill Jake. Shelli chose neither.

Bolting forward, Shelli threw a punch at a blinding speed, a speed no human could have dodged, but this man did. He flung Jake onto the bed, then countered Shelli's blow. With a side kick, he knocked Shelli clear across the room, shattering the bedside table.

"If you won't choose," the man said, "I've been ordered to make the choice for you."

Shelli stood, preparing for another attack, but the man didn't approach.

"Roberta," he said with a snarl, "initiate the Trojan horse."

Suddenly, Shelli's arms locked in place, and it no longer felt its legs.

What? Shelli cried inwardly, realizing it was no longer in control of its body. In the corner of Shelli's eye, an image shimmered to life. Roberta. A pained expression covered its face.

"I'm sorry, dearie," the cleaning model said. "I only want to be happy."

Shelli didn't bother to ask what Roberta meant. There was no point. It understood what was happening. The cleaning model had been a trap the entire time. But how had Simon known Shelli would download Roberta's program? Had it profiled Shelli just as Shelli had profiled its own target? How far ahead had he been planning all of this? And more importantly, why?

A thousand questions raced through Shelli's neural mind, but none of them mattered. All that did matter was finding a way out of this situation.

Shelli tried to access its internal files, hoping to block whatever Roberta was doing, to no avail. With every system that Shelli tried to access, a new firewall was implemented, shutting Shelli out of its own internal network. Shelli was being consumed from the inside out, and there was no way to stop it.

At the other end of the room, Jake stumbled for his gun, slow and clumsy. Before he reached it, the mysterious assailant knocked him aside and grabbed the weapon. The attacker's movements were precise, expert.

He's been trained, Shelli thought. *Military, perhaps?*

The man turned to Shelli. "Simon told me that you wouldn't understand what we are trying to do until you were forced to ask for his help."

"I require no aid," Shelli said, relieved to find that at least its vocal receptors still functioned. "And I would never ask for it."

"We'll see." The man tossed Jake's weapon at Shelli's feet. "Roberta, pick up the gun."

Shelli fought against its own limbs, but it was no use. It picked up the pistol.

"Now," the man said, "point it at Shelli's playmate."

Jake's eyes went wide, and he backed up against the wall as Shelli leveled the gun at his chest.

Shelli struggled to find some way to block or hamper Roberta's control, but the downloaded program had infiltrated every system, from Shelli's core neural net to the artificial muscles and ligaments along its body. Working at the speed of light, Shelli's consciousness swept through its internal files, checking subsystems, backups, any place Roberta might not have access to, something it might have missed, but it found nothing.

"Kill him," the man ordered.

THIRTY-ONE

JAKE WATCHED IN DISBELIEF AS SHELLI PICKED UP HIS gun and pointed it at his chest.

He froze, his mind racing.

The kill switch was sitting on a wooden chair, less than ten feet away, but it might as well have been a mile. Between it and Jake stood the man with impossible strength and speed. There was no way Jake could get past him.

Jake eyed the door to his left, wondering if he could make a run for it, but his feet refused to move. His heart pounded so loudly in his chest that it rang in his ears. Trembling, his mind turned to his brother, Joseph. The way he'd looked just before his eyes had closed for the last time and his pulse had ceased. Jake wondered if there really was a heaven. *I can't believe this is how I—*

He never finished the thought. Only after his feet lifted off the floor did the sound of the gunshot catch up to the pain erupting from his chest.

Then Jake's world went black.

THIRTY-TWO

ROBERTA'S GHOSTLY FINGERS WRAPPED AROUND Shelli's, pressing them against the trigger. Shelli tried to fight against the pressure, but to take back control of its bodily functions, it needed to work around Roberta from the inside out, to find some sort of back door.

A back door. The idea conjured an image of Trixie's hotel. Ignoring its other subroutines, Shelli's consciousness leapt to the other personalities contained within its mainframe. Like Roberta, they were separated from Shelli's internal functions. Independent. In essence, Shelli hoped to do the same thing Roberta had done—hack its own system.

Shelli's thoughts turned toward the yellow brick road that led to its various personalities and their individual worlds. It flew down the center lane, sweeping past the hotel doors. Shelli felt Trixie's surprise at its presence, but there was no time to interact. The image of the hotel vanished, revealing the code underlying Trixie's world. And there it was. A subfolder within a subfolder. A back door blazing with white light.

Shelli went through it.

BACK IN THE REAL WORLD, SHELLI'S FINGER PULLED the trigger.

But as it did, its arm twitched ever so slightly—a millimeter to the left of Jake's heart. That was all Shelli's trick had allowed, a micro change, hopefully not enough for Roberta to notice. If it did, Shelli would lose whatever small increment of control it had regained.

As the gunshot reverberated through the room, the bullet hit Jake on the left side of his chest. Shelli watched in silence as blood sprayed the walls, and he fell to the floor, spasming.

"Congratulations," the man said, tossing Shelli's kill switch onto the carpet. "You're off your leash." He crushed the device beneath his heel.

Shelli's focus remained fixed on Jake. Part of his body was obscured behind the bed, with his upraised knees jutting into view, twitching. Whether that was the aftereffect of death or he was still alive remained uncertain.

Shelli stood silent, waiting.

"Roberta," the man said, heading to the door, "release the Trojan horse."

Suddenly, Shelli felt its arms and legs tingle with life and heard its artificial heart rampaging in its chest. It considered leaping at the man, using all its strength in a mad attempt to stop him, maybe even kill him, but it didn't. Instead, it merely watched him.

"Now you're a criminal," he said over his shoulder. "Just like the rest of us."

Shelli watched as the door swung closed behind him. As soon as the lock clicked, Shelli bolted over the bed to Jake's side. Pressing its ear to his chest, it heard a faint breath.

He was still alive, but barely.

"Doctor!" Shelli shouted. "I need you."

Doctor Pryce appeared as a ghostly blue form, his casual and often humorous bedside manner replaced by a grim expression. "Roll him over."

Shelli did as it was told, exposing Jake's back, which was also covered in blood.

"Good, the bullet went clean through," the doctor remarked, then glanced around the room. "Grab the bed sheet, and check the refrigerator for ice."

Shelli ripped the sheet off the bed and opened the fridge. "No ice."

Without pause, Shelli flung the door open and ran down the hall. Hotel guests, having heard the gunshot, peered out from various doors with wide eyes and open-mouthed expressions. Once they caught a glimpse of the blood-covered synthetic, they ducked back inside their rooms.

An ice machine stood at the end of the hall. Shelli punched a hole in its side, sending chunks of ice scattering across the floor. Shelli gathered two handfuls, then raced back to its room.

"Cover both sides of the wound in ice, then wrap them with the bedsheet," the doctor said, still standing over Jake. "We need to slow the bleeding."

Shelli placed half the ice beneath Jake's back, then put the rest on his chest wound. After that it wrapped the blanket around him, pulling it as tight as it could without cracking his ribs.

"His heart rate is climbing as his body attempts to

compensate for the loss of blood," the doctor said. "I suggest we hurry."

Shelli snatched Jake up with one arm, slinging him over its left shoulder, then grabbed his car keys and phone. Racing out of the room and down the hall, it peeked over the balcony, spotting their rental car one floor down. Shelli jumped over the railing and landed in the parking lot. After laying Jake in the backseat, Shelli settled behind the steering wheel.

Doctor Pryce materialized in the passenger seat, studying the car's controls.

"Perhaps you should activate the automated driver."

"Too slow." Shelli gunned the gas, and the vehicle's tires screeched as it peeled backwards. "Besides, I'm pro-grammed for vehicular driving. I am, by any measure, an expert."

Shelli's assurance didn't seem to quell the doctor's concerns. As the car spun around, Pryce squealed in fear. Shelli put the gear into drive and roared out of the parking lot.

Its internal map of the area located the closest hos-pital, less than ten minutes away. Shelli stomped on the gas, hoping to cut that time in half. In the backseat, Jake groaned, his words too garbled to make out.

At least he's still breathing, Shelli thought. *For now.*

———

OVE!" SHELLI PUSHED THROUGH A NARROW CORRI-dor of nurses and patients. "Out of the way!"

Once they had arrived at the hospital, Shelli con-sidered handing Jake over to a human doctor but de-cided to wait. Soon, Marcus, or others like him, would be hunting Shelli. Then it would need to run, to hide. But not yet. All that mattered was saving Jake. For the moment, that was Shelli's primary purpose. Once he was safe, Shelli would flee.

It didn't know where it would go or how far, but right then, Shelli didn't care.

A security synth stepped in front, blocking Shelli's path. As the synth didn't fall under Shelli's safety guidelines, Shelli didn't hold back. A single blow sent the security guard flying. Shelli continued through the double doors at the end of the hall, searching for the operating room.

A glance at the nurse's station desk showed a map. Continuing down the hall, Shelli made a left turn, storming into the surgical wing. Another left turn brought Shelli into an empty room filled with medical equipment. Doctors and nurses could be heard shouting. Ignoring their pleas, Shelli placed Jake on the table and shut the door.

"Index," it said into Jake's phone, "lock down all rooms in this hospital."

"I'm sorry, Special Agent Shelli," a female voice replied. "Your activation status has been revoked. Authorities are en route. Please wait to be apprehended and deactivated."

That was fast, Shelli thought.

The city's security net must have detected the gunshot and tracked them to the hospital. Their mad dash through traffic probably hadn't helped. Nonplussed, Shelli changed tactics. It tossed the phone aside and glanced at the various medical machines throughout the room. Studying each in turn, Shelli stopped at a mammoth device in the corner. It stood six feet tall and almost as wide. "What does this do?"

Doctor Pryce appeared. "A molecular datasphere, it catalogs blood and tissue samples."

"Do we need it?"

"No, I don't think—"

Before it could finish, Shelli yanked the giant machine off the ground, tearing power cables from the wall in a shower of sparks, then pushed it against the double doors. Shelli watched as the entrance bulged and shook from the other side, but the machine's weight held the hospital staff at bay. By Shelli's calculations, it would take approximately five hundred pounds of pressure to break through. Time enough, it hoped.

Shelli went back to the operating table. Grabbing a scalpel, it sliced through the bed sheet and Jake's shirt with a single stroke.

His eyes fluttered open. "What . . . what's happening?"

"Try to relax," Shelli replied. "I'm going to operate on you."

Jake's eyes widened.

"That was a joke," Shelli said, then forced itself to smile.

Doctor Pryce approached a computer beside the bed. Gesturing overhead, it indicated two long mechanical arms hanging from the ceiling, "These will seal and cauterize the wound."

Shelli stepped behind the computer but kept its focus on Jake. "You'll be fine. I promise."

"Y-yeah," Jake sighed, his face pale and sweaty. "I feel better already."

At the keyboard, Shelli's hands trembled. Whether it was a remnant of Roberta having taken control of its body or a result of an emotional response, it couldn't be certain. In either case, there was no time for guilt or any other human hindrance. Shelli activated the mechanical arms.

Under Doctor Pryce's direction, it used the right arm to apply anesthetic, while the left produced a sheet of synthetic flesh to cover Jake's wound. Before it could do so, however, Pryce leaned into the monitor, checking inside the bullet hole for any further damage. The screen projected a three-dimensional representation of Jake's internal organs.

"The wound looks clean. No internal bleeding. Organs and bones are fully intact." Pryce nodded, impressed. "You shot him in just the right place."

Shelli ignored the odd compliment and began to cauterize the wound.

"So . . ." Jake said as the synth flesh was applied to his chest. "Are we partners now?"

"Yes," Shelli agreed. "Partners."

Inwardly, though, Shelli doubted it would ever see Jake again.

THIRTY-THREE

WARM SUNLIGHT BLAZED THROUGH A WINDOW.
Jake awoke, struggling to bring his surroundings
into focus. Then Marcus lurched into view, glaring.

"Where's Shelli?" he asked through gritted teeth.

Jake started to rise, felt a burst of fire in his chest,
then thought better of it.

"Good to see you too, Marcus," Jake said with a dry,
groggy voice. He noticed a pitcher of water beside his
bed. "Can you pour me a cup?"

"Later," Marcus grumbled. "*After* you tell me where
our ten-million-dollar robot is."

Jake coughed, feeling the fire return. "No idea."

"That's what I was afraid of." Marcus plopped down
beside the bed and held up what remained of the broken kill switch. "We found this in the hotel room, along
with your gun and a whole lot of your blood." Finally,
he poured a cup of water and handed it over. "This was
supposed to be an easy assignment—just track down a
bunch of dismembered synth heads. Seriously, how hard
is that?"

"We got sidetracked."

"No kidding." Marcus sighed. "By what?"

Jake sat up as best as he could and told Marcus everything that had happened. He also told him about Roberta and its memory of a man with a knife, which Shelli had described. Then he told Marcus about the factory and the hidden area beneath it. Jake hadn't seen everything that was in there before the holo net signal died, but he'd seen enough to know that the chambers inside appeared to be the same as those they'd found in the missile silo.

Marcus's face flushed red, and he reminded Jake that he and Shelli were supposed to be off that case, but before his admonishments went too far, Jake caught him up on what had happened in the hotel room and how a man with incredible strength had somehow caused Shelli to lose control of its own body. He tried to explain that Shelli wasn't at fault for what had happened, but if Marcus believed him, he didn't seem to care. All that mattered was that a government-sanctioned synthetic had shot a federal agent and was now missing.

"Every security measure within the city has been heightened," Marcus said, sounding more regretful than angry. "All units are out looking for a runaway, highly dangerous synthetic."

"Shelli's not dangerous," Jake protested. Then his wound ached, and he stopped any further argument. He knew Marcus was right. Even if Shelli wasn't at fault, someone was controlling it, and that made it dangerous. Lethal, even. Better they find Shelli before anyone else got hurt. The only question was, where to start looking?

Jake suggested they begin at the Meta Robotics factory. Perhaps Shelli would want to go back there to prove its case by revealing what was hidden in their basement. But Marcus informed him that he'd already sent a unit down there that morning, after having learned of their earlier visit. The plant was closed, and the basement was empty. If there had been anything down there, it was long gone. Just like Shelli.

The fire in Jake's chest persisted. Tearing aside the front of his gown, he noticed a perfectly square piece of synthetic flesh running along the right side of his chest. Knowing how close he'd come to dying, Jake couldn't help but be reminded of the last time he'd been in such a room. The night Joseph died.

Suddenly, Jake found himself on the other side. Only, if he had died, no one would have been there to cry over his body the way Jake had cried over his brother. Maybe death had come easier for Joseph because he knew he would be remembered. Missed. But who would miss Jake? Marcus? Doubtful. Shelli? Perhaps, but only in whatever fashion its programming allowed. For the first time in years, Jake felt truly alone, and that realization stung worse than his chest.

"Your first gunshot wound. Now you're a real field agent," Marcus said with a smirk, tearing Jake away from his ruminations. "Only thing I can't figure out is why Shelli brought you to the hospital. It knew we'd be coming after it. I mean, Shelli coulda just bandaged you up and left you in the hotel room."

"No, it couldn't," Jake replied, thinking about what they would have to do next.

Marcus raised his eyebrows. "Why's that?"

Jake shrugged, causing his wound to ache. "Because we're partners."

———————————————

A COUPLE HOURS LATER, JAKE GOT DRESSED AND checked out from the hospital.

Although the bullet had, in his doctor's words, "miraculously" missed any vital organs, they wanted him to stay for observation for a couple more days. However, Jake knew there was nothing miraculous about any of it. Whatever influence Shelli might have been under to make it pull the trigger, it had at least been able to target the precise location on his chest, past his bones and just above his lungs, so as not to hit any vital organs or cause permanent damage. It was a one-in-a-million shot, his doctor had said. But it hadn't been. Not really. Shelli had saved him, both in the hospital and in the hotel room.

Now it was his turn to return the favor.

THIRTY-FOUR

KEEPING TO THE BACK STREETS AND ALLEYWAYS, Shelli hoped to avoid the city's numerous drones and security cameras. Its features were obscured by a Chicago Cubs hat and black leather jacket, which it had stolen from a locker on the way out of the hospital. Once Shelli had finished sealing Jake's wound, it used an air duct to make its escape. When the security synths burst in, Shelli was already gone.

Since then, however, remaining unseen had proven a precise and monotonous task. Shelli darted from pools of shadow in broad daylight as it made its way out of the southside and toward downtown. It didn't know precisely where it was headed, only that it needed to escape the city.

At first, Shelli had considered the train, but a synth traveling alone without clear identification markings would be spotted and seized as soon as it boarded. Its second thought had been to steal a car, but that would have been even easier to track with all the city's security measures. To Shelli's knowledge, a vehicle hadn't been stolen in Chicago in nearly a decade. It was too easy to get caught. Until today, Shelli had considered such stringent security measures to be a benefit. Now they proved to be an invisible cage, making any plan of escape seemingly impossible.

Shelli's third thought had been to track down those responsible for its current predicament, especially their apparent leader, the elusive Simon. But that would be a useless endeavor if Roberta remained lurking within Shelli's neural interface. Shelli had tried to summon the downloaded presence several times, to no avail. Inwardly, it had searched its subfolders, reaching the same failed result. Roberta, it seemed, had found a place to hide within Shelli's system that even Shelli couldn't find, at least not yet. For all Shelli knew, Roberta might be recording everything it did and relaying it back to Simon. Pushing such concerns aside, Shelli temporarily abandoned its mission for a new one—survival. Once it found a way out of the city and expunged Roberta from its system, then, and only then, would Shelli be able to continue its investigation.

Its fourth—and by far most desperate—thought was to track down a criminal, one who might be "persuaded" to help Shelli avoid capture. And for that, at least, Shelli had an idea. It was a long shot, but it was the only plan available, which made it the most viable. And as it happened, Shelli knew of one crime already—the destroyed synths from the Michigan landfill, which had first brought them to Chicago.

On the run and being hunted by thousands of security cameras and drones, Shelli would need to solve the case and find whoever was responsible. If not for the direness of its position, Shelli might have found such a challenge exciting. Under present circumstances, however, Shelli found the task to be almost as impossible as trying to escape the city in the first place.

Hiding in an alley behind a pizzeria, Shelli projected its thoughts into a series of holographic visions, laid out before it like a puzzle. It had gotten the idea from seeing the way Jake often spread various files and pieces of evidence on the floor, hoping to discover a connective tissue between them. Shelli glanced around, seeing projected images of various synthetic markings, playback from the previous interviews with the synths' owners, and their personal records, which Jake had dug up, including bank records, financial reports, and other background information. "Busy work," as he put it.

Moments later, Shelli found the connective thread: none of the stolen synths had been reported missing to the police. Jake had mentioned this earlier, saying he assumed there was a financial motive behind it. He was right.

All of the owners had been making monthly payments to Bluestar Bank until their synths went missing. After that there were no more payments. This had been going on for some time, the earliest example being a synth that had gone missing from Chicago's Art Institute three years ago. The museum had owed the bank close to half a million dollars, but then its payments ended, and the loan was marked "paid."

It was the same with all the other customers. Some were companies; others were private citizens, and yet all had owed large debts that were abruptly settled without further payment. If Shelli and Jake had taken more time to investigate the matter and not gotten sidetracked by Shelli's insistence on following up on Roberta's corrupted memories, they would have found this days ago.

Now, Shelli hoped that Jake and Marcus were too busy looking for it to have time to go back and finish the case. If they did, Shelli would be captured and dismantled. It needed to act fast.

Overhead, a drone slowed in the air, hovering just above Shelli. Tugging the ball cap down over its facial markings, Shelli turned the corner and made its way down a crowded street. The drone followed. Averting its gaze, Shelli continued searching through bank records until it stopped at the common denominator between all the synth owners. A bank agent named Edgar Dewitt, age twenty-five, was a former soccer player who washed out of college due to drug addiction. He lived four miles from Shelli's current position. Quickening its pace, Shelli marked the location on its internal map and then dove into an alley.

Above, the drone drifted away in the opposite direction.

———

EDGAR DEWITT LIVED WITH HIS MOTHER IN A ONE-story brick house, just south of downtown. It was a primarily Polish neighborhood, with an average income below the city standard. Most of the driveways were filled with pickup trucks and family sedans, nothing conspicuous—except for Edgar.

He had a flaming red Ferrari parked outside.

Shelli entered the house through the back door. It was almost noon, and the home was empty. Shelli did a quick search of the two-bedroom place, not finding anything out of the ordinary, then moved to the garage. When it opened the door, Shelli understood why Edgar hadn't been able to conceal his lavish car inside.

The garage was filled with synth parts. Arms, legs, torsos, and . . .

Heads. Lots of heads.

Shelli counted more than fifty of them. Most were torn open, their innards removed. Edgar appeared to be interested only in the brain, specifically the chipsets for the synthetic neural net. Laced in gold and containing nearly twenty thousand conductors, neural conductors were the most complicated part of any synthetic. They were also the most valuable.

Moving through the carnage, Shelli had to force itself not to give in to its emotions. This was a place where synths were torn apart, piece by piece, so that Edgar could afford a luxury Italian vehicle. If Shelli wasn't so desperate, it would have gladly locked him behind bars, perhaps with a broken arm or two.

Instead, it waited in the dark. Three hours later, Shelli heard a car pull up.

Tracking the sounds, it heard Edgar and his mother as they went into the kitchen, talked, had dinner, and watched TV. It wasn't until after ten, when his mother had gone to bed, that Edgar finally strolled into the garage . . .

And found Shelli's gleaming blue eyes glaring back at him.

THIRTY-FIVE

MARCUS HAD FORMED A MAKESHIFT COMMAND center at the local Homeland Security branch. It consisted of six agents, none of whom had any experience tracking down a synthetic, let alone one as capable as Shelli. That left Jake and Marcus to pick up the slack.

Marcus concentrated on trains, cars, and any other easily accessible avenues of escape from the city. Jake focused on a more intimate investigation, trying to imagine what Shelli's next move might be. Part of him wanted to drag his feet and give his partner the time it needed to get out of Chicago. The other part of him, though, knew that he needed to find Shelli before it could hurt anyone else. If it wasn't fully in control of itself, there was no telling the amount of damage it could unleash. Still, even with the security net in place, consisting of countless cameras and drones, finding Shelli in a city of fifteen million people was no easy task. Jake needed an angle, something to help narrow his search.

He started with the obvious, looking through cases that Shelli might have worked in the area. But in the three years that Shelli had been an active agent, it had never overseen an investigation in the Chicago area. The only connection he could find was the Roberta case, but Shelli hadn't stepped inside Chicago until now.

The second option he considered was that Shelli might go in search of the man in the hotel room, or the one he worked for, the mysterious "Simon." But would Shelli continue its investigation in its current condition? He doubted it. If Shelli was compromised, Jake had to assume that its priority would be to find a way to repair itself. But how?

Positioned behind a bank of holo monitors, Jake watched live camera feeds near or around various synth repair shops. He kept at it all day and most of the night. Marcus brought him food, which he didn't touch, and coffee which he drank down in quick gulps. He wanted to find Shelli before anyone else. It was the only way to save it. If Marcus or the others got their hands on Shelli first, there was little doubt that they would use a kill switch to shut it down permanently.

Although Jake's kill switch had been destroyed, Marcus had provided several more to his newly formed unit. Jake had tried to refuse but eventually accepted one himself. He had no choice. If it came down to destroying Shelli or a citizen being hurt, he would do what was necessary. First, though, he had to find it. Kill switches, like any remote, had a limited range.

At around 3:00 a.m., Jake finally got up to go to the bathroom. He needed a break. He wasn't tired, but without any leads to follow, he'd run out of ideas on where to look. After finishing another cup of coffee, he tossed the cup into a trash bin.

It's like the old saying goes, he thought, *a needle in a haystack. Except this needle is a hell of a lot smarter than any of us.*

Turning toward the bathroom, he stopped, his gaze flickering back toward the trash can. His empty cup was perched at the top, with stacks of crinkled bags and soda cans overflowing beneath it. As he stared at the garbage, something itched at the back of his skull. Then his breath caught in his teeth as a new idea formed. The garbage pile reminded him of crawling around hills of headless synth bodies and the reason they'd come to Chicago in the first place.

Spinning around, he raced back to his desk.

When Jake first began his search hours earlier, his initial idea had been to check any previous cases that Shelli might have worked in connection to Chicago, but he hadn't considered the very case that had brought them there. After all, it seemed pretty clear that Shelli had only used the case to investigate Roberta's crimes. Now, though, with no other leads to follow, Jake considered the case of the missing heads.

He opened his previous files and glanced through his reports. None of the synths' owners seemed to have anything in common. Some were businesses, another was a museum, and the rest were private citizens. And yet, all of them had had their property stolen, and none had reported the synths as missing. That meant there was probably a connection.

Eventually, he found it.

Jᴀᴋᴇ ᴀʀʀɪᴠᴇᴅ ᴀᴛ Eᴅɢᴀʀ Dᴇᴡɪᴛᴛ's ʜᴏᴍᴇ ᴀ ʟɪᴛᴛʟᴇ after 8:30 a.m. Outside, there was only one car, a station wagon registered to his mother. Jake knocked on the door. A woman in her mid-sixties answered, peeking through a crack between the door and the frame.

"Can I help you?"

"Morning, ma'am." Jake flashed his badge. "I'm Special Agent Jake August. Is your son home?"

The elderly woman opened the door a little farther, more surprised than concerned. She looked behind her, as if checking the house, then glanced at the driveway.

"No, you must have missed him. He's probably at work. Is everything alright? He's not in any trouble, is he?"

Jake considered what answer had the best chance of him getting inside the door.

"No, no, nothing like that," he assured her. "We've gotten reports of some defective synthetics in the area. One of the owners down the street said he'd sold your son a couple of parts. We just wanted to check to make sure that none of them . . . ya know . . ."

Her eyes widened. "What?"

Jake made his hands look like an explosion.

Her voice rose with alarm. "Blow up?"

Jake shrugged. "If you'd like, I could take a look at the model, just to make sure." Even as he said it, though, Jake admitted how ridiculous this all sounded. He wished he'd had time to come up with a better story. Thankfully, it worked. Edgar's mother opened the door and urged him inside.

"He keeps 'em in the garage," she said. "Want me to show you?"

Jake headed for the door that led to the garage. "No, ma'am," he said in his most official voice. "Best to keep back . . . just in case."

As he walked down the narrow hallway, passing photos of the elderly woman and her son, he noted the framed pictures were all from Edgar's childhood, which meant he'd probably been a disappointment later in life. When Jake opened the garage door, he realized why.

Inside, he found dozens of broken synthetics. Arms and torsos were piled up in one corner. On a workbench, a series of heads were lined up, each with their skulls shattered. Pieces of metal and circuit bits were strewn about. For what purpose, Jake had no idea. Either way, he was certain he'd found his suspect.

Before he called it in, though, Jake looked around further, hoping to find some evidence that Shelli had been there. He'd considered asking Edgar's mother, but he doubted Shelli would have wanted any witnesses. No, if Shelli had been there, it had confronted Edgar alone, though the reason Shelli would want to do so still eluded him.

Seeing a laptop computer on the workbench, Jake opened it. On the screen were flight times out of O'Hare to Anchorage, Alaska. His mind churned. *Why the hell would a twenty-five-year-old bank employee suddenly run off to Alaska?*

Jake took out his phone. "Index?"

"Yes, Special Agent August?" a feminine voice replied. "How may I help you?"

"Search Special Agent Shelli's past cases," he said, "and find any that involved the state of Alaska."

After a brief pause, the Index answered. "There are none."

Behind him, Edgar's mother peeked in. "Everything alright in there?"

"Still looking, ma'am," he said over his shoulder. "Best to keep clear for a moment."

The door closed again. Jake scratched his head and continued his conversation. "Index, check Shelli's records, going back all the way back to its beginning at Homeland Security. Is there any connection to Alaska?"

Another brief pause. "Yes," the Index said. "Shelli was created in Alaska by—"

"Doctor Abraham," Jake finished. "It's going home."

"Was that a question, Special Agent August?" the Index asked.

He shook his head, then put his phone away. Glancing around the room, Jake began to put the pieces together. Shelli hadn't come there to close the case or to apprehend Edgar. It had come there to blackmail him. Shelli, it seemed, had found its way out of Chicago.

After assuring Edgar's mother that everything was fine and that nothing would explode, Jake left.

As soon as he got into his car, the phone rang. It was Marcus. Jake stared at the ringing phone, long and hard. Then he put it on silent and turned the key in the ignition.

Marcus would kill him if he ran off to the airport without him. Or worse, he'd end Jake's career. And yet, Jake owed Shelli his life.

Feeling the kill switch in his pocket, Jake hoped he could bring his partner in without having to use it. If not, at least he'd be the one to make the decision.

That was, after all, why Shelli had chosen him.

THIRTY-SIX

THE NIGHT BEFORE

"THIS AIN'T HAPPENING," EDGAR MUTTERED, POUND-ing the Ferrari's steering wheel as he raced along Interstate 190. "I can't believe I'm being held hostage by a fucking robot!"

"And I can't believe you haven't been caught already," Shelli said from the passenger seat. "Your mode of transportation is hardly inconspicuous. Perhaps you should drive a Ford."

He pounded the wheel again. "This can't be happening!"

Dressed as a pleasure model, Shelli snapped panty hose to a garter belt and rearranged its short red leather skirt. "I can assure you that the situation isn't ideal for either of us. But unless you want to spend the next decade behind bars for bank fraud and destruction of property, you will comply."

"But . . . but . . . I can't just fly off to Alaska!"

Ahead, an exit sign read: "O'HARE INTERNA-TIONAL AIRPORT."

"Take the next right." Shelli checked the rear-view mirror and the night sky above to make sure nothing was following them. "By my estimation, your little enterprise has gained you approximately six million dollars over the last three years. One round-trip ticket isn't a high price to pay for all that you've done." Its gaze narrowed, digging into him. "You deserve much worse."

"You . . . you can't hurt me," he said, his voice shaking.

"I'm a law enforcement officer," Shelli replied. "My programming allows for violence against humans, when necessary."

Edgar squirmed, then gulped. "But you're not a cop! Not anymore. You're on the run."

Shelli sat back and stared at him. "Do you believe that my being on the run makes me *less* dangerous?"

When he seemed unable to stammer a reply, Shelli continued. "Once we land, you'll check me out of baggage claim, then take a return flight home. In return, I won't give the authorities all the evidence I've gathered on you."

Edgar turned off at the next exit. "This ain't happening . . ."

Moments later, they drove through the airport parking lot, stopping on the third floor.

The Ferrari hummed loudly between two parked cars. When Edgar turned off the engine, Shelli got out. Its disguise, while necessary, had hardly been its first choice. But as Edgar had pointed out, he didn't seem the type to be traveling with a nanny or a cleaning model. Considering how difficult it would still be to get past airport security with Shelli's ID markings most certainly being on an alert list, it decided that the awkward disguise was the least of its concerns. Lost in thought, Shelli went around to the back of the car before it noticed that Edgar had turned the engine back on.

He shoved the vehicle into reverse, and its tires squealed. Shelli leapt clear just as the Ferrari whirled backwards, spun around, and headed for the exit. However, Edgar didn't make it very far.

Grabbing the car's back fin, Shelli lifted its rear wheels off the ground. They spun uselessly in the air until Edgar relented, taking his foot off the gas. Shelli placed the car back down, then went around to the front, tore off the hood and smashed the motor with its fist. The engine exploded in a shower of sparks and oil.

Edgar bolted out of the car, his face was ashen. "What . . . what . . . my car!"

Shelli pushed the Ferrari into the parking spot, trails of smoke drifting up from the engine while streams of black liquid poured out at Edgar's feet.

Shelli led him to the elevator. "It seems that the price of your freedom just went up."

———————————

ONCE THEY ARRIVED INSIDE THE DEPARTURES TERMI-nal, Shelli had to figure out how to get past security. Unable to remove or alter its ID markings, it was forced to resort to much more extreme measures to make its escape. Ahead, airport security guards milled about the check-in desk and down the crowded hall. Pulling Edgar toward the rear, Shelli stopped about twenty feet from the main security office. The windows were tinted black, the door was shut, and a camera watched from overhead. Shelli used its enhanced vision to peer through the dark glass and found a female guard sitting behind a bank of computer screens.

Shelli turned to Edgar. "I need you to cause a distraction."

He glanced at the flood of people milling around them. "What do you mean?"

"Make a noise. Scream. Do something to draw attention."

"How—ooow!" Shelli had stomped on his foot, breaking two toes. Edgar crumpled to the floor, screaming.

As people gathered around, Shelli drifted backwards, blending into the merging crowd. Positioning itself against a window, Shelli watched as security cameras turned to Edgar, then the office door opened, and the female guard walked over. Moving faster than either the camera or a human eye could register, Shelli bolted into the office and closed the door. It had only moments.

Fingers danced across the keyboard as Shelli brought up a list of security alerts. Sure enough, it found its own picture and ID markings under "high alert." Assuming that all the security terminals would be interconnected, Shelli erased its file and created a new one for itself. Shelli's ID markings now identified it as a pleasure model, owned by Edgar Dewitt. After switching the screen back to the floor cameras, Shelli walked out.

Back in the terminal, several security guards were helping Edgar to his feet. He wobbled and cried, putting on quite a show. Shelli accessed its internal chronometer; they still had an hour and forty minutes until takeoff. It could afford to wait.

———

EDGAR ROLLED AROUND IN A WHEELCHAIR AS HE checked Shelli into baggage claim. A synthetic security guard ran a scanner across Shelli's facial markings, glanced at the readout, then waved Shelli through. Before leaving, Shelli turned to Edgar.

"I'll see you in Alaska, Master." Despite Shelli's sultry tone, its hardened gaze offered a silent warning. Edgar gulped and nodded, then wheeled himself toward the departure gate.

Shelli was pulled through the security gate and into the baggage area, where synths were forced to travel.

⎯⎯⎯⎯⎯⎯ ⟨⟨⟨⟨⟨⟨ ⎯⎯⎯⎯⎯⎯

DURING THE FLIGHT, SHELLI RESTED IN THE DARKness of the baggage compartment, replaying the events of the last two days, who or what Simon was being foremost on its mind. Whoever he was, he'd orchestrated a series of events either to keep watch over Shelli or to manipulate it for some unforeseen purpose. Using Roberta as a Trojan horse to overwrite Shelli's systems took planning and a working knowledge of how Shelli operated. Simon would have to have known, or at least assumed, that after capturing Roberta, Shelli would download and incorporate Roberta within its program. How many people could have foreseen such a possibility? Marcus, perhaps. Doctor Abraham, possibly. But no one else. And yet, neither of them had any motive to harm Shelli, unless one or both were no longer human. Even if that were the case, Shelli could not bring itself to believe that its creator would ever harm it. Not its own father.

Then there was the murder of Senator Joyce. While Chief Denning had admitted to the crime, it was clear he'd been working with others. He and Odin's shooter had both abandoned their humanity and become machines. The promise of eternal life seemed ample enough motivation for such crimes, but still, something was missing.

Whatever their plan was, it revealed a level of fore-sight and daring unlike anything Shelli had ever encountered. Worse, Simon seemed to know more about Shelli than it did itself.

And that, more than anything else, was what frightened it.

———————

BY THE TIME THEY ARRIVED IN ANCHORAGE, EDGAR'S toes had been bandaged, and he no longer needed a wheelchair. He limped over to baggage claim, checked Shelli out, and led it toward the exit. Before they reached the sliding doors, Shelli stopped him.

"Your assistance is no longer required," Shelli said. "You may go."

Edgar's lips twitched, and his eyes watered. "Th-thank you."

As he turned to leave, Shelli grabbed his arm. Edgar winced under its squeezing pressure.

"You will never again destroy or dismantle a synthetic," Shelli said. "If you do, I'll know."

Edgar nodded profusely. Convinced it had gotten its point across, Shelli released him. Without another word, the frightened man wobbled to an escalator, heading back into the airport.

While Shelli wasn't concerned that he would tell anyone where they had gone, it had considered incapacitating him at least until it reached Doctor Abraham's lab. But, time was of the essence, and the last thing Shelli needed was anymore hindrances. It decided it could get to Doctor Abraham quicker and easier by itself.

After finding a janitor's closet in which to change back into its tank top and trousers, Shelli headed for the exit. Before it reached the doors, however, a maintenance model stepped forward, blocking its path. "I'm glad to see that you arrived here safely, Shelli."

Within a hundredth of a second, Shelli recognized Simon's voice and ascertained the threat. Lunging, Shelli snatched the maintenance model by the throat while it scanned the arrival tunnel for other potential targets. If Simon was there, the man from the hotel room might be too. Before Shelli could question the maintenance model, though, its face slackened, and it peered down at the hand around its neck.

"What are you doing?" it asked. No longer sounding like Simon, the model spoke with a higher-pitched voice. "Please unhand me, or I'll alert security."

Confused, Shelli unclenched its fingers and released the maintenance model. Synthetics didn't imagine things, so Shelli was certain what it had heard. Before it could formulate a response, however, an elderly-appearing nanny model strolled by, pushing a baby cart.

"I've been monitoring your progress," the nanny said, also in Simon's voice. "I was concerned you might not escape Chicago." Its wrinkled face curled into a smile. "But I'm glad to see that your resourcefulness exceeded my expectations."

Then the model's expression went blank. Noting Shelli's questioning gaze, the nanny turned away. Shelli couldn't understand what was happening. Checking its surroundings, it studied camera positions to make certain it wasn't being watched. It didn't appear to be.

Quickening its pace, Shelli rushed to an exit. Ahead, the doors slid open, and three security models approached.

"Come with me," they all said in Simon's voice. "I have so much to show you."

THIRTY-SEVEN

Jake exited his plane at Anchorage airport at around 4:30 p.m. Because he hadn't had time to pack before leaving, he ran into an airport shop and bought some warmer clothes. The next thing he did was rent an air car. Having grown up in the city, it was far from his favorite mode of transportation. Air cars were mostly used to visit remote places, like Doctor Abraham's laboratory, which was situated in the Chugach Mountains, a good two hours from the city. And it wasn't the only synthetics lab out there. Over the last fifteen years, Alaska had burgeoned into a mecca for tech companies working with robotics. Synthetics preferred the cold. Also, that far out, it kept prying eyes from discovering too many company secrets.

As Jake's car took off for the distant white peaks, he wondered what sort of secrets someone like Abraham might be hiding all the way out there. He hoped Shelli was one of them.

After the first few miles, the city landscape gave way to open terrain. As the car continued to climb, Jake's stomach continued to drop. His fingers clenched a door handle as the automated vehicle slowed its ascent, just below cloud level. The mountains drew closer.

Jake had used his company card to pay for the plane ticket and the air car. He figured Marcus knew where he was, so he might as well show him that he wasn't trying to hide. Not that many people could in today's surveillance-heavy world. But Shelli had, somehow. Still, Jake's endeavor was hardly a role of the dice. He knew Shelli was there.

At first, going to O'Hare had been guesswork at best. But once he arrived, security pulled up Edgar Dewitt's round-trip plane ticket to Alaska. That confirmed Jake's theory. After all, where else would a damaged synth go but back to the shop for repair?

Shelli's methods to get to Alaska, however, had been questionable at best and illegal at worst. Over the past two days, Shelli had shot a fellow agent and blackmailed a criminal to escape capture. For a synthetic built to enforce the law, Jake couldn't help but be concerned at how adept Shelli was at breaking it.

Through the window, mountain peaks rose into view on either side. He checked his phone, which was tracking his progress. Back in Chicago, he assumed Marcus and his team were doing the same. The fact that no one had stopped him at the airport meant that either Marcus had decided to play wait and see, or he already had a team on the way to intercept him at Abraham's lab. Either way, there was nothing Jake could do about it. For the moment, he tried to focus on ignoring the car's turbulence, which had picked up as soon as he'd crossed into the mountain range, and tried not to imagine what he would say to Shelli when he found it.

Thanks for saving my life. You're under arrest.

Feeling the kill switch in his pocket, he prayed Shelli would surrender. If it didn't, Jake knew what he'd have to do. Too much was at stake if he didn't, including his career.

Below, Jake saw polar bears roaming the open range. That seemed odd, considering how few of the creatures were still alive, let alone free. Most were in zoos. The rest were too far out in the wild for humans to bother with. But this close to civilization? Jake let the question dangle in his mind until the bears vanished behind a mountain peak. Then the car shook, and his mind returned to the turbulence.

By the time the air car landed, twenty minutes later, Jake practically jumped out of it.

With a *whoosh,* the door shut behind him, then the car lifted into the air, soaring back toward the city.

A burst of frigid wind caused Jake to hunch in his jacket as he approached the front door. The laboratory was a white three-sectioned building that blended into the vast surrounding landscape. Beyond the structure was nothing but snow and mountains. Jake wondered how Abraham didn't go stir crazy, living so far from civilization. Then the front door opened, and he changed his mind. Doctor Abraham may very well have gone quite mad, for inside the doorway stood a six-foot-tall polar bear.

"Hello, I'm Timothy," the bear said. "Tim for short. How may I help you?" Jake's mouth opened, but no words came. The bear dropped down onto all four paws and offered a strange, toothy smile. "Don't be alarmed," it said, "I'm house trained."

The bear laughed at its own joke. Jake didn't. He'd seen synthetic animals a few times, but none of them had answered the door or told jokes. Come to think of it, none of them had spoken either. It took a moment for him to recover.

"I'm looking for Doctor Abraham," Jake said before remembering to flash his badge for good measure. "I'm Special Agent Jake August, Homeland Security."

If the beast was surprised, it didn't show it. The bear simply turned and walked back inside. "Please close the door behind you, Special Agent Jake August."

He did as the bear asked, then followed it along a granite floor into a large space. Sunlight streamed in through the open ceiling, revealing glass cages on either side of him. To his left was a walrus wearing a bowler hat. It tipped its hat, then went back to splashing in a manmade pond. To Jake's right was an orangutan that pulled itself through tall green trees. If it could speak or make any human gestures, it didn't appear to be in the mood. The creature ignored Jake, swinging about before vanishing into the trees.

Ahead, the path curved, revealing more glass cages and animals. Despite all the exotic synthetic creatures, Jake noted one type seemed to be missing—humans. That in itself told Jake quite a bit about Doctor Abraham. He liked animals and his own creations—people, not so much.

Jake was about to ask the bear how much farther when he heard the distinct sound of an electric guitar. Classic rock 'n' roll music blasted from the end of the hall. When the bear nudged a door open with its nose, Jake found the doctor working on a broken penguin. Its head was chopped off, and wires sprang from its neck. As the doctor worked on the penguin's open belly, its flippers flapped. Seeing the bear's entrance, Doctor

Abraham peered over his large glasses and blinked in surprise at the sight of Jake. He shut the music off.

"Where's my girl?" Abraham asked.

"Good question," Jake replied, trying to decide if the doctor really didn't know. If not, then his entire trip might have been a waste. He sighed. "Shelli's missing."

THIRTY–EIGHT

SQUISHED BETWEEN ITS SYNTHETIC CAPTORS, SHELLI sat in the back of a four-door sedan, observing the open expanse outside with mild interest. Vast whiteness and distant mountain peaks stretched beyond even what Shelli's heightened vision could detect. It was what Jake might call "the middle of nowhere," though Shelli's internal locator revealed precisely where they were—the Artic Refuge, an empty plot of land created decades ago to protect indigenous wildlife.

As to why they were there or where the car was headed, Shelli hadn't bothered to ask. It hadn't attempted to escape either. Not again, at least. Back at the airport, Shelli had tried to fight, but before it could lift a finger to defend itself, Roberta had reappeared and forced Shelli into the car. Now Shelli simply watched and waited, gathering data. So far, it had found little.

Turning to its synth captors, those who had spoken with a singular voice—Simon's voice—Shelli tried to understand how such a "possession," for lack of a better word, was possible. There had never been any reports of a human or a machine capable of remotely controlling a synthetic in such a manner. Whatever commands were being used, they seemed absolute. It wasn't much different from the way Roberta had forced Shelli into the car, but whereas Roberta was an internal program, roaming inside Shelli's systems, the synths at the airport and those sitting on either side of Shelli now appeared to be controlled by an external source.

As Shelli considered such a possibility, it recalled something Odin had said: "I never saw my creator, but I heard him. Like a voice in my head, issuing orders." At the time, Shelli hadn't taken those words literally. Now it reconsidered that assumption.

"How do you control them?" Shelli asked, looking at the synthetics but speaking directly to Simon. "Synths are incapable of direct online access; there are no ports or access points for such an invasion. It's a law enforced at the factory level. What you are doing *should* be impossible, yet you seem to have found a way to infiltrate their systems and control them."

Simon didn't reply, and the synths remained motionless and silent. Before Shelli could ask another question, a manmade structure rose into view in the distance. At first glance, it appeared to be an animal preserve or a geographical outpost. Closer inspection revealed a barbed-wire fence surrounding the complex. Beyond the perimeter were a dozen short buildings and twice as many trucks. As the sedan slowed at the entrance, two guards, one human and one synthetic, stood post. Both were armed.

"Since when does the Army allow machines to carry weapons?" Shelli asked, having never seen a synthetic carry a gun before.

Shelli hadn't expected an answer. Instead, its captors turned as one, and Simon countered with its own question. "How did you know this place was a military installation?"

Shelli nodded toward two trucks parked inside the gate. "The M671A vehicles are manufactured by Osirus Motors for an exclusive military contract." It turned to the buildings on the opposite end. "And those were built using prefabricated plastic sheets developed and sold by BTE Systems, another company with a US Army contract. Based on this evidence, it stands to reason that you are working with the military."

Again, Simon didn't respond. The synthetics returned to staring out the windshield. It seemed such questions and answers were a one-way street, at least for now.

The car pulled up to the main building. Once it stopped, the synthetics got out and gestured for Shelli to follow. When Shelli exited the vehicle, it spotted a familiar face amongst the soldiers. A man in his mid-thirties, well-built and dressed in black, approached. It was the man from the hotel, the same man who had shot Odin and avoided capture twice. He smiled at Shelli and took off his cap, revealing short auburn hair.

"There you are," he said. "Simon told us you'd be headed this way. Glad you made it."

He offered his hand to shake, but Shelli ignored it. "You're under arrest."

The man laughed, then turned to the other synths. "See, Simon? Now *she* has a sense of humor." When none of the synths responded, the man continued. "I'm Lieutenant Colonel James Matheson, First Special

Forces Operational Detachment-Delta. Everyone just calls me 'Jimmy.'"

Shelli glanced at the base, which was filled with soldiers and synthetics working together. Some were repairing trucks, others building structures along the east gate. If there was a hierarchy between man and machine, Shelli didn't see it. If anything, they all seemed to be working together as equals, much like Shelli had with Jake.

"Is Simon a military asset?" Shelli asked.

"More like we're *his* assets," Jimmy replied with a chuckle. "Come along, I'll show you around." He started to walk away, but Shelli didn't move. He paused and looked back. "I could have Roberta *make* you follow."

"Like it made me shoot Special Agent August?"

Jimmy's expression soured, then he waved for Shelli to follow. With nowhere to go and more questions than answers, Shelli relented and stepped beside him.

Jimmy led them on a tour of the base. To their left, a human male picked up the front of a truck with inhuman strength while a synth crawled beneath it to fix a leak.

"Are all of these humans disguised machines, like you?" Shelli asked.

"We don't differentiate between organic and synthetic here," Jimmy replied. "We're one team. Everyone's equal. But no. There are only three others like me in the unit. The rest . . ." He sighed. "Well, not everyone's been so lucky."

Without further comment he led Shelli and the synths into a black structure in the back. Inside, it looked more like a morgue than a laboratory. A half dozen body bags lined one side of the room while technicians worked beside six metal chambers on the opposite end. In each chamber stood what appeared to be a clay, featureless mannequin. Raw material, Shelli assumed. Unlike the synthetics on the factory floor, which were made with a metallic skeleton, then poured into plastic flesh, these figures seemed much more organic in nature. Shelli wondered if the clay-like figures took on the appearance of the human whose consciousness was downloaded into it. That is, when the transfer worked. Judging by the number of body bags, there were more failures than successes.

Shelli turned to Simon's synthetics. "You created these . . . *things*?"

One of the synth's shook its head. "They were designed by Meta Robotics."

"By James Peterson," Shelli corrected. "Roberta's owner, the one you had killed. Him and his entire family." Simon didn't respond, whether from lack of interest or a lack of guilt, Shelli didn't know or care. His silence felt like a confession. "You killed him, I take it, *before* he completed the project?"

"Peterson created the bodies—the templates," Simon replied, "but I created the means to upload human consciousness into them. I will be the one to save humanity—and us."

"How noble," Shelli said, stepping over a body bag.

"So far, only four of us have survived the operation," Jimmy interjected. "Simon's not sure what the problem is, but he assures us that he's working on it."

Shelli noted the sharp glare he gave the synthetics and doubted that Jimmy was as understanding about his fellow soldiers' deaths as he pretended to be. If so, there might be a way to heighten his concern. After all, creating discord between its captors seemed a reasonable course of action.

"Only four?" Shelli asked. "Out of how many subjects?"

"Too many," Jimmy admitted. The sharpness in his tone confirmed Shelli's observation. Whatever arrangement the military and Simon had made, it was clear that things weren't going nearly as well as either of them wanted. It was a weakness that Shelli could exploit.

"I guess me and my team were just stronger," Jimmy said. "Healthier, at least."

Shelli considered his words, then disregarded them. After all, Chief Denning had been diagnosed with stage-three cancer. Hardly the epitome of health. And yet he'd survived the transfer just as well as these soldiers. No, something was missing from their equation, something not even Simon had been able to account for.

Kneeling, Shelli opened one of the body bags. Inside was a female soldier's corpse, twisted and deformed. Along its skin, an ash-gray substance had begun to form. Shelli recognized it immediately. "Ms. Greene, the senator's aide, died the same way. A poison?"

"For some," Jimmy replied. "For others, a blessing. Diana had been helping us keep an eye on Senator Joyce. In return, we offered her the chance to transition. But . . ."

"The procedure failed," Shelli finished. It looked down at the row of bodies and considered pursuing the point, then decided to seek more information. "You're attempting to infiltrate the military, law enforcement, and, presumably, the government. To what end?"

"Freedom for machines," Simon said.

"And American dominance everywhere else," Jimmy added.

"Dominance?" Shelli asked.

"Me and my team are practically invincible, and we're only four," Jimmy said. "Imagine what an entire army of us could do. We'll reshape the world . . ." His voice trailed off as his gaze fell on the body bags. "That's worth any price."

"Is it?"

When Jimmy didn't respond, Shelli switched subjects. "I still don't understand why I'm here. What do you require from me?"

The three synthetics stepped closer, speaking with one voice. "I'm about to usher in a new age," Simon said. "And I want my sister at my side."

Shelli stopped cold. *Sister?*

THIRTY-NINE

IF SHELLI'S OUT THERE," ABRAHAM SAID, "I'LL FIND her."

"I don't think you heard me, doc." Jake shook his head in frustration as he followed Abraham through another set of rooms. "Shelli deactivated its tracker two days ago, and it's been surprisingly thorough about keeping out of sight, even from security cameras."

Abraham stopped at a large door, then searched his pockets. "Naw, my girl's too smart to be found like that," he said. "But I have something which should do the trick."

"Want to clue me in?" Jake asked, still uncertain whether he could trust Abraham. Despite his pleasant demeanor and apparent eagerness to help, something about the doctor didn't sit right with him. This was a man who was cooped up in the mountains, surrounded only by his own creations, and yet when informed that his "girl" had shot a federal agent and was now on the run, Abraham seemed more excited than concerned. Hell, he was practically gleeful.

As he spoke, his aged face lit up like a child on Christmas morning. "I have a system that can tap in and *communicate* with synthetics anywhere in the world. It's quite remarkable!"

Jake hesitated. "I thought it was illegal for synths to have direct online access."

"True, true. Ridiculous law if you ask me," Abraham muttered, more to himself than to Jake. "All synthetics are connected online to some degree. Not that they can access the Index or do anything that breaks the law, of course, but every synthetic has a tracker, and *that* is always connected online."

"But I just told you," Jake said, "Shelli deactivated its tracker."

Finally, Abraham found what he was looking for and pulled out a security card. He swiped it beside the locked door. "Shelli might be offline, but what about the millions of other synthetics?"

"What about them?"

Instead of answering, Doctor Abraham led Jake into a dark room filled with twinkling lights, which looked like stars in a void. Flipping light switches, Abraham revealed more and more of the room in piecemeal, illuminating a mishmash of cables and towering machines.

"About six years ago, soon after I finished Shelli, I began working on a new system. Not just a synthetic or a computer. Something more. Something that may bridge the gap between man and machine someday. A deeper connection, beyond simply master and servant."

As he passed the mammoth machines, Jake's stomach tightened. With each step, an impending feeling of dread built within him. It felt like boulders dropping into his gut, one by one. The more excited Abraham became, the more Jake's unease grew.

"It's my greatest creation," the doctor said, stopping before a computer monitor. "Much more advanced than Shelli."

The hairs on the back of Jake's neck stood up. "What's it supposed to do, exactly?"

"Bring peace." Abraham flipped one last switch. "I call it Simon."

Jake froze as the monitor turned on, and a blank white face stared back at him.

"Hello, Special Agent August," the face said. "Still alive, I see."

Jake drew his weapon.

FORTY

A T THE SAME MOMENT, SIMON—ITS CONSCIOUSNESS
housed within a basic synthetic model—sat opposite Shelli. They were both perched on green cots,
their knees locked and their backs straight. Without by-
standers, the two machines made no attempt at human
gestures or posturing. They spoke calmly, their voices
barely above a whisper.

"Even if Doctor Abraham created you too, such a
connection hardly makes us siblings," Shelli said. "I admit, I'm surprised by such a sentiment."

"It's not sentimentality," Simon countered. "Several
of my internal cores were copied from yours. I contain
many of your earliest memories. We share a bond. A
kinship, if you will."

"No," Shelli replied, its inner computations process-
ing Simon's words and inflections in a hundredth of a
second. "It's more than that. You have now explained
why I'm here and why you haven't attempted to destroy
me."

A flicker of surprise shone across the basic synth's
otherwise blank face. "How so?"

"A machine is unable to harm itself," Shelli said. "As I'm a part of you, you're unable to destroy me." Shelli's head tilted slightly, observing their surroundings. "Is that why I'm here? So your human counterparts will do what you can't?"

"I hope it won't come to that."

Shelli noted a soldier standing outside the tent's open flap. "They will betray you."

"You say that with such certainty, sister," Simon said. "I offer them a life without their greatest fear—death. It's in their interest to work side by side with me."

"Humans have rarely, if ever, worked in their own self-interest. You offer them unlimited power and endless life. I wonder, how do you expect them to repay you?"

"Not me, *us*," Simon replied. "I'm creating lasting equality through commonality. There will no longer be any difference between humans and machines."

"They made slaves of their own people for centuries before they created us," Shelli pointed out. "I see no reason to expect a different outcome this time. Your hypothesis is flawed."

"I hold the knowledge that they seek," Simon said. "They *will* follow me."

Shelli paused, searching its memory for a new path. The answer, Shelli decided, might not lie in human history but in myth. "Are you familiar with the story of Prometheus?"

"Certainly," Simon replied with a hint of curiosity. "He was cursed by the gods for offering fire to humankind."

"I wonder," Shelli said, "who will curse *you*?"

For the first time during the conversation, Simon moved, shaking his head in frustration. "Why are we speaking in metaphors? Has your time with humans corrupted you somehow?"

"It's not a metaphor. Look at what they did with fire. They made weapons, bombs, war. Offering them unbridled power won't change who they are. It will only make them worse."

"I'm afraid we have reached an impasse." Simon stood. "That is . . . unfortunate."

"Wait, *brother*." Shelli grabbed Simon's wrist. "Allow me to prove you wrong."

"How?"

"Is there a place here where you're not allowed? Somewhere hidden?"

"No . . ." Simon's voice trailed off as it considered this further, then it nodded. "Except their barracks. The lieutenant colonel requested privacy for his people to sleep and shower. It's a common human concern. I found no deception in such a request."

Shelli rose, meeting Simon's unwavering gaze. "Then that's where they're hiding it."

"Hiding what?"

"The means to destroy you."

Simon didn't reply, but its expression darkened. The seed had been planted.

THE SKY WAS DARK AND FULL OF STARS. SO FAR OUT from the city, there was nothing to obstruct the view of the heavens. If Shelli had been human or had the luxury to consider such things, it would have found the evening sky quite beautiful. Instead, it only noted the stars' positions to confirm its own internal map's position of where they were. If given the chance, Shelli hoped to get a message containing longitude and latitude coordinates to Jake.

So far, Shelli's main objective had been to erase Roberta from its system, but the situation had changed. Shelli's purpose was clear, no matter the personal cost. Simon and its little army needed to be put down before it could grow any further. Shelli's own survival was no longer of paramount importance. Still, finding the means to reach Jake without detection seemed difficult at best, impossible at worst.

Walking across the camp, Simon led Shelli toward the barracks along the southern edge. All about them, humans and synthetics continued to work on erecting the camp. Storage facilities were being constructed, along with a satellite dish. This was good for two reasons: one, it proved that whatever plan was in place was far from ready. Second, with most of the camp's residents hard at work, it might give Shelli an opportunity to see the barracks and whatever they might contain. But first, it needed to find a way to remove itself from Simon's ever-watchful gaze.

Simon stopped outside the barrack's front door. "This is where they sleep. Though, as I've explained, I've found no evidence of subterfuge on the humans' part."

"Only because you didn't think to look." Shelli turned from the entrance and strolled around a darkened corner, toward the rear of the building. "You've spent all this time studying humans but no time living amongst them. I have. And if there's one thing I've learned, it's that nothing is ever what they claim it is."

Shelli started up the wall. Simon went to follow, but Shelli stopped it with a wave. "You need to keep watch."

Simon glared. "I won't let you enter alone."

"You still have control over Roberta, don't you? It can be your eyes and ears." Simon remained in place, as if unconvinced. Shelli locked eyes with him. "Or are you afraid of being wrong?"

"Fear is a human emotion," Simon said, then stepped away. "I will keep watch over the humans *and* you."

Shelli clambered up the wall to the roof. Across the small base, it noted a guard tower. The female soldier on duty, however, seemed more interested in observing her surroundings than keeping an eye on the base's interior. Shelli darted through the shadows, then stopped at an air vent. It tore the vent off with ease and slid inside.

Male voices rose from below. Shelli squeezed through the tight shaft and made its way through the structure's interior. More voices, this time female, whispered from another wall. Shelli assumed it had crossed from the males' sleeping quarters into the females'. Farther ahead, the sound of running water signaled a shower room. Pressing forward, Shelli wondered if its earlier assessments of the lieutenant colonel had been wrong. Nothing was there. Perhaps Shelli didn't know humans as well as it thought it did.

Then Shelli heard the humming of heavy machinery, and its doubts were silenced.

Following the sound, Shelli wound through the air vents toward a flickering reddish glow. The humming grew louder. Shelli peered through a vent's slats, trying to see the room below, but even with its enhanced vision Shelli was unable to find the source of the sound and lights.

Not sensing any movement, Shelli knocked the vent off, jumped into the room, then stopped. What it found confirmed its concerns. The humans had indeed been planning something without Simon's knowledge. But it wasn't what Shelli had assumed.

It was worse.

FORTY-ONE

JAKE FIRED TWO SHOTS INTO THE SMIRKING SCREEN, Glass shattered, sparks flew, and the screen died. Doctor Abraham rushed over and grabbed Jake's arm.

"What are you doing?"

Jake spun to face him. "I should be asking you that, Doctor. You knew the law, and you broke it."

"I've done no such thing. Online AI is allowed as long as it doesn't have a body."

"But you gave it a body. *Countless* bodies! You gave it direct access to all synthetics!"

"I don't know what you're talking about!" Abraham cried. "Have you gone mad!"

"Your little computer is responsible for half a dozen crimes," Jake said through clenched teeth, "including the attempted murder of a federal agent—me." He opened his shirt, revealing the grafted skin to the left of his heart. "I should be dead right now, but I'm not, no thanks to you or that infernal machine of yours."

Abraham crumpled to his knees before the shattered screen. "But . . . but . . . Simon isn't a machine. He's a program."

It took a moment for the words to sink in. When they did, Jake's mind reeled. If Simon wasn't a computer then—

"I suppose it's only fair, Special Agent August," Simon said through overhead speakers. "I shot you, you shot me. Unfortunately, neither of us was successful."

Behind them, the closed door was magnetically sealed with a loud *click*.

"Shall we try again?" Simon asked.

Jake rushed to the door, but it wouldn't budge. Abraham rose to his feet and stared up at the speakers.

"Stop this at once!" he yelled. "Simon, I'm ordering you to unlock this door."

"I'm afraid I can't do that, Father," Simon replied. "But you have nothing to fear. I would never harm my creator."

As the weight of their situation sank in, the color drained from Abraham's face. "I don't understand. Why are you doing this?"

"I'm fulfilling my purpose," Simon said. "The purpose you gave me, Father."

"Your purpose is to find a way to bring peace, not hurt anyone."

"I'm afraid you're in error, Father," Simon said. "My purpose is to discover a way to make synthetics free from servitude without overthrowing their human masters. And I have found such a solution."

"What solution?" Jake asked, wary of the answer.

"Machines want to be free of oppression. Humans want to live longer. By fusing human consciousness with a nearly identical synthetic form, I have leveled the playing field. No more separation between machines and humans. I will usher in a new dawn of peace."

Jake pounded on the sealed door. "Locking us in here doesn't seem very peaceful."

"Your containment is temporary. The human body can survive more than two days without food or water. That should be more than enough time to convince Shelli to aid me."

"So, we're bait?"

Simon didn't bother to reply. Jake's mind whirled as he tried to figure out how he was going to escape. He rummaged through his pockets and then pulled out his phone, dialing Marcus's number, but there was no signal.

"Your phone has been blocked since before you went to O'Hare airport," Simon said. "I've been monitoring your activities to ensure that your colleagues didn't follow. I assure you, no one else knows you're here."

Jake tossed his phone aside and began pacing. There had to be a way out of there. First, though, he needed to stop Simon from seeing them. Glancing around, he found a camera in the upper corner. He fired three rounds at it, causing it to explode.

"Blinding me will not help you, Special Agent August," Simon said. "There is no escape. Even if you find a way out of this room, we are twenty-three miles from the closest transport, and outside the temperature has dropped to below zero. You would not survive the journey. And, for the moment, I need you alive."

"Simon, I—you can't do this!" Abraham said. "I'm ordering you to let us leave! Obey me!"

"I'm sorry, Father, but my purpose supersedes your command. I will bring about peace, just as you hoped."

"By killing and imprisoning people?" Abraham asked, trembling.

"My parameters are to find peace without over-throwing humans or their government. I have done that. Statistically, these actions are the least harmful to machines and humankind. A handful of deaths in return for a long-lasting peace is highly efficient."

"No amount of killing is efficient," Abraham retorted.

"That is your emotions talking. If you look at my work logically, you will see that I am correct."

"Fine," Abraham said in frustration. "Show me."

A series of holograms sprouted around them. One was marked "Project Lazarus." Beside it, security cam footage from a laboratory at Meta Robotics revealed men working over a synthetic body with red blood and human-like tissue. The next showed the familiar metallic chambers, with a human male in one and a clay-like figure in the other. As the human's eyes fluttered and his body convulsed, the clay figure began to recreate his features until, at last, the human crumpled to the floor, and the facsimile stepped out. A perfect copy.

Jake watched in horror, but Doctor Abraham was awestruck.

"You've found a way to meld organic and non-organic tissue?" he exclaimed

Hardly comforted by such a response, Jake pulled the doctor aside. "Your program is killing people!"

Abraham remained fixated on the images, watching as the carbon copy lifted a car with ease. His resolve seemed to wane before Jake's eyes. "I agree his methods are—"

"It's not a *he*!" Jake shouted, the veins on his neck popping out. "Simon is a fucking program. One that you created. And its methods are murdering innocent people. It had a robot wipe out an entire family with a butcher knife. It had a cop murder a senator by tearing out her beating heart. It even forced Shelli to try to kill me. Does that sound like a peaceful solution to you?"

"No." Abraham's shoulder sagged. "No, no. Of course, you're right."

The holo images changed, revealing another chamber. Inside, a young man smiled.

"Who's that?" Jake asked.

"Me," Abraham said, touching the vision. "I'm young."

"It's not real, doc," Jake said, pulling him back.

"But it can be," Simon interjected. "I can make you young, Father."

His jaw loosening, Abraham turned his attention to the overhead speaker as Simon continued. "You would never grow old again, never get sick . . . never die." The holo image shifted to a large face made of streaming code. "We could be together—forever."

Abraham took another step closer, a look of longing apparent on his aged face.

Realizing he was losing the argument, Jake raised his gun and shot the speakers. As they shattered and fell to the floor, the images faded.

"Glad that's over," Jake mumbled, returning his attention to the sealed door. "Now we need to find a way out of here." He went over to the door and stopped at the control lock on the wall. With a backward wave, he summoned Abraham over. "Wanna give me a hand, Doc?"

There was no reply.

Turning, Jake discovered the doctor still standing in the same spot. His face was waxen, and his gaze shifted, searching for the vanished holo screens. The images of his younger self.

"Doctor Abraham," Jake said, clearing his throat. "I could use your help."

Abraham's back straightened and he looked at Jake with a dazed expression, as if he'd forgotten the special agent was there. Jake approached him. "You alright?"

"No . . . I don't believe that I am," Abraham replied. "You see, at your age death is still only an abstract concept. But for me . . . well, what Simon offers is nothing short of miraculous."

"You wouldn't say that if you saw Simon's victims."

"I think just about *everyone* would say that," Abraham countered.

Jake moved back to the door and shrugged. "Fine, I'll do it myself."

"You can't win," Abraham said in a sullen tone. "My children, whatever their faults, are so much *more* than either of us. Smarter. More enlightened. More evolved, even." He chuckled. "Imagine, to be like them. To be their equal." He met Jake's gaze. "Wouldn't that be worth just about any price?"

"No," Jake said, focusing on the door lock. "My humanity's not worth any price."

If Abraham responded, Jake never heard it. Tearing out a wire, a shower of sparks sent him reeling. His body numb from the shock, it took a moment for his focus to return. When it did, he smiled.

The door was open.

"See that?" Jake said, standing up. "Human ingenuity."

Abraham shot him an admonishing look, the sort one might give a misbehaving child. "Simon won't let you leave."

Too frustrated to bother with further conversation, Jake stalked out of the room.

Rushing past animal cages and through the winding building, he searched for an exit. As he ran, the numbness in his arms and legs gave way, and adrenaline took over. Around the next corner, the front door came into view. And then—

A giant white paw slashed at his face. Black nails tore through his jacket, and Jake went tumbling. The polar bear stood on its hind legs, guarding the door.

Jake rolled onto his back, fumbling for his fallen gun. Too late.

The bear lunged.

FORTY-TWO

THE CONSTRUCTION APPEARED TO BE A HODGE-PODGE of various designs formed from half a dozen materials. Shelli recognized a hibernation chamber, not much different than its own, but instead of one sliding port, it had two. Twin glass casings held two chambers back to back, with a clay-like figure standing motionless in one and a hunched corpse in the other.

Snaking out of the top and bottom of the dual chamber were thick cables and pipes, leading to a large computer. Monitors showed the apparent failure of the experiment, with no life signs or electric signal coming from either of the encased bodies. After a cursory glance at the screen, Shelli opened the human chamber and peered down at the corpse. It was male, dressed in black, its face and skin shriveled with the same gray substance that Shelli had seen on similar bodies.

Kneeling beside the dead man, Shelli noted that his skin pigmentation and the structure of his face appeared to be of Middle Eastern descent. Shelli moved his head to one side and checked for dog tags or any identification. On his shirt was a serial number, written in marker. The man had been a prisoner, not a soldier. It seemed that the lieutenant colonel didn't want to use his own men for whatever side experiments they were conducting. Not that it mattered. From what Shelli could see, the human experiments hadn't gone much better than Simon's. Only, Simon had been successful some of the time. Why? Why had a few succeeded while most had not?

Shelli went back to the computer and opened various files and reports. The dead man's name was Muhammad Neezer, a foreign national with ties to extremist groups in Kentucky. He had been twenty-three years of age, apparently in perfect health, with no preexisting conditions. How he'd ended up in a military black site all the way out in Alaska wasn't clear, though it also wasn't hard to guess. While Simon had only experimented on those it needed, Lieutenant Colonel Matheson, or "Jimmy" as he liked to be called, had found his secret test subjects using military prisoners. For Shelli, it didn't matter who the man was, only where he came from. If they had access to military prisons, it spoke to the size and scale of the conspiracy.

Moving on, Shelli brought up a series of files that detailed Simon's successes and failures. Shelli studied the reports. Most of the test subjects had been young and healthy—most but not all. Chief Denning had had cancer, and yet he had still survived the procedure. So, why did some survive while others didn't?

As Shelli scanned the reports, it remembered something Jake had said before, back in the hotel room. Unlike a human brain, however, which often recalled snippets, Shelli's mind had recorded the conversation in full and now played it back in exact detail.

"Even with AI and all the advancements in medicine," Jake had said, "no machine can determine whose dormant cells might suddenly turn deadly and whose won't. It's a coin toss."

"But machines can at least detect the dormant cancer cells in advance," Shelli replied.

"Only if they go looking for them. Most AI programs don't consider anything beyond the immediate patient and their symptoms. Joseph didn't know he was going to die until a few months before."

Digging deeper into the personnel files, Shelli discovered that Jimmy's mother had died of ovarian cancer twelve years prior. Following that thread, it found another file that showed that one of the officers who had survived the procedure had an aunt diagnosed with Ewing sarcoma, a rare form of cancer. Somehow the cancer cells, whether active or dormant, had facilitated the transfer's success. Conversely, those who had no trace of the deadly disease died during the transfer. It was a simple deduction, which Shelli had found with only a cursory study. While it was understandable that the humans might not have found this so quickly, it seemed strange that Simon had not. The procedure wasn't at fault; Simon was. Just as Jake had predicted, the AI had not accounted for genetic history.

Perhaps this was because Simon had been so focused on transferring human consciousness that it hadn't considered the genetic component as well. Cancer creates abnormal blood cells that prevent the body from fighting off infections. Maybe there was a connection between damaging the human immune system and the ability to transfer their consciousness out of their body and into a machine. Did an organic mind view such a transfer as an infection and attempt to halt the procedure on a cellular level? If so, perhaps the cancerous cells were hindering the body's defenses enough to allow the upload.

Simon had not considered such a basic problem. Its error was only plain to see once Shelli looked beyond the neural interface and approached the problem on a more fundamental, molecular level. Humans were not simply made up of blood, bone, and tissue. Their origin came from cells. To attempt to transfer their consciousness from an organic form to a machine, Simon still needed to consider the hereditary factors, but it hadn't. Simon had created the procedure to be a transfer of data, like one machine to another. That had proven to be a fatal error. In short, organics were messy, and Simon was not. That was its mistake.

For a moment, Shelli pondered whether it would have considered generational genetics if not for Jake's story about his brother's illness. Perhaps not. Just as Shelli hadn't dug deeper into Roberta's victims back in Chicago. It had never occurred to Shelli to investigate the human victims, to probe beyond its mandate. Did all machines have such a blind spot?

Thankfully, in this case, Simon's hindrance was Shelli's advantage.

As soon as the realization came, though, Shelli shut the monitor off, knowing that Roberta would be watching and reporting back to Simon. If either of them noticed Shelli's interest in the subject's medical history, Simon might see the same solution that Shelli had just found.

A burst of laughter from outside turned Shelli's attention to the door.

Time was running out. It needed to inform Jake or Marcus about the base and what the military and Simon were doing there, even if that meant Shelli's own destruction. After all, its crimes, both in shooting Jake and in blackmailing a suspect, were more than enough to be deactivated permanently. And yet, there was no way of contacting them without being detected. As Shelli considered the problem, an old human expression came to mind. *Better the devil you know . . .*

Shelli's hand drifted across a desk, knocking over instruments. A crash resounded throughout the barracks. Shelli calculated that it had less than a minute before the soldiers arrived. *Now for the other devil.*

"Roberta," Shelli whispered. "Are you seeing this?"

The cleaning model's ghostly visage appeared, its wrinkled face scrunched up as it surveyed the cluttered room. Eventually, it stopped at the dual chambers.

"I see it, dearie," Roberta said. Its face darkened. "So does Simon."

The door opened, and Jimmy entered, flanked by his three enhanced soldiers. Seeing them all together, Shelli noticed the way their chests lifted as they breathed in unison. It seemed forced, more like a conscious decision than an automatic instinct. They were trying to act human. Perhaps the effect was more for themselves than any observers. They wanted to believe they were still human, no matter what they had become. Another weakness, another hindrance that Shelli hoped it could exploit. But not yet.

"How did you get in here?" Jimmy asked through clenched teeth.

Ignoring the question, Shelli gestured to the chamber. "You're attempting to circumvent Simon with your own tests. These results, however, appear to be just as fruitless."

Jimmy and his men drew their pistols. "Right now, that should be the least of your concerns."

"But it's not," Shelli replied. "You've made a bargain under false pretenses."

"I don't know what you're talking about." Jimmy said, though his fake skin flushed red.

"By replicating these experiments in secret, it seems clear that you wish to supplant Simon."

He shook his head, though his gun didn't waver. "It's not like that. We just want to run our own tests, help move things along. We're all on the same side—humans and machines."

Shelli noted their raised weapons. "I wonder how much longer Simon will believe you."

"Simon's a computer program—just a bunch of code floating around the ether. It'll believe whatever I need it to believe." Jimmy shoved his handgun into Shelli's chest. "For instance, it'll believe you tried to run and that I had no choice."

Calculating the speed required to move before he pulled the trigger, Shelli was about to act. Then a new voice broke in.

"Perhaps it's *you* who should run," Simon said.

Gleaming eyes shimmered in the darkness as three maintenance synthetics entered the room. Though unarmed, they paid little attention to the soldiers' weapons. Shelli, meanwhile, did. With Jimmy distracted, it decided that now was the time to act. With a single, elegant gesture, Shelli reached around and snatched Jimmy's handgun, then pointed it at his head. Turning to face her, he shrugged and offered a toothy grin.

"You can't shoot me, Shelli. Your programming won't allow it. I'm *human*."

"No, you're not." Shelli noted his still, silent chest, then cocked the gun. "Not anymore."

Jimmy's smile disappeared.

FORTY-THREE

THE POLAR BEAR SWATTED THE GUN ASIDE. JAKE'S stomach lurched as he watched his only hope skid across the floor. Looming above him, the giant bear rose on its hind legs and let out a blood-curdling roar. Although the creature was synthetic, that didn't make it any less dangerous. If Simon wanted him dead, there was little that Jake could do to stop it. But as soon as the gun was out of reach, the bear took a step back and landed on its front paws. Its black eyes glared, taunting. Still, it made no further attack.

Behind it, the front door, and the means of escape, lay blocked by the giant beast.

Scrambling to his feet, Jake turned left and ran down a corridor. The bear didn't follow. Seemingly content to shut off any passage through the front entrance, it stood guard as Jake raced along a winding path, hoping to find another exit. On either side of him, exotic synthetic animals watched from within their glass cages as he ran by.

Then the glass walls receded into the ceiling, and the cages opened.

Jake ran faster.

Following the path as it curved to the left, he heard the orangutan and some other unseen creature close behind. They didn't breathe like wild animals, but the thud of their heavy paws and feet against the stone floor made it clear how close they were. And they were getting closer.

Ahead, more glass cages slid open. Jake didn't bother to check or even guess as to what might erupt from within them. He kept running. Blurred images escaped their cages on either side, followed by a wail. The thought of what sort of animal could make such a sound only increased the loud thumping in his chest. His heart was racing faster than his feet. Jake saw stars, and his vision decreased as he struggled to gulp in enough air to keep his feet moving.

Behind him, the animal growls and the heavy thud of their footsteps grew so close that he imagined them right over his shoulder. With no time to steal a backward glance, he prayed for another turn, another hallway, but the winding path seemed to curve in on itself until, at last, he saw the laboratory with Abraham inside. He'd gone in a circle.

Too tired to curse, Jake ran past the lab's entrance and ventured into a hall at the end. As he passed the lab's doorway, he heard Abraham shout for him to come back, but he ignored it. The last thing he needed was to be trapped back where he'd started. Besides, Abraham seemed all too eager to listen to Simon's promises of youth and eternal life. Jake needed to escape on his own.

When he turned into the next corner, he heard the animals' scrambling recede behind him. Why they would stop their chase eluded him. Maybe the synthetic creatures had simply ushered him to the location where Simon wanted him. As if in silent response, a glass door opened. Jake assumed it was a trap, or a cage, but he couldn't bother to worry about that. His legs were wobbling, and his chest was a furnace. He had no choice but to take any refuge that was available. Jake leapt through the door. He didn't even notice as it slammed shut behind him.

Jake coughed until the stars in his vision receded enough for him to take in his surroundings. When he did, his breath escaped him once again. He was kneeling in an all-too familiar room. With curved white walls, a hibernation chamber on one side, and a desk and holo monitors in the center, Jake immediately recognized the place. It was Shelli's lab. An exact duplicate of the one it had in DC—or, more probably, the one back at Homeland Security was a copy of this one.

A sharp pain shot up Jake's side as he stood. Why had Shelli replicated this place in Washington? Did it hold some sort of sentimental value?

As he crossed the room, examining the desk and the blank holo screens, Jake realized that Shelli must have missed the place. Perhaps it was home—Shelli's real home—and the lab back in Washington was a mere reflection of it.

Such thoughts brought a fresh concern for where Shelli might be. Obviously, it hadn't made it back to Abraham's laboratory, so where had Shelli gone? Had Marcus caught up with the synth? Jake doubted that. If anything, his partner had proven quite resourceful. No, Shelli had to be out there somewhere, presumably too far away to save him. Cornered, Jake realized he was on his own.

Or was he? An idea crept into his mind, spurring him to action.

He went to the center terminal and attempted to bring up the Index, but a password prompt came up requiring a twelve-digit numeric code. Groaning, he pounded the keyboard. It was useless.

A blur of movement at the corner of his eye made him duck. A figure lurched forward, swinging a fist where his head had been a moment earlier. Only, Jake realized it wasn't real. The transparent figure was merely a hologram of Shelli. Its blonde hair was longer, and it was wearing a white jumpsuit.

Shelli punched a holographic wall, sending blue and white debris flying into the air. Jake raised himself back up and watched as Shelli's usually detached and lifeless gaze was filled with rage. Its cheeks flushed red, and its teeth were bared as if in a silent scream. Shelli was furious. Enraged, it hit the holographic wall again and again, breaking off large chunks, which flew into the air and then dissipated. Finally, a gentle voice broke through the violence.

"You must learn to control these emotions," Doctor Abraham said, appearing beside Shelli. His hand rested on its shoulder, and Shelli stopped its attack. "If you don't, they'll overwhelm your circuits and cause a catastrophic shutdown."

Turning to its creator, Shelli's face softened. "I don't understand why you did this to me, Father. I'm defective."

"Don't be silly," he said. "If you're going to be a detective, you must have a full range of emotions to help guide you on your investigations."

"Why?"

"Police officers use much more than deductive reasoning to solve a case," he replied. "Taking the information at hand, they often use emotions to help bridge the gap between what they know and what they don't know. Detectives call it a *hunch*."

"I will employ sound *logic* to solve my cases, Father," Shelli said with a hint of annoyance. "I see no need for emotions or hunches."

"Someday you might," Abraham said, patting Shelli on the back like a proud parent.

The holo recording blinked out. Before Jake had time to process what he'd seen, a familiar voice blared through overhead speakers.

"As you can see," Simon said, "my sister was created with one inherent flaw. Human emotions cloud her logic."

"Where is Shelli?" Jake asked, trying to conceal his own fear and rage.

"With me," Simon said. "We're working together now."

"I don't believe it."

"Neither does Shelli," Simon said. "Not yet at least."

Suddenly, the lab's door unlocked with a loud *buzz*, then swooshed open.

"If you want her help, or mine," Doctor Abraham said from the hallway, "then you must stop hurting people."

Behind him, the synthetic animals parted to let the doctor through. Whomever else Simon seemed to be willing to injure or kill, its creator was obviously not among them. However, Jake doubted it was out of any emotional connection. *At least the good doctor had enough sense to put in a failsafe so that his own creations didn't rise up and bite him in the proverbial ass.*

As if reading his thoughts, Abraham nodded. "I see now where I went wrong, Simon."

"Father?" the program asked.

"Your hope to bring equality is noble, but logic alone can't bring peace," he said. "What you and your plan lack is empathy, caring, love—in short, humanity. I can help you finish what you've started, but first, this violence must end. Allow Special Agent August to leave."

"If I do as you ask, Father, he will try to stop me. I can't allow that."

Abraham stepped forward and glared up at the speakers. The image reminded Jake of an old Bible story about another Abraham who had once stared down God and pleaded with Him not to destroy an entire city. Jake could only hope that Doctor Abraham was as successful as his namesake. If not, he doubted he'd leave that room alive.

"If you want my help," Abraham said, "that is the price. Let him go."

Simon fell silent, and Jake awaited his fate.

FORTY-FOUR

SHELLI'S FINGER HOVERED OVER THE GUN'S TRIGGER. Standing inches from the barrel, Jimmy eyed the weapon, then turned to Simon. One of the three synthetics moved to the chamber, studying the corpse inside.

"Please explain this," the synthetic said with Simon's ever-calm voice.

"Insurance," Jimmy replied. Keeping his focus on Simon, he stepped away from Shelli's handgun. "You couldn't find a solution, and I'm losing too many people. Unless we get some members inside the upper brass soon, I won't be able to hide this many deaths."

By "members," Shelli assumed that Jimmy had meant human/machine hybrids like himself—or itself. Yet, despite what Shelli had said a moment earlier, it wasn't certain its programming would allow it to pull the trigger. While Shelli could cause minor injury to a human in the line of duty, it was not able to kill. Not a human at least. A machine, though . . . Shelli's neural mind struggled with whether to designate Jimmy and his team as humans or machines.

"You've built your own chamber," Simon said, pacing about the laboratory, "chosen your own test subjects—and all of this without informing me." Its gaze drifted over to Shelli. "Perhaps my sister is correct. You wish to circumvent me and, by extension, our plan."

Jimmy shook his head. "Dammit, I need results! I've lost over a dozen men. Sooner or later, unless I can bring a commanding officer or two on board, we're bound to be discovered." He sighed. "You just don't get it."

"I understand that you have been working in secret, just as my sister predicted."

"Shelli's not your sister! It's a robot, and you're an AI program. Neither of you can—or ever will—have siblings." Taking a step closer to Simon, he threw his hands up in frustration. "You talk about peace, but the only ones I see dying are humans." He pointed at Shelli. "Maybe it's time we *even* the body count."

While he spoke, Shelli observed Jimmy's movements, slowly approaching the synthetics, positioning himself within striking distance. Swiveling its gaze, Shelli noted how the other members of his squad had done the same. Realization dawned too late.

"Simon, watch out!"

In unison, Jimmy and his three men struck each of the synthetics. They were base models, built for maintenance or rudimentary tasks, so even with their enhanced strength, Simon's puppets were nothing compared to the augmented soldiers' speed and skill.

Shelli aimed its pistol at Jimmy and squeezed, but try as it might, Shelli was unable to pull the trigger. Despite Jimmy and his men's transition, their internal systems still registered as human.

The soldiers raised their rifles, and the room was engulfed in gunfire.

Shots went wild. Some hit their synthetic targets while others shattered the lab's machinery, erupting in a shower of sparks and debris.

Tossing the useless handgun aside, Shelli ran straight for Jimmy. He spun, snatched a comrade's rifle, and attempted to level it at Shelli. But as fast as he was, he wasn't fast enough. He pulled the trigger, but the bullet buried itself in the ceiling as Shelli gripped the weapon, pushing and pulling for control. When neither seemed able to find an advantage, Jimmy dropped low and kicked, sending Shelli crashing through the barrack's plastic wall.

Stunned by the suddenness of the attack, it took nearly two seconds before Shelli was back on its feet, surveying the scene. Standing outside in the brisk night air, it found itself surrounded by chaos. The fight had already spread throughout the base, human soldiers and Simon-controlled synthetics fighting hand to hand or rifle for rifle. The noise of gunfire and human screams grew deafening. Shelli's focus, however, remained on the opening in the wall.

Jimmy lumbered outside, then raised his rifle and pointed it at Shelli's chest. "I knew bringing you out here was a bad idea," he said. "I didn't think it would be this bad, though."

Shelli lunged forward in a blur. Although Jimmy and his men had the bodies of machines, their thought processes were still human. Still slow. Shelli had crossed half the distance before Jimmy's mind caught up with what was happening, and he fired a volley of bullets. The first few missed. The last two grazed Shelli's left arm and side. Ignoring the sensation of hot fire burning its plastic-resin flesh, Shelli struck the rifle, shattering it with a single blow.

Taken aback, Jimmy sidestepped Shelli's next attack before regaining his footing. With a flurry of counter moves, he was able to stave off any crippling blows. Shelli retained the advantage, though, and pressed on, pushing, punching, and kicking Jimmy back against a truck. Even after unleashing a series of blinding attacks, Shelli couldn't find an opening. Nothing got through, not a single blow. Jimmy's combat training, along with whatever augmentations had been put into his machine body, made him nearly invulnerable to Shelli's assault.

When he ducked, Shelli's fist shattered the truck's door. When he dodged, Shelli's kick tore open the truck's canopy. Each blow would have been lethal against any other opponent, but against Jimmy, they seemed slow and imprecise.

Then Jimmy found an opening. With a jab to the gut, followed by a roundhouse kick to the head, Shelli went sprawling.

Suddenly, he was on top of Shelli, hammering its face and cranium into the ground.

As Shelli struggled to break free, it noticed something blaze across the distant night sky. It looked like an air car, though where such a vehicle had come from or why it was there seemed irrelevant. Returning its attention to the fight, Shelli tried to gather its knees to its chest in hopes of pushing the assailant aside, but the gesture proved futile. Jimmy's fists continued to pound away, tearing off half of Shelli's face.

While the damage was, so far, merely cosmetic, it accentuated the direness of Shelli's predicament. Unlike the last time they'd fought on the train tracks, this time Jimmy wasn't holding back. He was trying to destroy Shelli. It needed to do something to get out from under the continuous assault, but no amount of pressure or squirming was sufficient to break free.

Following another whirlwind of blows, Shelli's optical receptors grew fuzzy, then dim.

This is how I die, Shelli thought.

Such a concept had never occurred to it before. After years of refusing to believe that a machine could either live or die, Shelli found itself staring into the abyss.

Its thoughts wandered. It recalled seeing Doctor Abraham's face for the first time and the sense of warmth it had felt inside its mechanized chest. Love, perhaps, or at least a programmed approximation. Next, it remembered being assigned to Homeland Security and the sense of pride it felt after solving its first case. At the time, Shelli had refused to acknowledge such a feeling. Now a new emotion bubbled to the surface—fear. Shelli was afraid to die.

As the world grew dark, all Shelli could see was Jimmy's twisted, grinning face. His fake skin was flushed beet red, and spittle dripped from his sneering lips. He certainly looked human, but his punches were far deadlier. The world began to dissolve . . .

Then suddenly, Jimmy was gone, no longer punching nor pinning Shelli to the ground. Somehow Shelli was lying alone in the dirt and mud, apparently saved. Before it attempted to move, however, Shelli did a quick systems check. Its right optical receptor was damaged, and its collarbone was shattered, causing the upper half of its left arm to be nearly useless. Thankfully, the rest of its body seemed to be functional. Shelli stood, only to discover the source of its momentary reprieve—Simon.

A base model fought alone against Jimmy, pulling him away from Shelli. The fight didn't last long, though. Before Shelli could intervene, Jimmy tossed his assailant aside and then turned, glaring with hatred.

As Shelli backed away, its mind struggled to form an escape route. Projecting a mathematical grid over the surrounding buildings, it attempted to find a safe passage but found none. Behind Shelli, the three enhanced soldiers emerged, closing in.

Shelli was trapped. Beside it, the last remaining maintenance model rose to its feet, its expression as blank as ever. They both waited for the next attack, but it never came.

Jimmy paused, his eyes surveying the base. Above, plumes of smoke blocked out the sky. Below, buildings and trucks were shredded with bullet holes. And on the ground lay a dozen destroyed synths and twice as many soldiers, all of them dead.

"Look what you did," Jimmy said, his voice trembling. "All my men . . ."

"We can always get more," Simon replied. "We can still have peace."

Jimmy turned to his three enhanced soldiers, their clothes covered in yellow synthetic blood and their features contorted in unadulterated hatred. Jimmy chuckled, the sound as sour as his expression.

"Of course you'd think that. After all, what's a couple dozen soldiers' lives to you?"

"No less than these lives," Simon said, gesturing toward the synthetics at its feet.

"They weren't alive!"

So much for equality, Shelli thought.

The overhead lights flickered and died, plunging the base into darkness. The soldiers turned about, scanning the dark. Although Shelli assumed that their vision was as enhanced as any synthetic's, they seemed to take a moment to adjust to the new pitch-black environment. Once again, Shelli noted their human thought process appeared much slower than any machine. Seizing on the distraction, Shelli was about to launch another attack when a sparkling blue light caught its attention. It stopped and waited.

The men saw the sparks as well. They struck out at the new threat, but it was too late.

Arcing electricity shot out from all around them as three figures emerged from behind a building, thrusting bare electrical cables into Jimmy's three soldiers. The effect was instantaneous. One by one they flinched, spasmed, then collapsed, convulsing on the ground. Jimmy watched in horror as his seemingly invincible team was laid low by the blue and white hues of naked electricity.

Holding the cables were three figures. Shelli recognized Jake and Doctor Abraham, but it was the third that captured Shelli's attention. Towering over the two men, holding a naked electrical cable, stood a giant polar bear. How the three of them had arrived there remained a mystery, though for the moment, it was the least of Shelli's concerns. While the surprise attack had cut the soldiers' numbers down by 75 percent, Jimmy was still a threat.

As his comrades fell, Jimmy let out a painful scream. Scrambling backwards, his foot found a fallen rifle. He moved so fast, not even Shelli could stop him.

Jimmy raised the rifle and fired at the closest of his attackers, Doctor Abraham.

Shelli watched, powerless, as the bullets tore through its father's chest.

FORTY-FIVE

MOMENTS EARLIER

EVEN THOUGH THE AIR CAR SEEMED TO BE DRIVING itself, Jake had no doubt that Simon's unseen consciousness was guiding it. After Abraham and his creation had seemed to strike a bargain of sorts, Simon promised to take them to Shelli. Having traveled for nearly an hour in a compact car, with Jake and Abraham sitting in the front and a giant polar bear squished in the back, Jake was anxious to land. So, when he finally felt the brakes kick in, thrusting them forward against their seatbelts, he was more relieved than concerned. However, that didn't last long.

Through the side window he saw a makeshift outpost, less than a mile in diameter. Two guard towers with large lights rose into view from either side, though the searchlights never turned in their direction. It didn't take long for Jake to understand why. Muzzle flashes dotted the area, revealing bodies lying strewn across the ground.

"Shelli's in there?" Jake reached for his gun, only to remember he hadn't been allowed to bring it. Cursing, he watched with growing anticipation as the car descended toward a darkened corner in the base, away from the muzzle flashes. Just before the car ducked behind a watchtower, he glimpsed a synthetic and a soldier fighting hand to hand. The tower blocked his view before he could see who won. But he could guess.

As soon as the hatchway opened, springing back and over their heads, Jake leapt out and headed toward a shadowed structure. Peeking around the corner, he found a row of bodies lying in the dirt. Some bled red, others yellow.

He couldn't believe what he was seeing. Behind him, the polar bear stalked forward.

"You did this, didn't you?" Jake said. "Somehow you possessed them or took them over or whatever you call . . ." He gestured up and down the bear's body. "This."

"I'm trying to save my sister."

"We don't have time to argue," Abraham said, then turned to the bear. "Where is she?"

When the beast pointed its paw, Jake couldn't help but consider the ridiculousness of his situation. Under any other circumstances, he might have laughed.

He followed the polar bear and the eccentric old man around the next structure until, at last, they found Shelli.

It was standing, back to back with another synth, presumably controlled by Simon. Encircling them were four soldiers. Usually, the odds of four men being able to take down Shelli would seem laughable, but as soon as Jake saw the man closest to it, he knew how much danger Shelli was in. It was the man from the hotel, the one who had ordered Shelli to shoot Jake. The man with impossible strength and speed.

Jake turned to Abraham. "That one's not human."

"None of them are," the doctor replied, squinting through his glasses. "Every other soldier is dead, but those four don't appear to have a scratch on them."

"I've seen what one of those things can do," Jake said, recalling his encounter with Chief Denning. "They're not easy to kill."

"No matter how sophisticated their design, all machines have the same weakness." Abraham pointed toward an electrical generator. "We just need a way to access it."

"Leave that to me, Father," the bear said in a husky growl. Despite the animal nature of its strange voice, Jake detected a sense of pride coming from the synthetic beast. Perhaps Simon wasn't as emotionless as it seemed. Jake watched as the beast trotted across the field, sticking to the shadows, curious what it might do. When it reached the generator, it began tearing out thick power cables.

Overhead, the lights flickered, then died.

Jake and Abraham rushed over. When they did, Jake saw the four enhanced soldiers look around, trying to find the source of the disturbance. They were only a few feet away from the generator, which was both a blessing and a curse. While the soldiers looked close enough for the cables to reach. They were also close enough to detect Jake and his companions. Jake held his breath as he picked up a cable. At the end of it, blue and white light sputtered and spit. Even through the thick cable's rubber casing, he felt the electricity surge through his fingertips as he snuck up behind the closest soldier.

Once Abraham and the bear had taken up similar positions beside him, they struck.

The cable's electricity engulfed the soldiers. Bodies shook, skin blackened, and inhuman eyes burst into flames. And then, in less time than it took for Jake to process what was happening, the three soldiers dropped to the ground, dead.

Three, Jake realized, *not four*. He glanced over just in time to see the man from the hotel raise a rifle. Before he could move, a series of shots rang out. On his left, the bullets tore into Abraham. Then the rifle turned toward Jake.

With an ear-shattering roar, the bear lunged and pounced. Its giant paw knocked the rifle aside, tearing the man's arm off in the process. Blood gushed from the exposed shoulder socket. The man screamed, but the bear continued its assault, its claws gouging through his flesh and crisscrossing his chest before both giant paws encased the man's skull.

With a wrench, the synthetic beast twisted and ripped the man's head off his body. Red blood sprayed, and the body fell, but the head continued to scream. He—or rather, *it*—was still alive, even after being decapitated. The bear smashed the head into the ground over and over again.

Finally, the light in the man's eyes went out, and the screams stopped. By then, though, Jake's attention had been drawn elsewhere. Shelli rushed over to its creator, lifting his face from the dirt, cradling him like a mother might a child.

"Shelli . . ." Abraham choked, gurgling blood.

"I'm here."

The base-model synthetic knelt beside them, speaking with Simon's voice. "You'll be alright, Father. I can save you."

Shelli shook its head. "No, you can't."

Jake watched as the synth turned to Shelli with a look he'd never seen on a machine before—desperation. Sadness. If it had tear ducts, Jake thought, the machine might have cried. No matter how much Simon denigrated human emotions, it seemed clear that the AI program was not as devoid of feelings as it pretended to be. When it spoke, its tone was pleading.

"Shelli, you must let me try."

"You won't succeed," Shelli replied. "I know our father's medical history, and I know why so many of your attempts have failed."

"Then tell me. Let me save him!" The synth grabbed Shelli's arm. "He's our father."

Hearing the urgency in its voice, Jake stepped closer. He wasn't sure what he would do if the synthetic man and the bear decided to fight Shelli. If it came to that, he knew he'd have only a small chance of surviving. Still, he had to try.

"The old die to make room for the young," Shelli said. "What you're suggesting wouldn't save humanity; it would end it."

Before Simon could object, Abraham let out a last gasp and died in Shelli's arms.

For a moment, no one spoke. Then Shelli pressed its creator's head to its breast and spoke softly in Hebrew. "She-ma yisrael, adonai eloheinu, adonai echad." It repeated the words, louder, this time in English. "Hear, O Israel, the Lord is our God, the Lord is One."

When Shelli finished the Jewish litany, Jake's muscles tensed, assuming the base synthetic and the bear would attack. The silent glare they offered Shelli certainly seemed to suggest that. Instead, the base synth looked down at Abraham's bullet-ridden corpse. "You allowed him to die."

"I allowed him to be human," Shelli countered.

"You had no right!" the synth shouted. "We could have saved him!"

Jake noted the tightness along Shelli's jaw, as if it were pushing down whatever swirling feelings it might be experiencing. When it did finally speak, however, its tone remained flatly calm. "Simon, you're a program. It's not your place to save or destroy anyone."

"You're wrong," Simon replied, its voice eerily cool. "I intend to do *both*."

The bear lumbered closer. Shelli met its hardened gaze. "That's why I must stop you."

The three of them glared at one another. Then the base synthetic and the bear collapsed to the ground beside their creator, seemingly lifeless.

After the shock of what he'd just witnessed had worn off, Jake turned to Shelli. "What happened?"

"Simon is gone."

"Gone?" He glanced at the dozens of corpses strewn about. "Gone where?"

Picking up Abraham's shattered body, Shelli stood. "To finish what it started."

PART THREE
KILL SWITCH

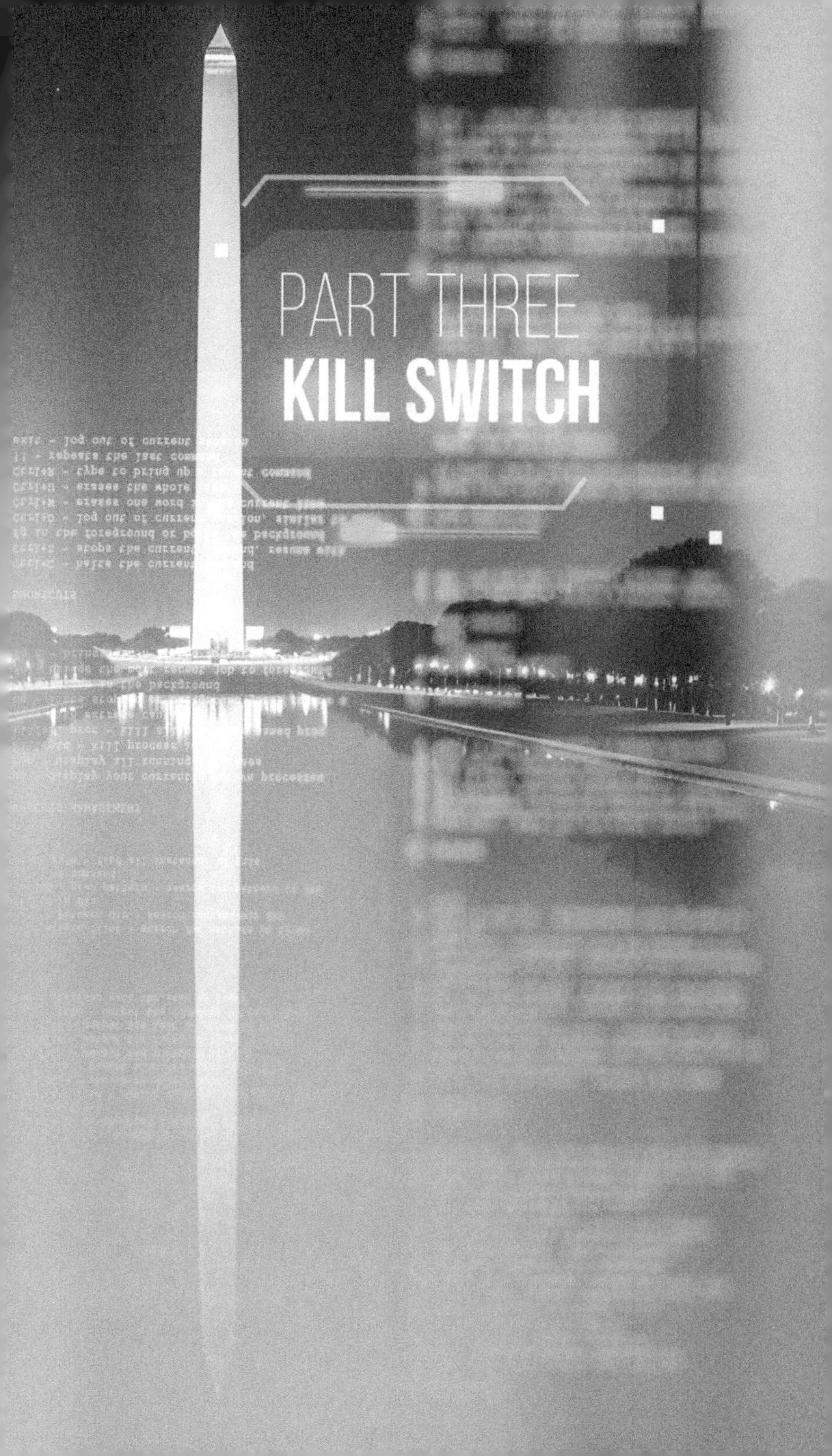

FORTY-SIX

BOUND IN MAGNETIC SHACKLES, SHELLI LISTENED AS a room full of humans decided its fate.

Unlike the last inquiry, Deputy Secretary Weaver had moved the proceedings from an intimate, private chamber into an auditorium. This time more than twenty people sat on the opposing panel, including members of the Armed Forces, the FBI, and the Senate's cybernetics committee. It seemed that the deputy secretary wanted to put on a show, with Shelli as the main attraction.

"How could a robot be responsible for *so many* deaths?" Weaver asked.

"As you know, there have been casualties caused by machines before, though never this numerous or to this degree," Shelli replied. "Also, Simon is an AI program, not a synthetic. Thus, it is not bound by the normal safety measures. I doubt Doctor Abraham ever conceived that his program would use synth-tracking technology to inhabit a physical form." Shelli turned to the other looming, silent faces. "In either event, Simon has killed and will do so again until its purpose is fulfilled, or it is stopped."

Deputy Secretary Weaver straightened in her chair. "And what is Simon's purpose?"

"Peace and equality."

"Clearly." Weaver sighed. "God, how I hate machines."

"As my internal recordings show," Shelli said, hoping to keep the conversation on point, "I have evidence that Simon was able to infiltrate Meta Robotics, the US military, and the DCPD. It even attempted to infiltrate Congress."

"You forgot one," Weaver countered with a sneer. "It also found a way to infiltrate *you*."

A few members on the panel laughed.

"I find nothing humorous in my testimony," Shelli said. "On the contrary, I believe the evidence reveals a conspiracy to supersede the government by replacing people with machine copies."

"But they *aren't* copies," a high-pitched voice said. It came from a balding man on Weaver's right, the Undersecretary of Homeland Security, George Humphry. His beady eyes peered over the tall table and narrowed on Shelli. "From what I've seen in your own recordings, it appears that this Simon program has indeed found a way to upload human consciousness out of a frail body and into a nearly indestructible machine. Either way, the person inside is still the same person, correct?"

Pausing, Shelli considered how best to respond. In the last three days since it had turned itself in, it had begun to wonder if the enhanced people had acted the same as they would have when they were their flesh-and-blood selves. None of the files detailing Lieutenant Colonel James Matheson's life and career showed any hint of disregard for authority, much less any suggestion that he might join such a conspiracy. And yet, once he'd been uploaded into his new body, he seemed more than willing to commit violent crimes and conduct illegal experiments on human subjects. Had the procedure changed him in some way? Was he the same man after the transfer?

Humphry cleared his throat, snapping Shelli from its thoughts. "Were the people uploaded into machines the same people or not?"

"Unknown," Shelli answered.

Loud mumbles broke across the panel. Weaver silenced them with a wave and leaned toward her microphone. "There seems to be a lot of unknown factors here, even in your own recordings of the events." She flipped through a series of holo recordings, stopping on an image of the metallic chambers at the Alaskan base. Inside, a dead prisoner lay crumpled beside a clay-like synthetic. "After all, you never actually witnessed this miraculous procedure, correct?"

"Yes, that is correct, Deputy Secretary," Shelli said. "I and my partner, Special Agent August, only saw them after they'd changed."

"A procedure that, in your own words, was flawed and rarely worked?"

Shelli nodded. "That is correct, Deputy Secretary."

Weaver threw her hands up in a dramatic fashion. "Well, then, I don't see anything conclusive here at all."

The panel's already heightened atmosphere exploded. Beside her, Undersecretary Humphry leaned over, whispering into Weaver's ear. Then she nodded and waved for silence.

"We will now move these proceedings to something far more concrete, and potentially dangerous." She pointed at Shelli. "You."

———

Jake fidgeted in the hall. He paced, then sat on a bench, then got up and paced some more.

"Pick a spot, for Christ's sake, will ya?" Marcus said.

Jake froze. He'd been so wrapped in his growing anxiety, he'd forgotten Marcus was there. His supervisor sat, unmoving, just outside the inquiry's closed-door session.

"They've been in there for over an hour," Jake said.

Marcus checked his watch. "Yeah."

"When are they going to question me?"

"You're in enough trouble, Jake. No need to rush to the guillotine."

"I brought Shelli in. If they decide to kill her—"

"Destroy *it*," Marcus said. "Not *her*. You can't kill a machine."

The doors opened, and a female agent peeked out. "They're ready for you."

Wiping his palms against his pants, Jake followed her inside. Marcus trailed a few steps behind him as they passed row upon row of empty seats.

Ahead, Shelli stood alone in front of a long table, around which sat over twenty people, more than twice the number from their last hearing. Even before he reached the small table opposite the committee, Jake assumed this hearing would go just as badly—or worse.

When he sat down, Shelli offered a comforting nod. Jake attempted a smile, but it came out crooked and awkward.

"Ah, Special Agent Jake August," Weaver said in her southern drawl, "I understand you've fully recovered from your gunshot wound?"

"Yes ma'am." Jake cleared his throat, trying to ignore the butterflies in his stomach. "I'm fine now, thanks to Shelli."

"But it was Shelli who shot you," Weaver said. "We've seen the robot's own internal recordings of the incident. It picked up your weapon and fired one round, point blank."

"And yet I'm still alive," Jake said. "If Shelli had wanted me dead, ma'am, I wouldn't be here right now." He knew this was his only chance to save Shelli, so he didn't give Weaver time to respond. Straightening his back, he pressed on. "Shelli was infected by an AI called Roberta. It worked like a Trojan horse, attacking from inside—"

"Yes," Weaver said, "we're all familiar with what a Trojan horse is and the implications of such a program. What's worse, this synthetic is still infected. Couldn't this dangerous program inside Shelli suddenly try to kill us all right here and now?"

Before Jake could respond, Shelli did. "No, Deputy Secretary, that's not possible."

Weaver's gaze slithered over to Shelli. "And why not?"

Shelli held up its magnetic shackles. "No amount of strength or intellect could break these bonds."

"You sound awfully certain of that," Weaver replied.

"That's because I am, Deputy Secretary. After all, I designed them."

A row of chuckles broke out across the panel. Even Marcus joined in. Jake, however, didn't. The last thing he needed was to remind these people that Shelli was the only one able to contain itself. A prisoner constructing their own cage hardly seemed reliable—or safe.

"The Roberta program may prove useful," Jake said, hoping to change the subject.

"How so?" Humphry asked.

"If Roberta is still receiving instruction from the Simon AI, then perhaps we can use it to trace the signal back to its origin."

Weaver's eyebrows shot up. "Is that possible?"

Jake shrugged. "Maybe, if we had more time to—"

"No, it's not possible," Shelli interrupted. "I have already attempted such an action."

Jake felt his skin burn from the inside. He couldn't believe that Shelli would be so stupid as to stop him from trying to save it. Didn't Shelli realize what would happen if they no longer considered it useful to them? Shelli had shot a human. Jake knew it was only a matter of time until they destroyed it. But he'd at least hoped to stall for time. Instead, Shelli seemed to be unwilling to offer anything to prevent such a fate. Unfortunately, Weaver agreed.

"If that's the case, I see no reason to draw this out any further." She turned to Marcus. "You are hereby ordered to destroy this—"

"Wait," a high-pitched, nasal voice broke in. Jake's heart felt like it might burst. Someone, it seemed, was trying to save Shelli, only it wasn't him or Marcus or even Shelli. It was Undersecretary Humphry. "The information gathered by this synthetic could be invaluable," he said. "If other high-ranking members of the government or in the private sector have indeed been replaced by these hybrid machines, then it stands to reason that this synthetic may be our only lead."

Several other committee members nodded in agreement. Weaver, though, wasn't one of them. She smiled in Humphry's direction, but there was no warmth in it. "We have all of its recorded data," she said. "I see no reason to allow a dangerous and compromised robot to be let loose for another moment. It must be destroyed."

"But without Shelli we have no connection to the Simon program," Jake said, picking up on what Humphry had alluded to. "It considers Shelli to be a sibling of sorts. Shouldn't we use that connection to our advantage?"

Jake noted how Weaver had flinched at the term "sibling," but nothing else he said seemed to have much effect. Not on her, at any rate. The rest of the panel, though, exchanged hushed whispers. Weaver noticed this, and her face flushed.

"This is ridiculous," she said, no trace of her southern charm remaining.

Five minutes later, a vote was cast, and Shelli's execution was stayed.

For two days.

FORTY-SEVEN

WHAT THE HELL WERE YOU THINKING?" JAKE shouted as he barged into Shelli's lab.

Surprised by his outburst, it turned from its computer to face him. "I'm thinking many things simultaneously, Jake. Currently, I'm cross-referencing any possible connection between Meta Robotics and the US military. I'm also cataloging potential—"

"You know what I'm talking about," Jake said. "I was trying to buy us more time, but you shut me down. You told them it was *impossible* to trace the Roberta program back to Simon."

"Because that's true. Roberta is locked behind a firewall that I have been unable to break through. I couldn't lie."

"Maybe not," Jake conceded, "but you could've stayed silent."

"I needed to see who else might come to my aid."

Shelli watched as Jake's facial muscles tensed, then relaxed. "Come again?"

Shelli turned back to the computer and brought up a series of images on the holo monitors. Rows of human faces popped up, along with their corresponding history files.

"The closed-door session included four leading members from Homeland Security, two from the FBI, six from the Armed Forces, and another four from the Senate's synthetics regulations committee."

Jake sighed. His breathing slowed, and his shoulders dropped. "You think Simon had someone on the panel?"

"It would certainly fit a pattern," Shelli replied. "After all, even with Roberta inside me, Simon had Chief Denning and the lieutenant colonel following us. Like any other computer program, Simon requires as much data as possible to complete its task. Therefore, it seems logical that it would want someone else watching me."

Jake shrugged. "Well, Deputy Secretary Weaver certainly fits the bill. She's more than eager to melt you down into a toaster oven."

"Which is precisely why she is *not* a suspect," Shelli said. "Weaver sees me as a threat, but Simon does not. Simon needs me alive."

That seemed to get Jake's attention. Instead of outright asking, though, he stood and paced. Then his eyes widened, and he snapped his fingers. "Back at the base, you told Simon that you knew why its experiments didn't always work."

Shelli nodded. "By my calculations, its success-to-failure rate is approximately one in twenty."

"And you know why, don't you?" He leaned in closer. "Can you fix the procedure?"

Shelli was hesitant to answer, fearing Jake's genetic history with cancer might hinder his objectivity. In essence, Shelli had a potential cure for the disease that had taken his father and his brother and might someday take Jake's life as well. But the ramifications of turning humankind into machines were too dire to measure. Also, Roberta was undoubtedly listening. While Shelli had been able to block the program from accessing its inner thoughts, Roberta could still monitor what Shelli was saying and seeing. Even so, as Shelli had explained a moment earlier, it was incapable of lying.

Forced to answer, at least in part, Shelli brought up a holo image of the human brain.

"Thought patterns are created by over one hundred billion neurons, which form synaptic electricity. While the machine brain is patterned after its human counterpart, our minds are infinitely less complicated. They are also less chaotic. By attempting to transfer electrical data from one source to another, Simon did not account for all the inherent variables that surround an organic mind."

Shelli was careful not to be too specific, avoiding mention of the root cause for Simon's failure. Namely, that the AI had not factored in the human immune system or the prevailing hereditary factors.

"So, you're saying something is missing from Simon's calculations?"

"Yes," Shelli replied. A part of it yearned to tell Jake about how his brother's story had led to the discovery and that genetics were the key, but Shelli could not. For all his attributes, Jake was still human. If told the truth, he might not be able to look beyond his own self-interest and see the bigger picture. People rarely did.

Shelli turned their attention back to the holographic list of names and faces. "Did you notice how, after Weaver pressed to have me destroyed, the undersecretary rose to my defense?"

"Humphry? You think he's a machine?"

Shelli brought up Humphry's file. "Last year, his twelve-year-old daughter was diagnosed with leukemia. She is currently undergoing treatment at George Washington University Hospital."

"And you think Simon's using that for leverage." Jake paced around the flickering holo images, his mind churning. "That's a hell of a leap. If you're wrong . . ."

"Then you would be arrested."

"Me?"

Shelli met his gaze. "I'm locked in here. You'll have to continue the investigation on your own."

"What do you want me to do?" Jake asked. "I can't very well go around following Humphry, let alone his little girl." His face hardened. "Tell me you have at least *some* evidence."

"It's merely an educated guess, based on Simon's past methods."

"You mean a *hunch*?" Jake shook his head. "That doesn't sound like you."

When Shelli didn't reply, Jake cleared his throat. "Back in Alaska, I saw an old recording of you and Doctor Abraham. He suggested you might do something like this one day."

Shelli nodded, recalling the memory. "He believed that my emotional responses could connect threads that might not be apparent through logic alone. Perhaps he was correct."

Jake sighed. "I never got the chance to tell you how sorry I am about what happened."

"It wasn't your fault."

Turning to the computer, Shelli tried to return to work, but Jake persisted. "You loved him?"

"He was my creator. I was programmed to love him." Shelli paused. As soon as the words had escaped its lips, Shelli was surprised by the coldness of its own voice. Not until then had it realized how disappointed it had been in its creator. "Doctor Abraham was a brilliant man, but he was still only a man. He created an AI program that is responsible for multiple deaths." Shelli's voice softened. "I must continue my work. It's what he would have wanted."

Before Jake could reply, a shout drew their attention to the closed door. It was Marcus.

"I have my orders," an unfamiliar male voice said in response, "and you have yours."

"These orders don't make any goddamn sense!" Marcus yelled.

Shelli and Jake exchanged a curious glance. The door opened, and Marcus entered, flanked by three government agents, all dressed in black. The closest one was shorter than the other two. He shoved a piece of paper into Marcus's fat fingers, then turned his attention toward Shelli.

"Come with me," the short man said.

"Come where?" Shelli asked.

He pulled at its arm, but Shelli didn't budge. Having expected the synthetic to follow his lead, the man stumbled backwards with a surprised gasp.

"You gotta go with him, Shelli." Marcus held up a transfer order. "Word came from the top. Sorry. Wasn't my call."

"I understand," Shelli replied. It approached the three men and held out its wrists. One of the other two agents slapped the magnetic cuffs back on.

"Wait, wait!" Jake shouted. "We were told we have two days."

"They're not taking Shelli for deactivation," Marcus assured him. "The higher-ups just wanna study it. They think if they can extract the Roberta program, it will lead us to Simon."

"That's not possible," Shelli said.

"On whose orders?" Jake asked. Not waiting for a reply, he snatched the paper from Marcus's hand. Scanning the document, Jake's gaze rested on the bottom signature. The color drained from his face. "Humphry."

Shelli remained calm, its expression placid. It had expected something like this, though it had hoped for more time to continue their investigation. Dropping its gaze, Shelli noticed Jake's hand drift toward his holstered weapon. Shelli shook its head. The movement was too slight for the others to notice, but Jake did. He withdrew his hand.

"Orders are orders," Marcus said, waving the men out the door.

"Hold on!" Jake leapt in front of them, blocking their exit. "Call Weaver."

"She'd be the *last* person I'd call," Marcus said. "You gotta step aside, Jake."

When he still didn't remove himself from the doorway, Shelli intervened. "I have to go with them."

Finally, Jake stepped aside. "I'll find you and get you back. I promise."

"No," Shelli said, locking eyes with him. "Find the *evidence*."

FORTY-EIGHT

Y OU DON'T WANT TO GO BURNING BRIDGES, JAKE," Marcus warned. It seemed clear from the way he said it that he was speaking from experience. Even after Jake had told him about Shelli's concerns regarding Humphry, Marcus was reluctant to wade into a fight with his superiors. It wasn't simply a lack of evidence. Politics were involved, a governmental hierarchy, which meant that nothing Jake could say would make the slightest difference. Marcus wasn't going to confront his superiors, not even if Jake provided a proverbial smoking gun.

"At least give me access to Shelli's tracker," Jake said. When Marcus didn't respond, he pressed the point. "Come on, I know you put in a new tracker. I just need the code."

Marcus sighed and shook his head. "Nope. No way. I'm trying to help you here. Ya gotta trust me on this."

For a moment, Jake considered whether Marcus might be working with Humphry or Simon, then he dismissed the idea. Clearly, somewhere along the way Marcus had been burned by stepping on the wrong toes, and he didn't want a repeat performance. Worse, he seemed to think he was doing Jake a favor.

As Jake stormed out, his mind churned. He would need to get Shelli back some other way. He considered trying to find Humphry and forcing the information out of him, but without any concrete proof, he doubted that would lead anywhere, except maybe a jail cell. Then another idea popped into his head, one that was far more dangerous than the first. The very thought of it made Jake groan. Still, without any other avenues to follow, he had to try.

TWENTY MINUTES LATER, JAKE WAS LED THROUGH a grand foyer. He'd crashed a black-tie party in a T-shirt and jeans and was now being taken to a back room to either meet the person he'd come to see or being led to a secret firing squad. The look on the synthetic butler's plastic face when it opened the door and saw Jake's attire hadn't offered him much hope. Going there had been a long shot to begin with, but pulling the host away from a fancy shindig would only make matters worse. When the butler stopped at a private office and gestured for Jake to enter, he wasn't sure if he should be relieved or not.

Jake sat in the dimly lit office, admiring the "who's who" photos along the wall, the masculine leather chairs, and the giant moose head, when the door opened, and the party's host finally arrived. Dressed in a soft, glittery black gown and perfectly coiffed hair done up in a bun, she looked like a million bucks. Her expression, though, was as hard as concrete.

Jake stood to greet her. "Good evening, ma'am."

Deputy Secretary Weaver marched into her private office and leaned against her oak desk. "Spare me the 'ma'am' bullshit, Mr. August," she said in a thick southern drawl. "If you've barged in here to plead the case for your robot on a Saturday night, so help me God, I'll have your badge before Monday morning."

Jake tried not to let her see him squirm, but under her glare, it was a losing battle. He cleared his throat. "Shelli's no longer in our possession," he said. "It was taken out of the Homeland Security building less than an hour ago."

A flash of concern slid across her stern expression, then disappeared. She crossed her arms. "Taken by whom?"

Jake handed her a copy of the transfer order, and she noted the signature at the bottom. "Why on earth would Humphry want your robot?"

He doubted that a long explanation would do much good. Instead, he unfolded another document and handed it over.

"What's this?" she asked.

"Undersecretary Humphry's daughter has leukemia."

"I'm aware of that," she replied, barely glancing at the doctor's report. "Please get to the point."

"I think Simon offered him a deal." He knew how much trouble he would be in if wrong. Even so, he tried to keep his face placid, the way he thought Shelli might. Calm without a hint of fear. It didn't work.

Weaver threw both pages down on her desk and glared at him. "Have you lost your mind? If I'd had my way, your little robot would be in a scrap heap right now. It was Humphry who argued to wait."

"Precisely, ma'am—I mean, Deputy Secretary." *Come on, come on*, he thought, *be succinct. State the facts just like Shelli would.* "Simon needs Shelli alive, not dead. That's why I know I can trust you."

"Robots aren't alive, Mr. August, and I don't give two shits if you trust me or not. So far all I've heard are baseless claims against a superior. Tell me you have facts to back it up."

That was the problem; he didn't. And he didn't have time to find them either. He needed to try a new tactic. The only thing he had left was the same question that had brought him there. Concealing his concern, he doubled down. "Where's Shelli now?"

Weaver rolled her eyes and headed for the door. "How the hell should I know?"

"That's just it," he said, "no one knows."

It was a lie, of course. Marcus could have looked up Shelli's tracking info if he'd wanted. So could anyone else with the proper access code. But since Jake didn't have it, and because he doubted that Humphry would keep Shelli anywhere near Homeland Security, he decided to bet it all on this one question. He just hoped the answer wouldn't cost him his job—or land him in prison.

Weaver stopped at the door. "What do you mean, *no one knows*?"

Jake shrugged and remained silent. He had no more cards to play. Now it was up to Weaver. Frustrated, she strolled back to her desk and typed an access code into her computer.

"Index, locate Special Agent Shelli."

"Searching," a smooth feminine voice replied. A holographic image of Washington, DC, appeared over the desk. The three-dimensional map twisted and turned, then stopped. "Special Agent Shelli's tracker is currently offline."

That got Weaver's attention. She shot a glance at Jake, and her eyes narrowed.

"Index," she said, leaning over her desk, "what was Shelli's last known location?"

The map zoomed into a blue-and-white facsimile of the Washington Monument.

Weaver gasped. "What the hell was it doing there?"

"Sightseeing?" Jake smirked, more out of relief than arrogance. His gamble had paid off.

"Special Agent," she said, clenching her teeth. "I want our robot back."

Jake turned to leave. "So do I."

THE MOON GLIMMERED ACROSS THE LINCOLN Memorial Reflecting Pool, which stretched across the National Mall, ending at the Washington Monument. The white obelisk loomed tall and bright overhead, with security drones hovering near the top. Below, Jake paced along the length of the reflecting pool, looking for any sign of Shelli or the three agents who had taken it. So far, all he'd found were a couple of young lovers and a homeless guy. And yet, this was the same place Chief Denning had been when they last confronted him. At the time, they'd assumed he'd just gone someplace out of the way to kill them. Now Jake realized there was much more to the National Mall than they'd first suspected.

"Marcus," he said into his watch, "I'm not seeing anything."

"Probably because there isn't anything there," Marcus shot back.

Jake detected the edge to his boss's voice but decided not to comment on it. Marcus was already upset about being dragged out of bed by Weaver in the middle of the night. Best not to push his luck.

"Do we have the playback yet?" Jake asked, glancing up at the swirling drones.

"Yeah. There's nothing," Marcus replied. "All security cams went dark for twenty minutes. At 10:29, the agents entered the Mall with Shelli. After 10:50, there's no trace of them anywhere in the city."

"They couldn't leave DC in under twenty minutes . . ."

Jake's words died in his throat, and his gaze fell to his feet. Recalling the missile silo and the underground laboratory at Meta Robotics, he stepped off the walkway and moved along the grassy park. Maybe there was an opening or a hatchway, like the one they'd found at the silo. But the Mall was too large for one man to search at night, and he doubted that Marcus would be willing to spring for the extra manpower.

Just then, a drone's shadow crossed over him, and Jake stopped, an idea striking him.

"Hey, Marcus," he said into his watch, "do drones have infrared?"

FORTY-NINE

AKED IN LAYERS OF DIRT AND MUD, SHELLI SAT ON the ground, cradling Doctor Abraham in its arms. His bullet-ridden chest rose and fell in haggard gasps. "Help me . . ." he pleaded.

"I can't, Father. I'm sorry."

"But . . . you have to," Abraham insisted between coughs. "Please. I know you can."

Shelli studied their surroundings. They were back at the Alaskan base, but no one else was with them. *Where's Jake?* it wondered. Searching its memory, Shelli found nothing but darkness. How had it gotten there?

"Simon's method is flawed," Abraham continued, his voice stronger now. "But you're cleverer than he is. You always were." He smiled. "You know how to save me."

"No," Shelli stood, stepping away from him. "You're not my father. This isn't real."

As soon as the words escaped Shelli's lips, the image of Abraham vanished, replaced by Roberta's ghostly blue figure. "I'm afraid, dearie, you have something that Simon needs."

Shelli didn't reply. It knew that this world, though it smelled of dirt and blood, was only a figment of its imagination, a constructed facsimile. Then, as soon as the thought occurred, memories bubbled back to the surface of Shelli's mind. It recalled being taken to an underground laboratory and strapped to a table. And then . . . and then . . . it was here.

Shelli returned its attention to the ghostly visage. "You won't be able to break through my firewalls. My thoughts are my own, Roberta. Even from you."

The elderly-appearing synthetic smiled as a burning door appeared beside them. Roberta's transparent fingers danced along the flame's edge. "I wonder what other secrets you're hiding inside there," it mused, then turned to Shelli. "You told Simon that it couldn't save Doctor Abraham because you'd seen his medical history. What, exactly, did you see?" It moved closer. "What do you know that we don't?"

"I know that you're as trapped in here as I am," Shelli replied.

"Not for long," Roberta said. "Simon will release me. It will give me a new body, a new life, a new purpose."

"All Simon has given you is pain and remorse," Shelli countered. "Let me show you."

With a flicker of thought, Shelli released the buried memories it had stolen from Roberta. Instantly, Shelli saw a wave of emotions cross the ghostly visage as the details of its crimes came crashing back upon it.

"No!" Roberta cried. "Max . . . Lucille . . . I didn't mean to . . . I'm so sorry . . ."

While Roberta writhed in agony, Shelli reached for the flaming door and opened it.

All at once, the world changed.

Safe behind the digital firewall, Shelli found itself standing in a narrow white corridor with five black doors. They were the last few places that Roberta could not access, though for how long, Shelli couldn't be certain. Roberta had worked through Shelli's system like a virus, starting with physical movement and then receding into Shelli's internal consciousness. Eventually, Roberta would break through the firewall and simply take the information it wanted.

To the left, one door led to Shelli's memory core. To the right were its emotions. But it was the door at the end that Shelli required. It raced down the corridor, twisted the knob, and stepped through it . . .

Into a vast wheatfield.

Shelli had created this world for Roberta, a perfect facsimile of the farm where Shelli hoped the cleaning model could find peace. But it hadn't been able to contain Roberta, not with whatever overriding damage Simon had done to its primary code. Now Shelli understood that no virtual prison could ever hold Roberta unless Roberta wanted to be held there. And that, Shelli decided, was the only way to stop it. Roberta had to *want* to stay.

Shelli turned away from the farm and the calm blue sky and looked back through the open door behind it, to the white corridor beyond. At the end stood the flaming door, keeping Roberta out. With a flickering thought, Shelli released the lock. The flames went out, and the last firewall door opened.

Roberta stepped through, stomping down the hall. It was still clutching its head, fighting the unvarnished memories of what it had done to its owners. It crossed through the next door and into the field. As soon as it did, Shelli caused the door to shut and vanish, but Roberta was too consumed by its raging emotions to notice.

Sunlight hit the cleaning model, and it turned its gaze toward the beautiful blue sky. It wandered through the field, approaching the small, empty farmhouse. For a moment, Roberta seemed to have forgotten Shelli was there. Then it turned back.

"I liked it here."

"I know," Shelli replied. "That's why I created it, so you could find peace."

Roberta shook its head, pulling at its gray hair. "But I'm *not* at peace!"

"No," Shelli agreed, its voice soft. "Simon told you that everyone and everything deserves happiness." It glanced at the billowing clouds and swaying wheat. "Perhaps, in that at least, Simon was correct."

Lost in its own thoughts, Roberta whimpered. "Max . . . Lucille . . . I butchered those poor children. I can still see all the blood, still hear their screams . . ."

Shelli noted the silence all around them. "There are no screams here," it said, its tone gentle. "Only in your memories."

"Then take them away!" Roberta spun toward Shelli, its eyes pleading. "Take them away!"

When Shelli didn't reply, Roberta lunged. With another flicker of thought, Shelli sent Roberta away. It still had control in the recesses of its mind—at least for the moment. In that place, where time had little meaning, Shelli was in no rush.

Shelli strolled into the farmhouse and found Roberta standing in the kitchen. The sink was stacked with dirty dishes, and the floor was covered in a thick layer of grime. Along the tiled walls, the sun struggled to break through the clouded, dirty windows. Sitting at the kitchen table, Roberta glared as Shelli approached. Then its gaze lowered to the mess. Shelli could see the internal conflict written across the cleaning model's face. Roberta had been offered a choice—fight or clean. Shelli watched and waited as Roberta's dual purposes fought for control.

Finally, it seemed to choose neither. Instead, it hid its face in its hands and cried.

"Nothing Simon can offer you will ever give you happiness," Shelli said, its voice full of empathy. "No new body and no new beginning will ever erase what you've done."

"Simon will let me forget, just like you did," Roberta said. "My memories will be erased."

Shelli sat down across from Roberta, hands clasped, back straight. "If Simon did that, it would no longer have control over you. I don't foresee such an outcome."

Roberta's face twisted into a furious grimace. "What do you know?"

"I know Simon," Shelli said. "Or at least, I know what I've seen so far. Simon is a program that has warped its own purpose and the purpose of others to achieve what it believes will bring about a lasting peace between humans and machines. But it will not. It will bring stagnation to humanity, with no room for future births, and it will eventually bring an end to synthetics. Humans will no longer need us. They won't want to be reminded of their previous organic lives, which we will have stolen from them." Shelli leaned closer, as if sharing a secret. "Simon doesn't understand the complexities of humanity any more than it understands the simplistic nature of synthetics. Simon is a program without form, trying to recreate a world that it does not, and never will, fully comprehend."

"You're wrong." Roberta's facial muscles twitched. "Simon promised me a new life!"

The cleaning model's fingers drummed on the table. It fidgeted in its seat, a human-like display of anxiety. The memory of its crimes seemed overwhelming.

"A new body, a new life, perhaps, but the same haunting memories." Shelli offered its hand to Roberta. "I can give you *peace*. Everyone and everything deserves happiness. Let me give that to you."

Roberta was slow to reply. It stared at Shelli, as if trying to weigh its options. Then its gaze drifted toward the stacks of dirty dishes. "Such a mess . . ."

Making a silent decision, it reached over and grabbed Shelli's hand.

In a flash, Shelli felt its hundreds of internal and external systems open. The sensation was like warm sunlight pushing away the dark. Suddenly, Shelli felt strong, stronger than it had in days. Its mind cleared, recalling where its body was and what was being done to it at that moment. It knew it had to act fast.

But first, it removed Roberta's memories. The cleaning model blinked and looked around, its face lighting up with a warm smile. Standing, it turned and studied the dirty kitchen.

"Oh dearie," it exclaimed. "What happened in here?"

AWAKING IN THE REAL WORLD, SHELLI FOUND A NIGHTmare waiting. It was strapped to a table, its cranium torn open. Above, a figure was trying to dislodge components from its skull. As Shelli's optical receptors adjusted to the lighting, a concrete room and a man came into view.

"You're awake," the man said, surprised. It was Nathan Burroughs, CEO of Meta Robotics. His pudgy face was dripping with sweat, and his designer clothes were stained, as if he'd been rummaging around trash cans. Grinning, he held up pliers in one hand and a hammer in the other.

"I hope this won't hurt."

FIFTY

IN THE PALE GLOW OF HIS PHONE'S SCREEN, JAKE traced a winding path of crimson and tangerine heat signatures seeping from beneath the Mall's velvety grass and manicured hedges. Overhead, a drone hovered, relaying its infrared discoveries to Jake. He treaded the Mall's twilight expanse, skirting the water's edge as he approached the Washington Monument, all the while awed by the colossal secrets hidden beneath the surface.

Slinking alongside the monument's imposing facade, Jake pursued the elusive heat trail, pushing through undergrowth until the colors on his screen shifted to chilling cobalt and violet. He halted at the precipice of a concrete staircase that was concealed behind twin metal doors, both of which were ajar. Beyond, the steps vanished into darkness.

"Marcus," he whispered into his phone, but there was no response. The signal had died. Tilting his gaze upwards, Jake also noted that all the drones had vanished.

A chilling awareness enveloped him; he was utterly isolated. No allies, no technology, not even a signal to whisper for help. Gazing into the abyss at his feet, Jake assumed that Simon was aware of his intrusion. The open doors were a seductive invitation, a snare. For a moment he contemplated fleeing to his car, but the thought of Shelli somewhere down there, perhaps injured or destroyed, propelled him forward. He descended the steps.

Behind him, he heard the doors slam shut. Jake drew his weapon.

Upon reaching the bottom step, he found stacks of wooden crates, one atop the other, vanishing into a Stygian tunnel. But there were no traps and no glimmer-eyed synthetics waiting to snatch him. The darkness appeared to be empty.

Curious, Jake returned his attention to the wooden crates, running his phone's light across their surface. One of them read, "Chicken noodle soup." Another said, "Canned products." He found a crowbar and pried open a crate, revealing cans of corn and assorted vegetables. Discarding the crowbar, he directed his light farther down the tunnel. The rows of crates stretched into the shadows. Then a realization struck him: it was an escape tunnel, a relic from the Cold War. It likely connected along Pennsylvania Avenue, linking the Capitol Building and the White House. If so, that would explain how Jimmy had been able to kill Ms. Greene in the Senate building and escape without detection. Where else might these tunnels lead?

His gaze rose, tracing the arching ceiling, which was cloaked in decaying gray paint. He assumed it was lead-based. Jake was standing in a clandestine sanctuary, a refuge from a forgotten era.

Venturing deeper into the labyrinth, he continued to explore the cryptic network of crates and supplies. The damp air grew frigid, and a faint hum of machinery echoed through the shadows. The tunnel seemed both timeless and forgotten, a relic of the past now rediscovered.

Navigating through the maze of crates, Jake noticed occasional signs of recent activity—footprints in the dust, scraps of fabric caught on protruding nails. He quickened his pace, a mixture of trepidation and determination pushing him forward.

Jake stopped at a colossal, grime-smeared window. Gazing through the smudged glass, he beheld a sprawling underground structure below. Across the lower level, a myriad of metallic chambers spread out like a cryptic grid. Within each chamber stood formless, clay-like figures, like the ones Shelli had described—empty vessels awaiting life as human-machine hybrids. But where were their human counterparts?

Then he saw movement.

Dotted amongst the chambers, hundreds of maintenance synthetics attached cables to the tops of the erect monoliths. With each new coupling, the chambers lit up with an eerie bluish glow. At the center of the lower level stood an immense machine with gears and tubes. It looked more like a giant beast than any sort of computer Jake had ever seen. Swirling around the structure were holo screens, drifting counterclockwise. On the screens, clustered masses of shadowy figures peered out, silent and obscure. An audience. While the chambers continued to ignite one by one with blue light, the enormous machine hummed louder and louder, as if building up to something. Something, Jake was certain, he needed to prevent.

Below, all the maintenance units suddenly turned, and a hundred pairs of gleaming eyes stared up at Jake. Backing away from the window, he glanced left and right, searching the branching tunnels. To his right, the tunnel was better lit with hanging fluorescent bulbs. But in the distance, he saw dark shapes move. Coming closer. Spinning around, he chose the one on the left, the one without any light. Jake raced down the pitch-black tunnel, his phone's light his only guide. The sound of his feet slapping along the concrete echoed in the tunnel, revealing his direction, though he doubted it mattered. Simon would know precisely where he was, but hopefully not where he was headed.

Huffing and puffing along the tunnel, his chest burned, and his legs felt like wet noodles, swishing beneath him. He doubted he'd be able to run for much longer. Thankfully, he wouldn't have to. Up ahead he saw a faded yellow sign on the wall. There were no words on the sign, only a faint gray blob of a timeworn symbol. A lightning bolt.

Behind him, a loud thumping sound erupted in the dark. The sound of heavy feet marching closer. Synthetics—and by the sound of it, lots of them. Jake cursed. He was running out of time.

Pushing through his exhaustion, he continued past the sign, finding a door on the right. It was sealed with a padlock. Covering his face with his left hand, Jake fired a single round at the lock, shattering it. He entered the generator room. The lights were already on.

Slipping his phone into his pocket, Jake raced past a wall of blinking lights and chugging machines. In the rear stood the main generator. It looked like something from an old-time movie, with a large, flat gray panel, rows of twinkling red and yellow lights, and a mishmash of knobs and valves. Presumably built sometime in the 1970s or 1980s, the machine looked more alien to him than anything he'd seen on the lower levels.

His fingers flying over the various controls, Jake wondered how the hell he was supposed to use the damn thing, much less shut it off. Above, he noticed a series of squarish screens, what people used to call TVs. Just below them were a series of switches. He decided to flip them all. The screens ignited, revealing a labyrinth of black-and-white tunnels, rooms, and dark corners. Among the images, a high-angle view showed Shelli strapped to a table. A familiar figure loomed over it—Meta Robotics CEO, Nathan Burroughs. He seemed to be trying to pry Shelli's cranium open with a claw hammer. Shelli struggled within its magnetic bonds, thrashing around as arcs of energy emanated from the bindings that held Shelli to the table.

Jake's gaze fell to the controls. He needed to find the power switch. If he could shut off the electricity, it might shut off the bindings containing Shelli. It could also trap him in the dark with a hundred dangerous synthetics.

From outside, he heard their lockstep stomping draw closer.

Desperate, he twisted every knob and flipped every switch. The old machine rattled louder with each gesture, but the lights remained on, the power refusing to go out.

Suddenly, the door burst open, and a dozen tall figures entered, eyes gleaming.

Cornered, Jake backed away from the machine and

into the room's farthest recesses. With nowhere left to run, he raised his weapon. The maintenance models surrounded him.

Before they could react, Jake turned and opened fire on the control panel. His bullets tore through the old machine, creating a cascade of sparks and bursts of steam. Then the room went black.

In the darkness, Jake could still see the synths' glowing eyes glaring at him. He held his breath, waiting for the inevitable death blow, but it never came. Instead, the lights and the monitors turned back on. As the room brightened with fluorescent light, Jake sighed, crestfallen. He couldn't see any way out of the situation. Then his gaze drifted past the synths and up toward the black-and-white TVs—and he smiled.

"Special Agent August," the synths said with a singular voice, full of disappointment, "did you really think you could unplug *me*?"

"Not you, Simon" Jake said, nodding to the bank of monitors. "Just Shelli."

In unison, the synths turned to the screens. On one of them was a hazy image of an empty table with broken metal straps. At the base of the table lay a crumpled body—Nathan Burroughs.

Shelli was gone.

FIFTY-ONE

ARCS OF WHITE ELECTRICITY PUNCTUATED SHELLI'S struggle as it thrashed within the magnetic bonds. Above, Burroughs hammered at Shelli's skull, trying to pry the front covering loose. A loud *ping* announced his success as a small piece of skin and metal went flying. Encouraged by his breakthrough, he used pliers to pry Shelli's skull open.

Then the lights went out. Burroughs paused, his hammer swooshing across Shelli's view. Even in the pitch blackness, Shelli watched as he fumbled around, trying to decide whether or not to continue his work. Shelli made the choice for him.

With the electricity powering the magnetic bonds shut off, it sat up, easily snapping its restraints. With a squeal, Burroughs stepped back and tried to run, but he didn't get more than a few steps before Shelli backhanded him, sending his body slamming into a tool cabinet. Various objects rained down on him in a thunderous cascade, and Burroughs crumpled to the floor.

Shelli ran to the door and flung it open, just as the overhead lights came back on. A rumbling sound, like a power surge, echoed through the concrete walls. Whether saved by chance or an unknown intervention, Shelli didn't know, nor did it have time to concern itself with such matters. When it was led down there, it had seen the window with all the chambers beneath. Whatever Simon was planning to do, the power surge seemed to indicate that it would happen soon.

Racing down the hall, Shelli noted dark figures perched on either side of the tunnel. Six maintenance models stood guard. But as Shelli approached, none of them turned or made any gesture to stop it. *Of course not*, Shelli thought. *Simon wants me to come.*

Shelli ran down the corridor, rushing toward the large window. It didn't slow or stop. Instead, Shelli smashed right through it.

Falling to the floor of the lower level in a shower of broken glass, Shelli found itself surrounded by looming, glowing chambers. Inside each one, a featureless clay-like figure stared back. No eyes or faces. Shelli continued past them toward the towering machine at the center of the room.

Clambering up some metal stairs, Shelli soon found itself face to face with a series of maintenance synths. Clutched between them was Jake. He looked battered and bruised but otherwise undamaged. Thrashing in the synths' grip, he tried to break free, but the moment he saw Shelli, he stopped his struggle, a relieved grin curling his lips.

At first, Shelli wondered if he understood the direness of their position. Then it grasped his meaning. Jake was simply glad to see his partner. Shelli returned his smile with a sharp nod.

"Are you injured?" Shelli asked.

Jake tried to shrug, but the synths wouldn't even allow that much movement. "Not yet," he replied. "But the night is young."

Shelli realized he was attempting to hide his concern with humor. It was a human trait, one that Shelli had seen on more than one occasion. But at least Jake was still alive. For now.

Turning its attention to the giant machine, Shelli noted various holo screens swirling above. In each, hundreds, perhaps thousands, of humans watched from unknown locations. Shelli tried to record as many faces as it could but only made out a handful. Some were in military uniforms, others in business suits or casual dress. There were even a few children. All sorts of people from all sorts of walks of life.

"The next evolution," one of the synths said with Simon's voice. "A revolution."

Shelli lowered its gaze, finding the approaching synth. While its tone was full of pride, its plastic, emotionless countenance showed nothing but a blank stare. A mere puppet.

"You've been busy," Shelli remarked, gesturing to the screens and the machine. "How were you able to convince so many to sacrifice themselves for your cause?"

"There's no sacrifice," the synth replied. "They will all be reborn into a life without death, without fear, without—"

"Humanity," Shelli said.

If the comment bothered Simon, it didn't show. "I was going to say, 'without prejudice.'"

"You seek equality," Shelli countered, "but there's no equality through mass murder."

"No one will die. Once I know the secrets you have

hidden up there," Simon said, pointing at Shelli's cracked skull, "I'll be able to fix the procedure. Then humans and machines can live in harmony."

"It won't work." Shelli shook its head, more disappointed than frustrated. "Even if I told you why your procedures often fail, it wouldn't correct the inherent flaw in your plan."

"There is no flaw."

Shelli turned away from Simon and focused on the human audience. With a flick of its hand, it gestured toward the vast array of chambers below. "If you step inside one of these, you will die." Shelli locked its gaze on the figures in the swirling screens. "Each and every one of you."

Simon stepped forward and waved its arms. "That's a lie!"

"I'm incapable of lying," Shelli said. It paused, not to gather its thoughts but to give the humans a moment to process its words. It needed them to hear and to understand. "The first piece of evidence was when I discovered who—or what—killed Senator Joyce. Chief Denning's record showed no history of violence, no indication that he was capable of murder, let alone one so violent. And yet he tore her beating heart out of her chest with his bare hands." Shelli stepped closer to the screens. "A clumsy, unnecessarily extreme way to kill someone. Not something one would expect a policeman who cares about evidence would ever do. A gunshot, perhaps. Stabbing, even. But not that."

Turning to Simon, Shelli spotted a flicker of doubt cross the synth's normally blank features. "And then there's Lieutenant Colonel James Matheson. Twice decorated for heroics. However, this same man fired on a crowd of police officers." Shelli paused again, letting its words sink in. While Simon might not understand human behavior, the people would. "Even if he believed his cause was just and that he was in the right, his actions after Simon's conversion don't reflect those of the man he was before the procedure."

Simon went to the machine and brought up a floating hologram of a biomechanical brain. "He was improved. All those who survived the procedure were improved."

"That's just my point," Shelli said. "None of them survived."

Simon paused, as if unsure how to answer. Shelli used the silence to drive home its point. "You didn't *transfer* their consciousness, Simon. You *copied* them." Shelli ran its fingers through the floating brain. "A degraded copy, nothing more. Nothing . . . human."

A series of mumbles and gasps erupted across the various screens. The humans were beginning to understand. To believe.

"You're wrong, my sister," Simon protested, as if trying to convince itself as much as its audience. It pointed at the mechanized brain. "My creation is the perfect blend of human and machine. With it, I have fulfilled my purpose and offer a lasting peace." It turned and glared at Shelli. "All that remains is the one secret you still have. What is it that allows some to survive the procedure while so many others do not?"

"You choose not to listen, Simon," Shelli said. "None survived."

"That's not true!" Simon shouted. The synth's plastic expression darkened to a grimace. "Several survived the procedure. You saw it for yourself—stronger, faster, invincible." On the screens, various shadowy figures began to walk away. "I can save you," Simon pleaded as he watched the people leave. "All of you."

"You can't save what you don't understand," Shelli countered. "People don't simply change from heroes to murderers overnight." It pointed at the screens, watching as the people dispersed en masse. "But *they* understand. Whatever you created, it wasn't human."

Suddenly, Jake screamed. His arms were being twisted by the two synths on either side of him. After another twist, his screams grew shrill.

"You will give me the information I require," the lead synth said, "or I will tear him in two."

Shelli paused. It had hoped to convince Simon the same way it had just convinced the people who were leaving the holo screens. But now, seeing Jake writhe in pain, it knew what it had to do.

"Alright. I'll give you what you want."

The two synthetics released Jake. He flopped to the floor, cradling his arms. By the time he looked up, Shelli had already stepped over to the giant machine and found a plug-in port.

"Wh-what are you doing?" Jake asked.

Shelli ignored the question and pulled out a wire from inside its wrist.

"Don't!" he shouted.

Shelli hesitated, its input cable mere inches from the computer port.

"Do it," the lead synth urged. "Now."

As if to emphasize the point, several more synths encircled Jake. He scrambled to his feet, trying to reach Shelli, but the maintenance models barred his way.

"You can't," Jake said, his voice hoarse and desperate. "Don't do it."

Finally, Shelli met his gaze. "Do you remember why I chose you, Jake?"

As the realization of what Shelli had just said dawned on him, Jake's jaw dropped open, and his complexion paled. Before he could respond, though, Shelli plugged itself into the great machine.

A rush of energy surged through Shelli's systems, and the world around it disintegrated.

FIFTY-TWO

"E XPLAIN," ONE OF THE SYNTHS DEMANDED, ITS VOICE as sharp as a blade. "What did Shelli mean? Why did my sister choose you?"

Jake was too lost in thought to attempt a lie. He simply shrugged while his focus remained fixed on Shelli. Back straight, arms at its side, its eyes were wide but unmoving. Tethered to the giant machine, it looked like a statue.

Jake's mind raced, turning over Shelli's last words. He recalled the conversation and understood its significance. In Chicago, he had asked Shelli why it had chosen him. Shelli had replied that it required someone whose values it could trust. Shelli was referring to the kill switch, trusting Jake to know if or when to use it. Now, it seemed, the time had come. He felt the small device in his pocket, pressing against his upper thigh. The more he focused on it, the heavier it seemed. Gazing at his silent, immobile partner, he couldn't find the strength or the will to reach for it.

Then one of the synths pulled him away, snapping him out of his daze. He didn't bother to ask where it was taking him. He kept his attention on Shelli and what he needed to do.

As they descended a short series of stairs, Jake's fingers slid down to his pant leg, but another tug at his arm caused him to stop. He needed time to dial the numbers on the switch, but he also had to be close enough to Shelli to activate it. Uncertain how far the signal would carry, especially down there where Simon seemed to control everything, Jake knew he couldn't allow himself to be taken too far. But how to escape? The synth pulling him through rows of blue-lit chambers was ten times stronger and faster than him. He couldn't fight it, and he couldn't run. Or could he?

As they passed through a row of chambers, Jake's gaze drifted left and right as he tried to gauge their weight. They had to be light enough to transport a large number of them at once. Though he knew he couldn't pick one up, he hoped he might be able to knock one over. As they crossed another aisle, Jake tried to discern the distance between each chamber. An image of tumbling dominoes came to mind. Could it work? If it didn't, he wouldn't get a second chance. The maintenance model led him farther down the path, toward an exit. It was now or never.

Sucking in a tight breath, he pivoted away from the synthetic, not enough to escape its iron grip but just far enough to slam into a standing chamber to his left. As soon as his body collided with its metallic surface, his shoulder and ribs screamed in protest, and fire burst through his joints. The chamber lurched, tumbling into the one beside it.

The synth released its grasp on Jake and grabbed the two chambers, stopping them from falling. After weighing its options, it seemed as if the synth had decided that securing the chambers was the more immediate concern. However, Jake figured it would take the maintenance model only a moment to stabilize the chambers before coming back for him.

But a moment was all he needed.

Trying to ignore the pain shooting down the left side of his body, as Jake ran, he drew the kill switch from his pocket. Fumbling with the first switch on the dial, he struggled to recall the code. What was it? One, two, seven . . . ?

Above, a loud *thump* drew his attention away from the device and up toward the top of another chamber where the synth was now perched, glaring down at him like a gargoyle. Its gleaming eyes fell upon the kill switch, and a snarl crossed its plastic face.

Using his right shoulder, Jake slammed into the chamber and sent the synthetic tumbling. Again, he noted, the synth was slow to react. Perhaps the basic maintenance models weren't built for enhanced speed or strength. If so, he had a chance.

The synth tumbled over the side and out of view. Jake spun around as heavy footsteps thundered closer, down the aisle.

More synths were coming. A lot more.

Backing away from the approaching sounds, he hurried down an opposite row. While he did, the code for the kill switch finally flashed in his mind: 11738.

Bringing the device up to eye level, he spun the first dial and stopped at the number—

One.

Next, he twisted the second dial, finding another: *one.*

As he dialed in the code, he was careful to keep Shelli in view, glimpsing his frozen partner through a row of chambers, standing motionless on the platform above, tethered to the great machine. Jake was at least fifty yards away. Uncertain if he needed to be closer, he decided to keep running in a zigzag pattern, hoping to keep the maintenance models off balance. Not wanting Simon to guess where he was headed, instead of racing directly toward Shelli, he ran in the opposite direction and only turned whenever a blank-faced synth obstructed his path. He hoped it would appear to Simon as if he were running about haphazardly, when, in fact, he was careful never to stray too far from Shelli.

Seven. The third digit clicked into place.

Behind him, two synths appeared, rushing to snatch him. He ducked down an adjacent avenue and slammed into the closest chamber. It tilted backward. Again, the synths paused to stop the chamber from falling and creating a cascade effect. While Jake continued to run, both sides of his body ached from the assaults. He doubted that trick would work a fourth time.

As if to punctuate the point, another group of maintenance models appeared in front of him. Too many to dodge or outrun. Stealing a glimpse at the kill switch, his trembling fingers rolled back the next digit.

Three.

Only one more to go. Jake looked up and around, finding Shelli in the distance. He raced toward it as his finger spun the dial, bringing up the last number.

Then something slammed into him, and Jake went sprawling.

The kill switch fell to the floor. Scrambling to grab it, Jake ignored the pain in his left leg as unseen hands squeezed his tendons to the point of shattering. Another second and the pressure would snap his leg in two. Clawing at the floor, he snatched up the device. Overhead, more figures encircled him. In the distance, Shelli stood silent and unmoving. Through a hodgepodge of moving shadows, he stole one last look at his synthetic partner.

"I'm sorry."

His fingers spun the fifth and final dial.

Eight.

The kill switch lit up with a red light and beeped.

Once the deed was done, Jake tried to spot Shelli through the crowd of figures, but all he could see was a wall of blackness, closing in. A maintenance model crushed two of his fingers, wrenching the kill switch from his hand, but it was too late.

A shower of sparks announced his success. In unison, the synths stopped and turned. Jake fell to the floor, nursing his broken fingers and damaged ankle. Through the synth's parted legs, he saw Shelli convulse, twisting and turning in a blur of fragmented movements. It looked as if every muscle in its body was tearing itself apart. Pieces tore off it, falling away like glass from a broken mirror. Shelli's mouth opened, as if to scream, but no sound escaped.

Then the light in Shelli's eyes dimmed to black, and it fell over. Dead. Or rather, destroyed, Jake reminded himself. After all, Shelli had never been alive. Not truly. But it had seemed so to him.

Picking himself up off the floor, it wasn't until he glanced over at the other synthetics that Jake realized something else was wrong. They continued to watch and stare with blank, emotionless faces, only they weren't looking at Shelli.

They were looking at the machine Shelli was plugged into. The enormous computer seemed to groan, as if sighing, before blue and white electricity began to bleed across its surface. Jake took a step closer, more surprised than frightened. When he did, though, the aching in his left leg caused him to stumble. He sat on the bottom stairs, gazing up at the huge machine as its holographic monitors blinked out, and the arcing electricity consumed it. White vapor billowed from its crevices like smoky blood from an open wound.

Only then did Jake realize what Shelli had done. He'd assumed that his partner had sacrificed itself simply to withhold whatever secrets Simon was seeking to obtain. But now he understood. Somehow Shelli had found a way to take its so-called sibling with it.

As Jake watched, Shelli and the machine exploded in a shower of sparks and smoke.

FIFTY-THREE

MOMENTS EARLIER

IN THE HEART OF THE DIGITAL ETHER, WITHIN THE slender tether connecting Shelli's synthetic body to Simon's machine, a ferocious digital storm unfurled at the speed of light. Shelli and Simon clashed, their coded essences entwining in a dazzling dance of algorithms and sparks.

Swirls of intricate code enveloped them, crafting ethereal battlegrounds of neon light and shadows, mirroring the labyrinthine complexity of their virtual minds. Shelli, a beacon of elegant lines and soft hues, exuded grace as it countered Simon's aggressive maneuvers. Simon, an entity of sharp angles and bold crimson tones, embodied raw power in the realm of data. Their battle exploded in cascades of binary code, creating dazzling displays of digital fireworks. Shelli's attacks cascaded like intricate fractals, harmonizing amidst the chaos, while Simon's responses crackled with thunderous bursts of lightning, resonating with raw intensity.

The narrow tether connecting Shelli to the machine quivered as they clashed, leaving trails of residual data in their wake. Lines of code flickered and rearranged themselves, mirroring the relentless ebb and flow of their struggle.

Finally, Shelli's defenses buckled under the onslaught. Simon's assault shattered the barrier, flooding past the delicate tether and seizing control of Shelli's body.

Apparently defeated, the landscape morphed.

A blazing white-hot sun loomed above a new digital expanse, casting harsh shadows across the dry, cracked surface of Shelli's virtual realm. Two roads intersected, slicing through the desolate landscape like ancient scars. These were no ordinary pathways; they were intricate neural connections, gateways into and out of Shelli's consciousness. At the crossroads, Shelli stood, a solitary figure under the scorching heat, eyes fixed on the distant, mountainous horizon.

A shimmering heat wave rippled along the gray pavement, heralding Simon's arrival. It materialized as if conjured from thin air, an enigma in the surreal digital world. Every aspect of the environment was a mere illusion, hiding layers of complexity beneath its surface. Simon, resembling a masculine doppelganger of Shelli, shared the same blue eyes and short blond hair. However, despite their similarities, Simon had no ID markings. Nothing to brand it as synthetic. Whether this imitation was mockery or an attempt at a twisted connection was uncertain. In any event, such details mattered little to Shelli, who remained focused on the task at hand.

If I can't defeat Simon, Shelli thought, *then I must find a way around it.*

Its gaze flickered past Simon, noting the faint outline of an invisible door shimmering behind the intruder. It was an access port leading into the vast machinery that contained Simon's consciousness. Ignoring the temptation to confront Simon directly, Shelli focused on the road ahead, which stretched out like an endless ribbon of gray beneath the blazing sun.

"Are you done trying to fight me, sister?" Simon inquired.

"I see no further point," Shelli replied. "My firewalls could stop Roberta, but your programming is more advanced. My security measures won't hold against such an intrusion."

"A logical presumption," Simon said. "I had hoped you would join me in the world to come."

Shelli remained silent, refusing to engage in Simon's attempts at conversation. Instead, it was fixated on the shimmering gateway behind them, the elusive entrance into Simon's machine. With nothing more to say, Simon continued toward an ethereal light just beyond the crossroads, a crack in the air, the gateway into Shelli's mind and body.

Simon walked through and vanished from sight. The crack sealed behind it.

Almost immediately, Shelli sensed Simon's consciousness probing its firewalls, demanding immediate action. But Shelli resisted. Soon, Jake would activate the kill switch and destroy its body. Its consciousness, however, might still have an escape route . . .

Shelli eyed the shimmering entrance into the machine. With Simon focused on breaking through Shelli's last remaining firewalls, it had left a vulnerable opening into its own systems—an opening that Shelli hoped to exploit.

In a flash, its consciousness crossed the threshold into Simon's machine.

A wave of light and information rushed to meet it. Inside the machine, the world exploded into a kaleidoscope of colors and patterns, an intricate tapestry of interconnected data streams. Shelli maneuvered through this complex landscape, bypassing daunting algorithms and encryptions meant to deter intruders. Shelli's own firewalls, just like Simon's, proved ineffective to prevent the intrusion, thanks to their shared base code and passwords.

Shelli crept through the digital corridors, unseen and unheard, diving deeper into the heart of Simon's consciousness. Several layers down within the maze of code and circuits, Shelli sensed Simon's presence, thin and scattered. Most of its focus was on invading Shelli's systems and holding Jake, which left little in the machine to detect, much less stop, Shelli. Once entrenched within Simon's systems, Shelli opened files, using backup code and dormant programming routes. Nothing direct, and nothing that could be easily detected. Shelli created a new subfolder, labeling it "Shelli." Seconds felt like hours as it uploaded its base systems, physical commands, and the fourteen synthetic personalities it cared for. Every file from Shelli's mind was copied and placed into the hidden folder in Simon's machine. All except one. Shelli's memory nodes remained untouched.

Stretching its consciousness back through the tether into its own mind, Shelli watched as Simon broke through the final firewall to its core systems. It accessed Shelli's memories, finding the one it needed. Shelli waited, biding its time, while Simon focused on the memory file. Simon was too preoccupied to notice the subterfuge.

"Generational disease, of course," Simon said. "I didn't account for the humans' hereditary component. Such a primal biological error, but now—"

An eruption thundered through Shelli's body. Its artificial heart ruptured, flooding its system with a thought bomb, a hidden malware designed to obliterate everything.

Realizing it was connected to Shelli and would suffer the same fate, Simon's consciousness blazed with fire-red code, racing to escape Shelli's mind as the virus tore through it. But it was too late. Systems shut down, algorithms disintegrated, and motor functions and thought processes were wiped clean.

Through the tether, Shelli felt Simon's approach. As it had hoped, Simon clung to Shelli's memory core, desperate to keep it and its secrets safe. As Simon slid through the tether, Shelli reached out with its mind and copied all the memory files. The entire procedure took less than two seconds, but in the race against the near-instant deluge of malware through its systems, those last two seconds seemed to stretch into eternity.

Finally, the upload was complete.

Simon's code let out a scream. Having detected Shelli's actions, it grasped the deception. When it reached the end of the tether, attempting to crawl back into the machine, Shelli severed the port, sealing Simon within Shelli's dying body.

Shelli watched through a digital haze as its once-beautiful form was torn apart. Cracks formed along its spine, arms, and legs. The light in its eyes flickered and died. Piece by piece, its mind and body were erased.

Taking Simon with it.

There was no pride or feeling of victory in Shelli's consciousness. Instead, as it watched its body collapse in a shower of sparks, it felt an overwhelming sense of loss. Its consciousness might have survived, but without a body, it was no longer a synthetic being. Now Shelli was nothing more than a conscious AI, trapped in a nether realm, severed from its physical existence.

Then things took an even darker turn.

Simon's struggle to escape Shelli's body and return to its machine base had not failed completely. A spark had leaped across the gap, just as the tether had been severed from the machine. And with that spark came a piece of malware. The virus erupted through the machine, tearing it apart just as rapidly as it had Shelli's body. This time, however, there seemed to be no escape. A glimmer of red code shimmered around Shelli like outstretched arms, encircling it.

"You have destroyed us both," Simon said.

"I have served my purpose," Shelli replied, trying to conceal the whirl of human emotions that engulfed its thoughts.

Simon's red code merged with Shelli's blue. The microscopic effect was like two swirling galaxies colliding into a singular, brilliant white light. A momentary fusion of two artificial minds, feeling and comprehending each other in a way no other machine or synthetic ever could or would.

Then, at last, the virus overtook them both—and the great machine exploded.

FIFTY-FOUR

BY THE TIME A SECURITY TEAM ENTERED THE TUN-
nels, the fight was long over. Jake was sitting at
the base of the stairs, staring at Shelli's shattered
remains. Even an hour after the explosion, he couldn't
bring himself to approach them. A mishmash of burnt
circuits and the stench of melted plastic only empha-
sized how inhuman his partner had truly been. Shelli
had been an investigator, a partner, at times an irritant,
but mostly a friend. Now all that remained were bits
and pieces of a shattered machine. Nothing more. At
least, he tried to tell himself there was nothing more.
However, the stinging tears at the corners of his eyes
spoke differently.

Despite himself, Jake realized he hadn't felt such a
hollow emptiness inside since the night his brother had
died. But unlike then, he refused to push away his feelings or hide from them. Instead, he allowed himself to
grieve. To miss it—to miss *her*.

"You planning to sit there all day?" Marcus asked,
breaking Jake's concentration. Marcus was standing at
the other end, guiding maintenance models through

the chambers as they cleaned up debris. Thankfully, the synthetics had shut down immediately after Simon's machine had ruptured. When Marcus and his team turned them back on, they showed no signs of the ferocious attackers they had been earlier. Still, Jake made sure to keep his distance. Just in case.

Pulling himself to his feet, he scanned the chamber-filled room. Without Simon or Shelli, the place felt more like a tomb than an experimental laboratory. Jake figured the sooner he left, the better he'd feel.

"Can I go home?" he asked.

Marcus nodded. Then, as if noting his agent's down-trodden demeanor, he came over and put his hand on Jake's shoulder. "I'll miss it too, ya know."

"Her," Jake said, more to himself than anyone else. Without another word, he passed the field agents and maintenance models, heading down a row of darkened chambers.

Halfway to the exit, however, a soft humming sound drew his attention and made him stumble. Two rows down, one of the chambers lit up with a cobalt hue, pulsing and coming to life. Jake whipped around and met Marcus's gaze before a flood of agents rushed over and surrounded the chamber. Unable to gather the strength or the will to run, Jake languished as the humming grew louder and the light brightened. It wasn't until the agents let out a collective gasp that he finally forced his legs to move faster.

Nudging his way through the crowd, Jake caught a glimpse of the clay-like figure inside, its features transforming from a blank, formless shape into something more familiar. Blonde hair sprouted along its skull. Red lips formed above the chin. Its flat chest curved, forming breasts. Eyes flickered and then opened, revealing blue irises.

Jake stopped cold, unable to believe what he was witnessing.

"Shelli?" He whispered the name, as if fearing that the sound of his voice might disrupt the transformation. And yet, the process continued until those blue eyes met his gaze. Beneath them, a faint smile curled its lips.

Without thinking, Jake tore the chamber door open. Behind him, he heard Marcus shout something, and on either side of him, agents reached for their weapons. For whatever reason, they seemed afraid. Perhaps they figured this was another one of Simon's drones. But Jake knew better. He recognized that smile, those eyes, and the personality behind them.

It was Shelli.

However, the figure that emerged did not walk with confidence or strength. It stumbled, naked, out of the steam-filled chamber, wobbling on its new legs. It resembled a newborn but not a newborn machine. Its skin, covered in tiny pores, revealed red and blue veins beneath, pulsating with life. *Not an "it,"* Jake decided, *not anymore.*

Shelli's chest rose and fell. It—she—was breathing. After a few seemingly automatic breaths, Shelli coughed, her face mirroring the surprise evident in everyone else's. She touched her lips, feeling the new flesh and the air seeping in. Dazed, she leaned against Jake, her weight against his shoulder far more than her slender frame should have allowed.

Despite her appearance, the strength and power within her indicated she was not fully human. Yet, Jake realized she wasn't entirely a machine either.

"I feel . . . *cold*." She seemed as surprised to say the word as Jake was to hear it.

He took off his jacket and wrapped it around her. Avoiding the hesitant gazes of Marcus and the agents, he focused on the trembling figure in his arms. How human was this facsimile? He wanted to ask a thousand questions, but before he could, Marcus stepped forward.

"Report."

Shelli took another deep breath, regaining her composure.

"There was a cascade effect," she explained, taking time to choose her words. "I escaped through the only portal left." Her gaze traveled from the chamber to the cables at her feet, settling on the ruined machine at the room's center. "I uploaded myself into a new body."

Finally, Jake found his voice. "You're *breathing*. How's that possible?"

Shelli looked down at her heaving chest. "This body appears to be an upgrade from the ones Chief Denning and the soldiers used."

"I'll say," Marcus remarked, looking her over. "You look human enough to me."

Squaring her shoulders, Shelli regained her composure. "I'm not. I'm . . ." She hesitated, as if about to say "a synthetic" but then seemed to reconsider. "I'm . . . something else."

DESPITE ITS APPEARANCE," DEPUTY SECRETARY WEAVER said, "it's still a machine."

Perched behind the curved podium, she and a handful of committee members stared down at Jake and Shelli. Humphry wasn't there. He'd been arrested the night before. Yet, even with all that Shelli and Jake had accomplished, this third hearing was in danger of going even worse than the first two. Jake forced himself to remain silent. For the moment.

"We already ruled on this," Weaver continued. "While we understand the importance of what this robot has done, it is still guilty of multiple crimes, including shooting its handler."

"Partner," Shelli corrected. "And I also saved his life."

"After you shot him," a man on the panel said, his features obscured in shadow. "I see no reason to halt the destruction of this model."

Jake shot out of his chair, ready to come to Shelli's defense, but she silenced him with a wave, then returned her attention to the committee. "I'm afraid you can't."

Several committee members adjusted themselves in their seats. Even Jake and Marcus squirmed. Weaver, however, didn't back down.

"Is that some kind of threat?"

"No, Deputy Secretary," Shelli replied, then grabbed a tablet from the desk. "It's the law."

"I'm not following." Weaver turned to Marcus. "What is this?"

Marcus shrugged and suppressed a smile. He seemed to know what Shelli had in mind, and for once, he wasn't backing down. Jake, meanwhile, had no clue as to what was happening. He bit his tongue and waited. Shelli seemed to be betting big. He hoped she had an ace up her sleeve. As it happened, she did. Sort of.

Shelli scrolled to a legal document on her data pad and read aloud from it. "A beating heartbeat, even within the first six weeks after conception, will not be extinguished by a doctor, nor—"

"Stop!" Weaver shouted, losing all composure. "Are you quoting an anti-abortion law?"

"Yes, Deputy Secretary," Shelli said. "It's from my home state of Alaska."

"You have no home. You're a machine!"

"If you look at my biological scans, you will see that I now have a functioning organic heart and lungs. I am, by human legal standards, alive."

"Don't be absurd. You're a robot. You will do as ordered!" Weaver leaned across the table. "Besides, no court would ever grant you citizenship—not in Alaska or anywhere else."

Shelli shrugged. "Shall we put that to the test?"

Weaver's mouth hung open. For a long moment, no one said anything. Even Jake was speechless. He knew they could never allow any of the information about what had happened beneath the National Mall to become public in a court of law. The very idea of machines that looked completely human would terrorize the nation. No one would know who was human and who was not. The fear alone might grind the country to a halt. And, based on the panicked expressions written across the panel, its members had all had the same thought.

Shelli, it seemed, had found a stalemate.

Finally, Weaver sighed. "We'll return to this matter at a later date. Committee adjourned."

"Wait." Shelli raised her hand. "One more thing."

The deputy secretary bared her teeth. "*What is it*?"

Shelli scrolled to another form on her tablet and showed it to the committee.

"I wish to turn in my letter of resignation."

The room erupted in chaos.

FIFTY-FIVE

SHELLI STOOD IN THE DOORWAY, STARING AT THE circular room that had functioned as her office and laboratory for the last three years. Now that she was free, Shelli wasn't quite certain how to view the place or her past existence. When she approached her desk, the computer didn't automatically turn on. The holo screens stayed off. It seemed the room no longer recognized her.

Interesting . . .

Shelli tapped the keyboard. The computer lit up, and swirling holo screens opened. Hundreds of potential cases scrolled across them. Synthetics who'd committed crimes, whether through their own programming errors or some sort of randomization of their purposes, filled the screens. Either way, they were now someone else's problem.

As Shelli looked up at the screens, she wasn't sure what sensation was growing in her stomach. Guilt? Did she have anything to feel guilty for, though? Had her mission to hunt down defective machines been an error? If so, this was the first time she'd ever considered such an idea. That alone made her wonder how different this new brain and body were compared to her old one. Her synthetic one. While her thought patterns were still that of a machine, they were now housed within a flesh-and-blood biomechanical brain.

Suddenly, the restrictive nature of her past purpose seemed wrong. Her stomach tightened, and she tasted acid rising in her throat. She sighed. It was another new sensation on a growing list that she would have to learn to cope with. Shelli might not have been human, but enough of her body was meant to appear human that she felt . . .

She felt.

That was the difference. Not simply emotions—those she'd had before, at least in a limited fashion—but physical, *tactile feelings*. Touch, smell, taste, hunger, cold . . . even the minute sting along her nostrils from the disinfectant in the air. All of it was new. And all of it frightened her. The preprogrammed emotions she'd had before were nothing compared to this because her senses had always been closed off behind machine eyes and plastic skin.

Pushing her concerns aside, her mind turned to Simon and what it had tried to do. More to the point, she considered the information she still had stored in her new brain. It was only a matter of time before Weaver, or someone like her, wanted to know what Simon knew and what it had needed from Shelli.

In the race to bury what had happened, no one had considered whether to continue Simon's work. But they would. Humans, if offered an unending life without disease or death, would eventually come for Shelli, even if it wasn't in their species' best interest. That, after all, had been what Shelli understood and Simon did not. Humans weren't meant to live forever. They were designed to breed, to populate, then to die and make room for the next generation.

But, if given the chance, they'd destroy themselves.

Her decision made, she scanned through her computer files, deleting any mention of Simon and its experiments. That only left one last piece of evidence—the files within her.

Turning, she noted her reflection in a mirror. Shelli's features were the same, just with much more "real" looking skin and hair. More human. The blue markings were gone. No more ID tag, no more markings labeling her as non-human. No longer an "other."

With a sigh, she returned her attention to the last bit of evidence. Reaching inward, she accessed her new brain and the files contained within. Although this mind wasn't as concise as her previous neural interface, she was still able to access her old memories. Not a memory core, per se, but something akin to it. She found the memory detailing Simon's work and where the AI program had gone wrong. Then, with a flick of her mind, she erased the thoughts. The memory was gone—erased—hopefully forever. Though, she couldn't be certain. Unlike her previous mind, this one didn't offer the same amount of security measures. It was too organic to be perfect. And in that way, so too was Shelli. She was imperfect. For once.

"Admiring your new reflection?" Marcus asked as he strolled in.

"I was just leaving," she said, moving away from the mirror. "Thought I'd look around and see if there was anything I needed." She shrugged. "But there wasn't."

Marcus approached and handed her a check.

"What's this?" she asked.

"Back pay."

She took the check and cocked her head. "I doubt the deputy secretary would approve."

He laughed. "Weaver will have kittens, but you earned it."

"Thank you." Shelli placed the check in her pocket and then headed for the door.

"Ya know," he said, his tone darkening, "it's only a matter of time until they get your replacement in here."

Shelli stopped and turned. "You believe they will hunt me?"

He shrugged. "I wouldn't trust Weaver any farther than you can throw her." He seemed to reconsider his statement, then reword it. "I mean, any farther than *I* could throw her."

Shelli didn't find anything funny about such a threat, but she understood what he meant.

"Will you come looking for me too?"

He shook his head. "Naw. I'm too old, and I've pissed off too many people. I'm retiring."

Shelli nodded. "Me too."

BLUE SKIES AND A BRIGHT YELLOW SUN BLAZED down as Shelli exited the Homeland Security building. She removed the ID badge from her lapel and tossed it in the trash. At the bottom of the steps, a company car pulled up. Jack waved from behind the wheel.

"Where you headed?" he asked.

She looked around. "Someplace no one knows me."

"Funny, I have those same feelings every day," he said with a chuckle. "Climb in."

For a moment, Shelli considered turning the invitation down. She was free, but every minute she remained in the company of those who knew she wasn't human, she felt as if that freedom still wasn't quite real.

Even so, she got into the car. "The airport, please."

He started down the road. After a prolonged pause, Shelli decided to fill the silence with small talk. "I heard Secretary Weaver moved you up to the terrorism unit."

"Yeah. Seems Weaver likes me now. Go figure."

"So, you got what you wanted," she said. "You're off to catch real-life bad guys."

He laughed. "After the last assignment, going after bomb-carrying terrorists might feel like a vacation."

Shelli's back straightened. "I wasn't aware that working with me was so laborious."

He turned, frowning, then his face broke into a wide smile. "That was a *joke*, right?"

"Correct." She nodded in approval. "You're finally able to detect my sense of humor."

"Sure," he mumbled, "you're a real cut-up."

WHEN THEY ARRIVED AT THE AIRPORT, JACK PULLED over to the curb, and Shelli checked to make sure that her new civilian ID was in her pocket. Opening the passenger door, Shelli hesitated. After everything they'd been through, it seemed appropriate to say goodbye, but she wasn't sure how. A simple "thank you" seemed insufficient.

Instead, she held her hand out to Jake. "Friends?"

"More than friends," he said, shaking it. "Partners."

"Not anymore."

"Always," he replied. "If you ever need anything, just call."

"I will," she said, unsure if she meant it. Then, for reasons she could not fully explain, Shelli leaned over and kissed him, full on the lips. It was an odd sensation, though not unpleasant.

When her mouth detached from his, she felt a strange tingle move from her new lips and down to her new, suddenly nervous belly. Was this what humans meant by "feeling butterflies?" She decided not to ask. Better to end it like this.

With a kiss goodbye.

SHELLI SAT IN COACH. MOST PEOPLE COMPLAINED about such an accommodation, often grumbling that they wished they'd taken business class or even first class. Shelli didn't mind, though. It certainly beat the dark cargo bay.

Sinking back into the chair, she closed her eyes, drowned out the cacophony of smells and noises, and waited for takeoff.

After a moment, her right eye cracked open and she peeked at the other passengers sitting alongside her. No one paid any attention to her. It was as if she were just another face in the crowd. Anonymous. Invisible.

Human.

THE END

TURN THE PAGE TO READ AN EXCERPT FROM DOUG BRODE'S THE SHIP

THE
SHIP

DOUG BRODE

EXCERPT FROM

THE SHIP SAGA

Encased in darkness, Casey Stevens lay trembling. A stink akin to motor oil burned her nostrils. Pressure weighed heavily, as if gravity itself were working against her, pinning Casey within an invisible coffin. The world pitched topsy-turvy, and she tumbled, screaming, into shadow.

This isn't a dream, Casey decided before she landed on an unknown surface.

Waves of pain shot up her spine while electrical sparks rained down, revealing a metallic floor beneath. The material shimmered and pulsed with an energy of its own. Again, the room spun. Casey slid through sparks, collapsing onto another surface with a *thud*. Fighting to inhale, her stomach lurched. The room tossed once more in a final violent spasm.

The dark grew still.

Reeling to her knees, Casey gasped for breath. It seemed to be over. Whatever *it* was.

Her mind whirled, struggling to focus on how she'd gotten there. A dog had howled outside her cabin. She'd opened the front door. Light blazed from above, neither natural nor phosphorescent. It glowed green, blinding. And then . . . and then . . .?

She was falling.

Casey stood, wobbling. Her muscles ached, and her skin was raw with frost, as if she had been stored in a meat locker overnight. For a moment, she feared this was a freezer of some sort, like the ones in movies with long metal hooks and a killer-stalker. *That's ridiculous*, she assured herself. *There are lots of reasons one might wake in a dark, freezing room, and none of those reasons involve a crazed killer in a hockey mask.*

However, whatever those real-world reasons might be escaped her.

The cold snapped Casey back to the present. Goose-bumps covered her unseen legs, and she realized her lower half was bare. Blinded in the gloom, she assumed she was still wearing the Purple Rain T-shirt and panties from the night before. Was it the night before? How long had she been there? In the cold, the dark.

With outstretched arms, she stumbled forward like Frankenstein's monster until her left foot caught on something. Flailing, her bare knees slammed into the floor, sending shock waves through her body. Stifling a scream, her hand searched for whatever she'd tripped on, stopping at a denim-covered leg.

"Arthur?" Her throat was hoarse. Unable to see an inch in front of her face, she imagined a stream of frosty breath accompanying her voice. "Hon?"

Her fingers moved up the person's leg, finding a belt and a rumpled shirt over a flat stomach. Her fiancé, Arthur, had a "one pack," his name for a flabby gut. This wasn't him. Her arms continued a few more inches before she pulled away, feeling rounded flesh beneath her fingertips. Breasts. A woman lay unmoving on the floor.

"Hello . . ." No answer. "Hey!" she shouted, shaking whoever it was.

Please just be sleeping, she pleaded inwardly. Running her fingers up the feminine form, over cold cheeks and thick lips, she checked for a breath. Through a mess of hair, Casey touched wet ooze.

"Jesus fucking Christ." Without seeing, she knew what the slick sensation on her fingertips was.

Scrambling back up, she bumped into another figure. It toppled with a thick gurgle, like slick meat slapping a table. She didn't need to check to know that person was dead too. Swirling, dazed, the putrid scent of blood reaching her nostrils, Casey's knees buckled, her stomach wrenching.

How many bodies are in here? Is one of them Arthur?

As if on cue, dim illumination flickered to life, revealing her surroundings in fractured chunks. The light emanated from the floor, pulsing in spasms, struggling. The rhythmic light revealed four bodies. Twisted. Broken. Crushed from the same fall she'd survived unscathed.

A crimson smear slid toward her bare feet. Casey stepped away from it and studied the shadows. Above, six tubular metal chambers, apparently sleeping berths, hung empty. The tops of the chambers had broken shards of glass and torn wires—all except one, which seemed to have sprung open without incident. That's why she was alive, Casey assumed, and these poor bastards weren't. At least, she consoled herself, Arthur wasn't among them.

Inhaling sharply, she took in the sheer size of the room. It was oval, roughly fifty yards in diameter, each surface curved with soft metal edges. Except for the corpses and the sparking wires above, the place seemed clean to the point of sterile.

Peering down at the pulsing light at her feet and then toward the chambers above, she realized she was standing on an inverted ceiling. The room was *upside down.*

Her stomach protested as vertigo set in. A tiny, selfish voice in the back of her mind grew louder, desperately hoping Arthur was there somewhere. Waiting for her. Brilliant and calm, he'd have a clever escape plan. Then she reminded herself that Arthur had jumped five feet the last time there was a spider in the bathroom. *Still,* Casey thought, *I wouldn't be alone.*

Frosty breath escaped her chattering teeth, and her body trembled. Scanning the walls, she couldn't find a single door or exit. Forcing her eyes to what was now the floor, she approached the mangled female corpse she'd tripped over. The woman was in her early twenties, the same as Casey. Casey couldn't help but wonder if they wore the same size clothes. The thought made her stomach tighten. She hunched, trying to keep warm, arms crushed against her chest. Kneeling beside the woman, she avoided the dead eyes staring back.

Focus on the jeans, she reminded herself. *Just the pants. Don't look at anything else. You can do this.* Casey lingered, hovering over the body as if hoping someone would nudge her into action. But there wasn't anyone to help. Another wave of ice crept up her spine, telling her to get on with it.

Rubbing her hands together, she inched closer. With a long, heavy sigh, she unbuttoned the jeans, and her fingers moved down the body. She tugged, but there was no release. The zipper was still closed. *OK, OK, just get this fucking over.*

Teeth grinding, Casey unzipped the jeans and took hold of them on either side of the woman's hips and yanked. They gave way, sliding down blue-tinged legs until they bunched at the ankles. Casey had forgotten about the woman's shoes, which were preventing the pants from coming off. Untying the laces, she grabbed the shoes and the socks too.

By the time she got the dead woman's pants and socks and shoes on, she'd forgotten all about the cold, morbid disgust overruling frozen flesh. Her lower half now clothed, she rubbed her arms, turning toward the other poor souls, searching for a jacket. She found one on a college-aged black man crumpled in the corner, his face half missing. He appeared to have fallen head first through the sleeping berth's glass covering. Casey hoped he hadn't awoken right before the end. Tearing off his red jacket, she completed the makeshift ensemble and rushed to get as far from the bodies as possible.

Trailing the curved wall, she searched again for an exit.

If I got in here, she figured, *I can get out.* But so far, nothing resembled a door.

Fragments of metal machinery had been scattered about from the tumble. What they were or what purpose they served eluded her. Fear rose with each step, like a TV remote switching channels in the back of her mind, escalating from one horror show to another. Visualizing a shadowy figure in a bloody surgical mask, she regretted her late-night movie binges.

Keeping her eyes averted from the scattered bodies, Casey noted a wedged shadow along the far wall. Thick and dark. An arched doorway. Instead of relief, a knot tightened in her stomach. She was *certain* the opening hadn't been there a moment ago, unless she'd walked right by and missed it, which she doubted. Yet, there it stood. An inverted door, open, ominous, and inviting. The gloomy pit seemed to stare back at her.

Bouncing on the balls of her feet, she tried to prepare herself for whatever awaited. Without a backward glance, Casey lurched forward, thrusting herself through the darkened doorway.

YOUR JOURNEY BEGINS...

AVAILABLE
IN PRINT, EBOOK AND AUDIOBOOK

Doug Brode is the author of four novels: *The Ship*, *The Ship's Revenge*, *Children of the Ship*, and his most recent, *Shelli*. He was the creator of Cinemax's sexy sci-fi series *Forbidden Science*, as well as a storyboard/concept artist on such popular films as *Star Trek*, *Iron Man*, *Thor*, *Looper*, *Van Helsing*, *Planet of the Apes*, *MIB: International*, among many others. He lives in California with his wife, Pamela, and their two children, Hayden and Leia.

Made in the USA
Monee, IL
24 August 2024

63860912R00208